DUCKRABBIT

HOWARD BURMAN

Master Arts Publishing

HOWARD BURMAN

DUCKRABBIT

Duckrabbit/ Howard Burman
1st ed.
Master Arts Publishing
ISBN 978-1-312-92673-8

www.howardburman.com

HOWARD BURMAN

DUCKRABBIT

Most people never have to face the fact that. at the right time and at the right place, they're capable of anything.

— ROBERT TOWNE

HOWARD BURMAN

CAST OF CHARACTERS

In order of appearance

STAATS
Chunky with droopy shoulders and a perpetually bemused look. Unkempt ponytail braids sometimes hang loosely down his back.

BRUNS (aka HOBSBAWM)
Square-built and bearded with sparkling china blue eyes full of mischief.

SINNOTT-SINSMYTH
Middle-aged with Art Garfunkelian hair.

ROSCOE
Gangly slab-sided with a gut headed toward paunchy.

CLETUS
Gangly slab-sided with a gut headed toward paunchy.

HYDE
Fireplug dumpy. Blinky-eyed and moon-faced.

TOOTSIE POPS
Hairless with a lean face, pitted, scarred and set off by prominent carbon-black eyes above deep grainy brown circles.

TRASHCAN
Top-heavy milksop with rotten teeth, rotten breath and a rotten crotch.

PADRE DICK
An avuncular basso profundo, self-proclaimed Trumpet of the Lord. A bellicose man, he speaks in uppercase. ALWAYS.

CHIP
Pasty man whose droopy belly is a perfect accompaniment to his droopy stash and even droopier personality.

HOWARD BURMAN

SISTER SARAH

Big, horsey-faced, muckle-mouthed with sharp cut lines.

SMUDGE

Reedy with a bad imitation Miami Vice look—more than a 5 o'clock shadow but less than a full beard only partially covering sunken pale, pitted cheeks.

MRS. SMUDGE

Hatchet-faced, liver-lipped with a dolichocephalic head and a kiwi-sized mouth out of which hangs a perpetually ash-tipped Vogue Menthol Super Slim cigarette.

FATHER JO

A little roly-poly butterball priest. A cherry-cheeked cupcake with collar.

BELINDA aka CHERRY

A gimlet-eyed snip of a woman, raven-haired with a crooked smile

LIEUTENANT OTT

Squinty James Dean eyes, dimpled Kirk Douglas chin, ski-jump Bob Hope nose, gap-toothed Ernest Borgnine teeth.

BIC BITTY

Diminutive swooshing force of dotage, determination and hair gel.

LIEUTENANT TRAXLER

A cement truck of a man, he bellows more than speaks. A real gum-bumper.

ALAIN

Right out of a GQ piece on French Canadian hip.

CHARLIE BROWN

Whiskery juicer whose flashing cornflower blue eyes belie his otherwise frowzy appearance.

LuTIMMOTHY JONES

Cheery Africa-American with a big smile that explodes into all teeth.

PART ONE

Duck

I'm a big fan of murder. I stare at a wall mirror looking deep into my eyes, and just slightly to the left of each retina I can make out the gates of hell. They are ajar.

HOWARD BURMAN

1

I can see it all as if in slow motion and I can see myself too as if I were watching myself in a movie. First person meets third person. A black and white movie about me with obligatory noirish low-key lighting, shadowy patterning from venetian blinds and banister rails, and lots of murky shots of people reflected in mirrors, and through rain-spotted glass. Pure chiaroscuro. Plenty of Dutch angle shots. Except whole sections have been snipped out: the loyalties, the connecting part of things, the explanations for things, and everything blowing in the grainy gray cinematic wind. I am another man it seems, a sneering spoilsport, a cynical wise ass. The creature who plays me is coarse and hard-boiled, cocky and reckless, a doofus tooting his own sardonic horn. I'm being played by Elmer Fucking Fudd. Looney Toons does noir.

2

Just tell me. If you got the guts that is.
— Staats Cotsworth, "Silent Night, Bloody Night"

As J. Alfred said, there will be time to murder and create, to spit out all the butt-ends of my days and ways.

These are my butt-ends.

She told me to keep it simple. Just the facts. The unadorned story sans self-serving adjectives, whether hyphenated or not she said. She was trying to mess with my mind, but my mind isn't messable.

Well, the story isn't going to flow without adjectives because adjectives won't hurt anybody unless they're super adjective sensitive like Stephen King, who said the road to hell is paved with those little suckers. But, Stephen King is going to hell for all the things he wrote so who cares about Stevie, beyond the reach of human range, a drop of hell, a touch of strange?

So here's the story with participles undangled, infinitives mostly intact and scores of adjectives, but then life ain't perfect, is it?

I should know.

For the un-official record: Some events in our past are and shall remain secrent—i.e., beyond secret, more secret than a secret, transcending the very concept of a secret. A secret so secret only a few even know it exists, let alone understand it.

It is my avowed intent to guard my secrets as if I were the Grand Wrabbit Wizard of the Mystic Society of the Memphi.

So, here's the story sans the secrent, at least for the nonce.

A sultry, dry bulb-hot Denton, Texas, night, the moon hanging low. Sometime after midnight. The police report says between 1:00 and 2:30, but it was later. No matter. People shop late in Denton, Texas, U.S.A. In case you run out of jalapeno peppers at 4:00 in the morning, the pig is there for you. Power to the pig.

I'm feewing wucky.

Cue the music: Fudd does "Ride of the Valkyries." Da da da da da.

His hair was red. Red like Lucy red. Out of a bottle red like it was fighting to be something else but henna-was-winning red.

He was fat ... ish. Domino fat. Blueberry hill fat. I'll-be-glad-when-you're-dead-you-rascal-you fat with shopping-bag eyes, bad teeth and a laugh between a snicker and a snort, but more snortish than snickerish.

He cut a lumpy stride in his flamingo pink flip-flops; a pumped up man of no determinate age in iridescent van dyke brown leather pants, denim jacket and a white rope belt—the nautical-ish look.

Got the picture?

He was coming out of the piggly part of Piggly Wiggly store number 4-0-something with a book under his arm: *The Food Guide Pyramid*. The pyramid can be your personal guide-no matter your age or lifestyle.

He also had a bag of Doritos Nacho Cheesier Flavored Tortilla Chips. Cheese the day. And a black murse messenger bag with wide straps, an adjustable flap close, and a spacious interior to house all his belongings. Worn with jeans and a cool shirt, no one mistakes this manly accessory for a purse.

I sat in my ultimate driving machine. Certified, pre-owned, ideas beyond expectations. Not quite telepathy but the next best thing Maxie, the little hair-lipped salesman had said/read. Candy-ass red. A plastic bag of dirty laundry in the back seat smelling like stale malted milk. The radio is on.

Kiww the wabbitt, kiww the wabbitt.

The xenon adaptive headlights lit up the littered tarmac showing the way for a little crawly multilegged creature of undetermined genus and a pile of soggy cigarette butts.

The motor is idling, but with valvetronic technology, the engine is breathing more easily than it might otherwise. So sayeth Maxie.

I didn't mind the scratching, didn't give a flying fuck about the pathetic Hoganish rasslin' holds, didn't care a lick about the bug eye popping, but I absofuckinglutely hated the screechy screaming. A guy could go deaf in a line of work like mine. Some rude assholes don't consider that, and nothing pisses me off more than rude assholes.

That's why I use Hearos in my ears. America's favorite ear plugs. Trusted since 1992, and that's a long time to trust ear plugs if you ask me. Consider it a lagniappe, no thanks necessary.

Good bye wabbitt.

I think he knew. I think he wanted it like he wanted Pop Tarts for breakfast. I know this because he had two of those sugary delights in his murse. I know a lot about Crazy Good Pop Tarts. For example the crust is 2 mm thick and popular flavors include (but are not limited to) blueberry, frosted strawberry, frosted brown sugar cinnamon, cherry, hot fudge sundae and s'mores. In 2001, our boys in the wild blue yonder dropped 2.4 million Pop Tarts in Afghanistan so that the rag heads would have the energy to beat the shit out of the Taliban. Worked, too. How many were the frosted kind remains a state secret to this day. Hail King Sharkara.

I emptied his fake New Holiday murse took his fake mini wallet with engraved Gucci script logo, signature web snap closure, eight card slots, bill compartment and zip-top coin pocket, and I took his faux man's 2T Silver Dial Beadset Rolex Datejust. Welcome to the world of Rolex.

I ate the strawberry Pop Tart which didn't need to be heated. In fact, they shouldn't be heated because strawberry Pop Tarts may be a cheap and inexpensive incendiary devices. Toasters which fail to eject Pop Tarts can cause the Pop Tarts to emit flames 10-18 inches in height.

Took the ring of the Nibelung.

It ain't about the money, pops.

What is it about, you ask?

3

--ShitIdunnno ... in a voice that rustled.

--I'm trying—

--To salve your own damn—

--to get a handle—

--need for whatever—

--to try to understand how someone like ... how someone could—

--the hell you think you can accomplish by—

--live with himself all this time thinking—

--by trying to intimidate me into—

--Intimidate? Is that what you think I'm doing?

--what?

--The truth. That's all. I'm trying to figure out what you did and why. I'm trying to figure out what was going on in your mind that you would do something so—

--Horrible?

--All right.

--Whatever. Make me a freak show like Siamese donkeys joined at the ass or the fat lady who can't get out of her chair.

--I want to get something on the record. Were you drinking?

--Nothing.

--You weren't drunk?

--Sober as Mr. Rogers.

--When was the last time you had a drink?

--Last night.

--I mean before the—

--I don't know. A couple of days before maybe. Maybe more. I don't know.

--What? What did you drink?

--Couple of beers.

--What kind?

--What does that have to do with—?

--Just trying to get a picture.

--Duckrabbit, if you have to know.

--Never heard of it.

--From back east.

--OK. You weren't drunk.

--I wasn't drunk.

--Drugs?

--I don't do drugs.

--A little grass maybe?

--Are you listening? Read my lips. I don't do drugs.

--Did you use to?

--A little.

--OK.

--Except you don't believe me.

--I'm just trying to get at the truth.

--Ah, the truth.

--Which I'm sure you want, too.

--I know the truth.

--So go on. Your parents.

--I didn't say anything about my parents.

--Were they supportive?

--They were my parents for christsake.

--What was your ... how did you feel about them? Your parents.

He finishes fitting the arm of the chair back where it belongs, leans away from it. --Nothing special. They were parents. You know, mother, father. You may have heard of them. A lot of families have them.

--Did you get along?

--If you're looking for an abused-by-father-ignored-by-drugged-out-mother story, try Oprah. You're not going to get it here.

--What kind of story am I going to get?

--I've got all kinds. What do you want?

--Just the—

--Yeah, I know.

--truth.

--Because you're going to come up with some bullhonkey theory that ties everything up in a neat little wiki screen shot.

--I'm not judging—

--Oh, don't make me laugh. Not judging? You want me to tell you the truth while you're lying your ass off to me?

--OK, I'll try not to—

--That's what you do.

--Let's get back to you.

--Judge anyway. Maybe the lying part, too. Probably.

--Your family… a brother—

--Two.

--Two brothers.

--You know all this shit. Why are you asking me? You know damn well—

--And a sister.

--One.

--I'm trying to find out what might have been on your mind when—

--I have no mind. I'm a complete idiot, haven't you heard?

--Now who's lying?

--That's what everybody is saying, isn't it? I must be a fuckwit to have done what I did.

--I didn't say that.

--Then you're the only one.

--I doubt that's true.

--Do you?

--I know it's not true.

--What don't you know?

--Why. I don't know why. Tell me.

4

Everybody has something to conceal.
      —Humphrey Bogart, "The Maltese Falcon."

I'll tell you the whole story, Morry, with a few whys and whens but first you've got to understand it ain't <u>just</u> a story. I want you to taste the goodness because it tastes good like a noirish life should. But remember, you can't trust that whisper stream because that stream don't run by everyone like it does by me. Just ask 17F. He stole my whole like-silk-blowing-in-the-wind bit in "Live and Let Die." I mean, what the hell can you expect from a guy with only half a lung? Of course I whisper, but I swear I never killed a chauffeur with a poison dart shooting mirror. That was all made up.

First things first, though, as Stevie Covey says, because there's a gap between the compass and the clock. You probably suspect I had a lousy childhood, that my father abused me and my mother was on coke, and I don't mean the diet kind. Good to the last drop kind of thing. T'aint so. I wasn't mistreated as a kid. In fact, I was barely treated at all. Mostly my parents ignored me, my brothers and sister. They couldn't be bothered. We were apparently sentient in our nuisancery.

Here's all the news that's fit to print about that: I was born and grew up in Wonderland, aka Levittown. As Allan Sherman sang through Harry Belafonte, "I'm upside down. My head is turning around. Cause I've got to sell the house, in Levittown." Although I wasn't planned, the community was. Thought-out, planned-out, mapped-out down to the last blade of fertilized Scott's lawns planted with weed control seeds just as I was. This was right after the war. (The one really worthy of the name.) Some Navy guy got the idea to mass produce crappy houses, with crappy materials, on crappy land, and sell them cheap to crappy returning servicemen who came home with little money but lots of raging hormones leading to lots of crappy kids.

Following in the fun-packed footsteps of "The Fuller Brush Man," Father got a job selling Jolly Boy Suckers that became the Good Humor family of products that captured the hearts of American consumers with unique treats reminiscent of the good things in life.

Now try to follow this: Father, aka Biff, hoped to marry his girl Margie, who worked as a secretary for Stuart, an insurance investigator. Margie wouldn't marry Biff, though, because she was the sole support of her kid brother, Johnny, a card-carrying member of the Captain Marvel Club. So Biff got involved with Bonnie, a young woman he tried to rescue from gangsters. But Biff's attempts to help her only got him accused of murder. When the police refused to believe his story, it was up to Biff and Johnny to prove Biff's innocence and solve the crime, which they did, and so Biff and Margie got married. End of "The Good Humor Man Story." Call it "The Bells are Ringing for You and Your Gal," or "The Only Comedy that Comes in Ten Assorted Flavors."

In the as-yet-to-be-penned sequel, Biff and Margie have four kids who grow up in Howdy Doodyland alongside Flub-A-Dub, Dilly Dally and Phineas T., before moving on to Hoppy and Windy.

Not only did my dipsomaniacal Father, Biff, not abuse me and/or my brothers (my sister is another story altogether), he didn't even know us. He was, however, on a first name basis with everyone in the firm of Daniels, Dickel, Beam, Walker and Jameson. The last barstool on the left at the Dew Drop Inn is permanently crumpled into the shape of his lazy ass. His yet-to-be-received authorized autobio *My Foggy Life* will be faxed in from cloud nine. It comes with a 30-day ironclad guarantee. Just pay postage and handling and UPS it to Abraham's Bosom. *What Can Brown Do For You?* Whether it's going celestial, seeing more, saving time or unexpected ideas, you can find out at the UPS Whiteboard.

Mommy dearest was gone most of the time, too. Someplace into the tangled maze of her Lucy-like red-haired noggin. She could sit all day in the Formica, fiberglass-rubber-melamine-aluminum-vinyl-plastic-kitchen with the black and white checkerboard vinyl floor and vacantly stare out the sliding aluminum glass door as if she believed in no goats, no glory. George Clooney had nothing on her. I don't know where the hell she was. She never said.

Mommy and Daddy named me after an otherwise easily forgettable actor—Staats Cotsworth—who was apparently well-known for playing Flashgun Casey on radio in the 40s but I'll have to take Daddy's generally unreliable word for that. Years later I came to know him as

DUCKRABBIT

Wilford Butler in the great noir classic *Silent Night, Bloody Night*, a man who returns home on Christmas Eve to find his house has been turned into a mental institution for the criminally insane. But on the day of his return, he is set on fire and dies. Then a serial killer escapes from another institution, finds refuge in the house, makes frightening phone calls, and kills anyone coming near. But what does the killer have in common with what happened to Wilford Butler years before? A question best left ...

My older brother was called Bruns after Philip Bruns who played Wilford Butler at another age in the same film. He went on to appear appropriately enough in the TV series "Just Shoot Me" and the film "Dead Men Don't Die" in which he does and then he is brought back to life by the voodoo spell of a cleaning woman so that he can go after his killer.

My other other brother was named Hyde after Grant Hyde Code who surprisingly enough played Wilford Butler as an old man in said same film.

My younger sister, who Daddy rather fancied—a lot. A little red-haired sprite everyone called Candy Darling after the eponymous Candy Darling, the actress in the family's favorite film—wait for it ... yes, of course, the aforementioned "Silent Night, Bloody Night."

Me and my brothers mostly lived a snap, crackle, and pop life by surviving on the crispy nuggets, each made from a single grain of rice, and occasionally on the unfeasibly delicious Birds Eye products featuring sweet-as-the-moment-when-the-pod-went- 'pop' peas poached from our GE Refrigerator—two door, right to left opening, 61 1/2" high by 30 1/2" wide with automatic defrosting. Because progress is their most important product, GE brings good things to life. Pure imagination at work.

In summer we rode a robin's egg blue Raleigh All-Steel Bicycle with the Sturmey Archer three-speed gear shifters made using the pioneering new brazing techniques to construct the frame. In winter, we slid our G Series Flexible Flyer with wooden seat slats bearing the distinctive red eagle trademark, wooden steering and handle bars, and steel runners with struts painted bright red. We played some ball, mostly the stick variety with Pensy Pinkies which were softer than Spaldeens and could be made to do movement tricks.

Sometimes we'd play Hyde and seek. Hyde ... well let's say he was more likely to win a Darwin award than a McArthur and leave it at that.

I didn't need, have or want other friends. I went through school with the bored gazes of audiences watching an Ali McGraw/Ryan O'Neal film. School was too easy, filled with imbeciles teaching morons how to do the idiotic. Once I asked my teacher why a pizza will get to your house faster than an ambulance and she didn't know. I asked her why there are handicapped parking spaces in front of skating rinks and she didn't know. I asked her if lawyers can be disbarred, why can't cowboys be deranged? She didn't know that either. School was useless.

I don't know what happened to my brothers. Hyde went into the Marine Corps and D.B. Coopered. Puff, all gone. As far as I can tell, Bruns disappeared into one of his own outré black-on-black paintings.

OK, here is where it gets … (adjective missing)

One fine afternoon in Little Boxville, Biff, an expert bimbologist and frequent winner at the Dew Drop's drunk olympics, was as blotto as Dudley when he decided, like Senator Teddy he needed company. Since it would be a long afternoon of strawberry Popsicle pushing he selected Betty Bimbo Bangs from a nearby stool and took her along. She was, according to various Dew Drop denizens, an accomplished Popsicle sucker and may have been doing just that when Biff, apparently mistaking our 10-year-old kid sister Candy Darling, for a parking place, turned her into instant road pizza by running her over, and then ran away. They found the truck in an empty lot but not good 'ol Daddy.

I guess Margie is long dead, but I can't say for sure and I don't want to tell you anything I'm not sure about because among the things I'm not is a liar. I am a veritable truth machine. All and nothing but. Polygraph me to your heart's content and that's what you'll get. If you've got a crappy haircut, don't expect me to say it's a snappy haircut. Then again, as Sir Winston Leonard Spencer-Churchill, KG, OM, CH, TD, PC, DL, FRS, Hon. RA once said, the truth is so important that it has to be surrounded by a bodyguard of lies.

5

--Why don't we just try to get at the truth ... of this situation?

--You keep using that word—truth—like you know what it means.

--Truth?

--What is that?

--You tell me.

--To you it means conformity to facts.

--To me?

--Sure.

--But to you ... what, something else?

--Yeah, conformity to an idea or emotion.

--How do you figure that?

--Artistic truth.

--Ah.

--Despite the never-ending trust we put in our eyes, things are not always what they seem.

--I suppose.

--That's the truth.

--So you see yourself as an artist ... someone who sees truth differently than—

--The difference between copying nature and making ideas and emotions visible ... or I suppose, oral ... is like the difference between copying a written page with careful penmanship and giving form to original thought in prose or verse.

--OK.

--Can I have a Coke?

--You want a Coke?

--I want a Coke.

--I'll see if we have any.

--Because you wouldn't want to deprive me of my rights.

--You think Coke is a right?

--Things go better with Coke. Or haven't you heard?

--I've heard.

--(singing) *I'd like to buy the world a Coke.*

--I'll get a Coke.

6

It's a dirty little world.
— Joan Bennett, "Hollow Triumph."

Throughout the high school years, whenever we had enough boodle we hightailed it to the Rexnor movie theatre. Not for just any movies though. Only film noir classics for us — "Double Imdemnity," "The Sweet Smell of Success," "The Postman Always Rings Twice," "Spellbound," "Out of the Past," "The Big Sleep," "The Killers," "The Maltese Falcon."

The noirier the better. No crypro, quasi, neo or pseudo noir. As far as we knew, Doris Day was either the name of an obscure holiday or the code name for the invasion of some foreign country. Skip the sugar-coating. No, we wanted to mainline the real thing and we did so for long dark popcorn and Dots fueled hours. It was glorious dingy realism, futility, fatalism, defeat and entrapment.

No Technicolor world where chipmunks and bluebirds do the washing up. Here were cheap gumshoes, cheaper gangsters, and people who weren't at home in places with carpets. A universe where the sun has died and everyone got by on neon. A world of rainy streets, shadows, chiascuro, lipstick, cigarettes, guns, dames with sordid pasts and heroes with no future.

Mitchum, Bogart, Lorre, were our idols. Crawford, Turner, Hayworth were our dreams. We imitated the Bogartesque shamuses—Fred C. Dobbs, Rick Blaine, Duke Mantee, Charlie Allnut, Sam Spade. Our heroes were the anti-heroes and there was no anti about it.

We couldn't take our eyes from the shadows and images so powerful that they burned themselves into our collective memories. I took to learning lines from these films as diligently as a Hafiz memorizes the Qur'an.

Old man Rexnor loved these films too, so they were always on his midnight showings. We were his best and sometimes only late night customers, but almost every weekend the four of us sat in the dark, watching the dark, relishing the dark. When we finally went home we didn't sleep comfortably because we knew there was nothing to be comfortable about.

We lived in the world of shadows, labyrinthine plot tangles and hopeless tones.

I would argue—and in fact have—that if you want to know the meaning of life, forget Shakespeare and Plato and their ilk. Everything you need to know about life you can learn from film noir.

Lessons learned at the Rexnor: Life is a cheap little game where everyone plays dirty.

7

--Where were you before?
Sipping a Coke--Like when?
--Immediately.
--The Piggly Wiggly.
-- Shopping?
--As opposed to what? Stealing candy bars?
--You tell me.
--Looking for jerky.
--Jerky?
--Lean meat, trimmed, cut, dried—
--I know.
--Won't spoil.
--So you bought the jerky and then …?
--Left.
--And then…?
--To go hunting.
--For what?
--Maybe squirrels or birds or something. Anything that would sit still long enough to plunk. Groundhogs. Rabbits really. I was hoping to see a

rabbit sitting up like a ... a sitting duck. A sitting rabbit.

    --So you had a gun, or a bow and arrow, or—

    --A 22.

    --Pistol?

    --Ruger. Had it for years.

    --Have a permit for that?

    --Nah.

    --You left the store with your pistol—

    --And the Jerky.

    --Then where did you go?

    --Started out the tracks.

    --Heading west along the tracks.

    --West? I didn't exactly check a compass. I don't know west. I left the Pig and turned right along the tracks. Is that west?

    --Westerly anyway.

    --I was going westerly.

    --Along the tracks.

    --The tracks, yeah.

    --Did you get anything? Hunting. A squirrel or anything?

    --Didn't have time.

    --You mean before the—

    --"Incident." That's what the papers called it, isn't it? "Incident." Sounds innocent enough doesn't it? "The incident on the tracks."

    --Did you fire at anything? Shoot the gun at all?

    --At a sign.

    --What sign?

    --With numbers on it.

    --A railroad sign.

    --Whatever.

    --No rabbits?

    --What does this have to do with—?

    --Just trying to get a—

    --Picture. Yeah, I know.

    -- Is that the only time you fired the—

    --Ruger.

    --Right.

    --Killed that sign stone dead. That was it.

--OK.

--Bam, bam, bam.

--I'm assuming you were alone. I should have asked you that before. You were alone, right?

--Actually there were three of us.

--Three?

--Me, myself and I.

--How original. But that's all?

--Who knows? Maybe the Holy Spirit or somebody. I don't know about things like that.

--But nobody corporeal?

--What?

--You weren't with friends or anything? Because if you were, everything would change.

--Nah.

--If you're protecting somebody else—

--I'm not.

--you're making a big mistake and sooner or later I'll find out.

--You won't because there wasn't anybody.

--All of a sudden I'm getting the impression you're hiding something … somebody.

--I'm not.

--Why do I think that—?

--I don't care what you think. I'm telling you.

--Nobody else.

--No.

--You're telling me—

--I'm telling you.

--OK.

--For now. About how long were you on the tracks before …

--The incident?

--We can call it that.

--I don't know. Maybe half an hour.

--Which would make it about three when you left the store.

--Maybe more. Forty minutes. I don't know. Forty-five.

--OK. It's not that important … you know that we—

--Then why did you ask?

--Because we know what time ... we know the time of the incident.

--So it doesn't matter what time I left the store.

--Unless you did something else first.

--I told you before. I left the store and headed directly down the tracks. Westerly.

--Not with anyone else.

--Do we have to——?

--Just making sure.

--go over this again? I've told you—

--Let's go on. What were you thinking?

--Nothing. A day off that's all. No classes. I didn't feel like studying so I ... went out.

--Was that what you were thinking about? School. Something in particular? A teacher you were angry with maybe. A fight you had with another student. Your girlfriend.

--Leave her out of this.

--Was she with you?

--I told you.

--Cherry, isn't it?

--This conversation is going to come to a fucking abrupt halt if you keep—

--Tell me what you were thinking about.

--Nothing.

--You were angry—

--Says who?

--at something or somebody.

--Whatever.

--Do you think I'm right? I'm right, aren't I? You were really angry.

--If that's what you think.

--At who?

--Whom?

--What?

--You mean at whom was I angry?

--That's what I mean. Who were you so pissed off at?

--Me.

8

I don't know a lot about anything, but I know a little about practically everything
— Vincent Price, *"Laura."*

To grow up when and where we did meant we were profoundly affected at a relatively early age by the Ruskie's development of the hydrogen bomb, Elvis, Sputnik, the Thunderbird, the Twist, the Nixon-Kennedy debate, the Bay of Pigs, the Cuban Missile Crisis, Muhammad Ali beating the bejesus out of Sonny Liston, Joe Frazier beating the bejesus out of Muhammad Ali, the civil rights movement, JFK's assassination, Martin Luther King's assassination, Malcolm X's assassination, Robert F. Kennedy's assassination, the Tet Offensive, the Days of Rage, the Strawberry Statement, LBJ's self-furlough, Jimi Hendrix's death, Jim Morrison's death, Janis Joplin's death, Duane Allman's death, Woodstock, "Easy Rider," "The Graduate," "2001: A Space Odyssey," Charles Manson, the breakup of the Beatles, the secret invasion of Cambodia, Watergate, Richard Nixon's resignation, fallout shelters, air-raid drills, hula hoops, acid, meth, speed, hashish, transcendental meditation and the words: "hassle," "pusher," "guru," and opinions, however slight or ill-conceived, about Patty Hearst, George Wallace, Jane Fonda, Sandy Duncan and "I am Curious (Blue)."

Those were the days when the phonies always showed up as soon as television cameras were within sniffing distance, always hammed it up, showing off at the sit-ins, burning their bras, scoring reefer, going off to live in the shaman's teepee to study Aramaic with a bisexual potter named Coyote. What they never did was play the accordion. They learned from the Jerrys—Rubin, Springer and Brown—to keep the target always moving.

Our history teacher, the one with more hair coming out of his nose than on his little head and a voice with a serrated edge that ostensibly distinguishes the Garrulous Ass (Pontificator Maximus) from the teeming masses, drove us nutzoid with nonstop blather about "contextualizing the New Paradigm," as if everyone's paradigm needed such contextualizing.

I for one never felt the burning urge.

Example of insightful question posed by said teacher/preacher:

"On August 3, 1962, Lee Harvey Oswald and Sirhan Sirhan are paddling a canoe down the Potomac at 12 miles an hour. Meanwhile, Charles Manson, James Earl Ray, and Mark David Chapman are hurtling toward them at 75 miles an hour. If the two boats collide just south of the Jefferson Memorial, which baby boomer hero will still be assassinated in the next few years: (A) Martin Luther King; (B) Bobby Kennedy; (C) John Lennon; (D) John F. Kennedy."

"The answer is John F. Kennedy," Hairy Nose assured us. "Since JFK was actually murdered by the CIA, working in consort with the FBI, the Cosa Nostra, Cuban exiles enraged by JFK's failure to provide air support during the disastrous Bay of Pigs invasion, and a cabal of shadowy New Orleans homosexuals, he would still be assassinated in Dallas on November 22, 1964. As everyone knows, Lee Harvey Oswald was framed."

So as one of the Yogis said, when you come to a fork in the road, take it. When I resentfully awoke from my four-year-long nap, they grudgingly gave me a diploma from what they laughingly call high school. (I called it the big easy.) I immediately got in my little deuce coupe, and aided by good vibrations, went California dreaming. Brian Wilson said that the West Coast has all the sunshine and the girls all get so tanned and who am I to argue with crazy Brian. I moved to bizarro Venice Beach, birthplace of the Doors where white men can't jump. For lack of anything better to do, I went to college for a while. Good golly, Miss Molly, what a joke! In the Golden State with the golden poppy I went to America West College which catered to morons, retards, idiots, imbeciles and the severely feeble-minded, only the college cherry-picked the euphemism treadmill and called them "mentally challenged," "those with an intellectual disability," and "students with learning difficulties and/or special needs." Good enough, just please don't ask me what they were doing in college.

Not that they lacked skills, however. They had elevated Scantron cheating to a high art and plagiaphrasing to a common art.

In my first and only semester, I took a biology class from a professor whose biggest claim to fame is that he invented a brand of sheep manure called "Baa Baa Doo." His class, as the ol' Bard might have said, was as tedious as a twice-told tale vexing the dull ear of a drowsy man.

One day I asked him for his position on Ernst Haeckel's theory that ontogeny recapitulates phylogeny.

"Are you trying to be a smart ass?" he said.

"Yes, professor Doo, I sure am" I said.

I don't know if the tear in his eye came from anger or embarrassment.

Adios and vaya con dios, I put the college in my rearview and like Zac Brown I stuck my toes in the water and ass in the sand.

I may no longer have been sitting in the ivy-covered day care center for young adults, but I was daily adding to my kaleidoscopic memory, learning a lot on my own including, but not limited to, learning what an autodidact was. I accumulated enough useless information to make me a college Dean—an otiose undertaking if ever there was one. For example, I know that the two earliest novels dealing with the idea of autodidacticism were the Arabic novels, "Philosophus Autodidactus," written by Ibn Tufail in 12th-century Islamic Spain and "Theologus Autodidactus," written by Ibn al-Nafis in 13th-century Egypt, both dealing with feral children living in isolation from society on a desert island, thus discovering the truth as they grow up without having been in contact with other human beings. I've read both.

I know a lot of things.

I know that cat-throwing studies show that if a cat is chucked off the seventh floor of a building it has about 30 percent less chance of surviving than a cat that falls off the 20th floor. It supposedly takes about eight floors for the cat to figure what the hell is going on so it can relax and correct the lousy situation. I know that armadillos are the only animal besides humans that can get leprosy, that a group of ravens is called a murder, that the IRS employee manual includes instructions on how to collect taxes after a nuclear war, that the Pope is an honorary Harlem Globetrotter, that men who are castrated are less likely to go bald, that between 1840 and 1960, every president elected in a year ending in 0 died while in office, that the world's termites outweigh the world's humans 10 to 1, that polar bears are left-handed, that apples are more efficient than caffeine at waking someone up in the morning, that 111,111,111 x 111,111,111 = 12,345,678,987,654,321, that here are 293 ways to make change for a dollar, that there are 318,979,564,000 possible combinations of the first four moves in chess, and that on average people fall asleep in seven minutes. I, however, average only 5 minutes. I've done the study. I know that there are 9.1 million digits in the longest prime number ever discovered and that took nine years and 700 computers to compute. I know that there are approximately 18,000 known murders committed every year in the United States.

Hell, I even know the difference between Troilus and Cressida, Monet and Manet, Herodotus and Thucydides. I know the distinction between macroevolution and microevolution. You can never tell when knowledge like that might come in handy.

I know that once upon a long time ago the Big Bang created an equal number of particles and antiparticles but the antiparticles seem to have disappeared which is a real shame because as an antimatter of fact, they should have been at least as popular. Even stevens. Oh where, oh where has my antimatter gone? It may not be on a par with searches for Judge Crater, Amelia Earhart, Glenn Miller, Heinrich Muller, Raoul Wallenberg, Michael Rockefeller, Jimmy Hoffa or Jack Lemmon's cinema kid, but it's obviously a matter of some import to some boffin nerds. (Not to be confused with Giant Chewy Nerds candy with the jelly bean center, and a bumpy, crunchy nerd shell sold by Nestlé under their Willy Wonka Candy Company brand.)

The apparent asymmetry of matter and antimatter in the visible universe is supposedly one of the greatest unsolved problems in physics, except I know the answer. A vicious pre-emptive strike by matter settled the issue. The thing is, the sides weren't evenly matched because for every billion atoms of antimatter there were a billion and one atoms of matter. So the bully matter won and it has been ever thus. No one ever asks what the antimatter is or says it doesn't antimatter that much. Life isn't fair, although it is fairer than death.

Holy Heisenberg, the problem is solved, although without the magic academic alphabet troika piled high and deep behind my name, no one takes me seriously. I have no need of the abracadabra bestowed by those with decanal authority, nor am I willing to parade my Marilyn vos Savant-ish mental gymnastics in tabloid Technicolor. I'm sort of a Little Man Tate meets John Nash meets William Sidis with maybe a smidgen of Bobby Fischer thrown in. So be it, or as the poet said, born in throes, 'tis fit that man should live in pains and die in pangs. So be it, then! Here's stout stuff for woe to work on. So be it, then.

Let there be no doubt about this: I was and am a bona fide information receptacle, not a seeker of knowledge, there being a significant difference between those two noun phrases.

Armed with all of this information and three bucks I could buy a Starbucks coffee blended with caramel brulée sauce, milk and ice topped with sweetened whipped cream.

However, alack, alas, I needed beaucoup pelf. Pelf in the sense of the Old French for *pelfre* meaning booty, stolen goods. Since I couldn't juggle chain saws and wouldn't swallow fire, I left funkytown and got a job with Big Blue IBM where I figured I could pilfer (from the Old French) their systems integrated money by doing as little as I possibly could.

"You understand, business is our middle name," said cock-a-hoop Bob—Not Bobby, Robert, Roberto or Bobarino he told me—just Bob, my putative boss.

"Gosh, golly gee, I never realized that," I said.

"Yep, just look at our logo."

"Oh, I sure will."

"See, it's right there. "Business" between 'International' and 'Machines.'"

"And to think, I never noticed that."

"Understand, you'll have to wear a dark or gray suit, white shirt and a sincere tie. It's all there in the manual I gave you. You'll want to read that carefully because it outlines our entire corporate culture and here at Big Blue we take that very seriously. Very seriously. It represents our organizational values, beliefs, and behaviors and you will want to make them your own."

Sure enough, Bobby was spot on. Right there in the manual it did say "sincere tie."

"Bobby," I said, "I've a problem right off the ol' bat. I only have insincere ties. A few might be meretricious or even a trifle obsequious, but oh, my goodness gracious, a little sincerity is a dangerous thing, and a great deal of it is absolutely fatal. Or so I've heard anyway never having been a proponent of either."

That was the highlight of my first day. There wasn't a second day.

I did, however, manage to land a job at Dirty Eddie's, a crummy bar in a crummy part of Slump City, aka San Diego, which is a redundant but accurate statement. They needed a guardian of morality, a preventer of immoral acts, a symbol of righteous conduct, and I met all of the requirements—I was big. They wanted a bouncer. These days, to be a bouncer, California requires a criminal background check including submitting fingerprints to the California Department of Injustice and the Federal Bureau of Misinvestigation. I would have flunked that test faster than Bonnie Tyler's speed of night. But back then the only test was the ability to say "get the hell out of here, kid," which I practiced a lot until I could get it right.

Nobody knew who Eddie was, how dirty he was, or when he opened the bar. As far as I could tell, the joint had either been around since shortly after the Big Bang or shortly after God created San Diego, whichever came first. The best word to describe it is nondescript, which I suppose is why people of the same ilk patronized it.

Apparently I was there to check legal age and refuse entry to the venue based on criteria such as intoxication, aggressive behavior or other ill-defined standards. Mostly I sat on my ass drinking Duck Rabbit full flavored dark beers, generally the Duck Rabbit Milk Stout a traditional full-bodied stout brewed with lactose (milk sugar). The subtle sweetness imparted by the lactose balances the sharpness of the highly roasted grains which give this delicious beer its black color. Besides, the brewers claim that during fermentation process they're so happy they dance and sing softly to the yeast which apparently renders the suds hard to resist. I'll have to take their words for that.

Paul Philippon, the founder of The Duck Rabbit Craft Brewery was a philosophy professor before deciding he could do more good for the younger generation by brewing beer than he could by teaching. Being a big fan of Ludwig Wittgenstein, he adopted Ludwig's duckrabbit diagram for his logo which looks like a duck or a rabbit, depending on the viewer's perspective and the amount of beer consumed.

How the brothers got the beer I never found out because it is normally only available in or near North Carolina. They protected the identity of their secret uniquely gifted social connector with a keen understanding of the subtle dynamics of a very fickle business (read fence) like it was the formula for Coca Cola.

DUCKRABBIT

All together now in Estudiantina Valse time:
My beer is Duck Rabbit the dry beer.
Think Duck whenever you buy beer.
It's not bitter, not sweet,
It's the extra dry treat.
Won't you try the Duck Rabbit beer?

The bartenders were Camel straight smoking twin brothers. Cletus and Roscoe, the Castor and Pollux of the tacky San Diego bar scene just waiting for shipwrecked sailors. The bar needed both brothers because they had to add up their IQs to reach triple digits. It was a shot-and-brew kind of joint so they didn't usually have to struggle with complicated cocktail recipes like martinis, but when they did they had the "Barman's A-Z Guide to Cocktails," a 320 page easy-to-use flip-card book and the ideal guide for anyone who likes to mix drinks like a professional. A comprehensive index helps to find the required drink in no time, with each recipe photographed in color to better show the final result. All recipes are easy to follow, with suggested garnishes.

The twins, Okie hillbilly rednecks recently dumped by the military, still wore their fatigues, saluted the regulars like they were choreographed Pattons addressing the troops, and poured drinks for them like they were George C. They had a tape player behind the bar that continuously pumped out country music—all three chords with repeats.

Topping the charts on their Motorola player with lifelike stereo were such classics as "I Would Kiss You Through the Screendoor But It'd Strain Our Love," "I Like Bananas Because They Have No Bones," and, "If I'd Killed You When I Wanted To, I'd be Out of Jail By Now."

The dump was Ne dark, lit mostly by the purplish neon glow produced when incident electrons with enough kinetic energy transfer that energy to the atom's outer electron causing those electrons temporarily to jump to a higher energy level.

An old television in the corner was always on but seldom watched except for "The Dukes of Hazard," when the twin savants had someone to explain the plots to them, and "Jeopardy."

"What's a terrafin?""

"I'll take assholes for one hundred, Alex."

I settled into a life of gatekeeper to the soon-to-be tottering and the underage aspiring totterers who came to call me "dude," "buddy," "man," or the highly creative, "door guy." It's a job neither requiring nor receiving respect unless you're Dalton, the best bouncer in the business. His nights are filled with fast action, hot music and beautiful women. It's a dirty job, but somebody's got to do it.

My life on a Hillsdale 32-Inch Montello Swivel Bar Stool, Patrick Swayze notwithstanding, was mostly as dull as a sculptured egg or a dead parrot, so to give my life a little life, I was often purposely rude to customers precisely because a little rudeness and disrespect goes a long way toward elevating meaningless interactions to a battle of wills and adding drama to otherwise endless benumbing nights. I specialized in alliteration insults, all of which consist of two words and begin with the same 1-3 letters. They are like the much-despised assonance insults but based on consonants instead of vowel sounds.

"Hey, shit shifter, you have ID?"

"Let's see your card, turd turner."

"Look, butt butler, you ain't getting in here with that phony card."

"Who gives a fuchsia fuck about you sweetheart?" (In this case "sweetheart' is the insult.)

Feel free to come up with your own. Try it, it's fun.

Cletus and Roscoe thought (if that's the word) that my insult-a-thon was either risible or innocuous without knowing what either word meant. They lived above and in the windowless bar as if fresh air was noxious, toxic and fattening. As far as I can tell, they knew absolutely nothing about the world outside their upstairs, downstairs quotidian world. Their idea of a long trip extended to the length of the staircase. If the universe went Big Crunch tomorrow they wouldn't know it unless it somehow messed with their tapes or sucked the kegs into a black hole.

And, by the way, the Big Crunch will happen tomorrow and nope, despite what it sounds like, it's not a new cereal. Rather, if our cozy universe is finite and the cosmological principle (not to be confused with the cosmological constant) does not apply, and the expansion speed does not exceed escape velocity, then the mutual gravitational attraction of all matter will cause everything that exists everywhere to go snap, crackle and pop, then come together into one big black hole. Then maybe another Big Bang leading to another universe with another Dirty Eddie's.

One day a physicist walks into a bar. Or does he?

9

--It's not exactly the end of the world, though is it? What I did.

--Maybe not yours, but his.

--And?

--You were angry at ... yourself, or is that just some ... I don't know, way of avoiding the reality?

--Not really.

--Someone in your family. They make you angry, don't they? Tell me about them, about your family. Growing up.

--Oh, I get it.

--What's that?

--You think that you can ... figure this out by some bullshit analytical ... something your read in a book you picked up at the airport—"How to Analyze Wackos in Ten Minutes."

--That's it. You got me. Found me out.

--OK, I grew up in a crappy pre-fabed town back on Long Island. That's in New York in case you didn't know.

--Yeah.

--But there's not a whole helluvah lot to tell you about that if you want to know the truth.

--Your brothers.

--You asking or telling?

--I just want you to tell me—

--We've been over that.

--Were you close?

--Once. Not now.

--Where are they?

--No idea.

--When was the last time you saw them?

--A long time ago. I don't know. Years.

--What happened?

--Nothing. We went our separate ways that's all.

--And you don't know—?

--I told you.

--But you've heard from them?

--No.

--Since one went into the Marine Corps? The youngest, wasn't it?

--If you know so fucking much maybe I should be questioning you.

--Well I know that much. He enlisted right after—

--You have a brother? Where the hell is he?

--college.

--If you say so.

--Graduate school.

--My brothers don't have anything to do with anything.

--I wasn't suggesting they do.

--So why the fuck do you keep bringing up ... asking about everybody else that have nothing to do ... oh yeah, I know that book. How much you pay for that anyway?

--Twelve ninety-eight. Let's go back to the—

--Incident?

--You were thinking about—

--Nothing. Mind as blank as my eighth grade algebra paper.

--I don't think that's possible.

--You didn't see the paper.

--I mean you had to be thinking about something.

--Why?

--A mind just can't turn off completely to ...

--Reality?

--everything.

--Is that some Zen-like bullshit? First there is a mountain, then there is no mountain, then there is a mountain, crap.

--Just my experience.

--Maybe our minds work differently.

--Maybe.

--Yours in perfect balance with the universe, mine all fucked up.

--Is that what you think?

--No, but I think it's what I think you think.

--Let's say you were walking along the tracks with a completely blank mind.

--A veritable cipher, a complete goose egg, nada, zilch.

--And you came to the switch.

--Or the switch came to me.

--Did you stop? Think about it? Think about the consequences? What would happen when—?

--Nothing.

--You must have ... obviously did ... come to a decision. Made a choice to—

--I just did it.

--But every action is preceded by... something either conscious or not, realized or not. Nothing comes from nothing.

--Read that in the book?

--You tell me what happened.

--I threw it. That's all. The whole enchilada.

--And you didn't wait to see the consequence. But you knew.

--Just went on. Went looking for rabbits.

--Then when you heard—

--Birds maybe. I dunno.

--It had to be loud enough to be heard for miles. In town people even said they heard it. Even over in ... you knew it was coming.

--I told you I didn't think about it.

-- I find that hard to—

--That's your problem, not mine.

--No, actually it's yours.

10

i want to tell you all about it because i should of a long time ago. me and my two brothers we all growed up together but then we kinda got seperated. i went into the marine core but they didnt. i had to go into the core if you want to know the truth on account of stuff that happened at home but that's a story i aint gonna talk about. its supposed to be a secrent.

11

"There's nothing like a good murder to give a bar a bit of character."
— Powers Boothe, "Red Wind."

One day whilst wiling away a night of smoky ennui with Mr. Pastry dropping his plates on smiley Sullivan's quasi-obligatory Sunday night snore-a-thon on the TV, I had a moment somewhere between Shakesperian and Seussian.

I was at Defcon 4. Through the Cutty mist and neon hum I watched a chemically inconvenienced old guy stagger lee out the door. He looked like a belt and braces no risk kind of a guy, living somewhere in a Baden Powell/Betty Crocker world. His Vitalis V7 hair was slicked back like it was spray-painted on by Saturday Evening Rockwell.

I followed the soaker skulking in the shadows because who knows what evil lurks in the hearts of men? The Shadow knows. I waited until the boozer was alone in a smelly place, dark if not dank.

Oh, dat scwewy wabbit!

Oh, Mister Game Warden, I hope you can help me. I've been told I can shoot wabbits and goats and pigeons and mongooses and dirty skunks and ducks. Could you tell me what season it weawwy is?

Why soitainly, my boy... it's hunting season.

Be vewy vewy quiet, I'm hunting wabbits.

I stepped out of the shadows, stopping him in his zigzaggy tracks.

"Mister Wabbit, before you die, you can have one wast wish." He valiantly tried to focus his booze-floating eyes, and grasp any part of the non-tilting world available. None was.

I gave him one shake, as in "to shake a lamb's tail" to come up with a wast wish which is exactly 10 nanoseconds or the time of one generation of a nuclear chain reactions with fast neutrons.

When he didn't: *"KILL THE WABBIT, KILL THE WABBIT!!*

I one-eight-sevened him, with an insincere tie I kept in my pocket should the urge to use it ever creep up on me, then I finished the job using my hands gloved in a pair of luxurious Italian wabbit fur driving gloves. Leather driving gloves protect your hands from a hot steering wheel while their ventilation holes keep your hands cool (and you'll look cool too).

Ah, yes, sweet death, the cure for life.

Don't for even one of those nanoseconds think he didn't deserve it.

I then scarpered back to the bar to accept the thanks of a grateful nation. Thanks, I might add that naturally were not forthcoming then, nor would they ever be. Blow, blow, thou winter wind. Thou art not so unkind as man's ingratitude.

Anyway, he was wery wucky. Wucky that he had lived to this point in his sodden life.

If his parents hadn't gotten it on to the exact nanosecond he wouldn't have been hanging around lousy gin mills, and if their parents hadn't done likewise, he wouldn't have been here, and if their parents … and so on back through thousands of generations. Going back say only eight generations to the time Honest Abe was assassinated, there were more than 250 people on whose couplings his existence depended. Moving back to the time Shakespeare— or more likely when the Earl of Oxford, Edward de Vere, wrote "Et tu Brute" into a scene about the murder of Julius Caesar—that number rises to some 16,384 precise fuckings. Twenty generations ago, when Giuliano de' Medici was murdered, the number rises to 1,048,575. Looking back 64 generations to the time when the real Julius Caesar was or wasn't crying out "Et tu Brute" while being murdered, his existence depends on about 1 million trillion precise unions of parents and parents of parents and their parents in a line leading directly to him.

Gee Jumpin' Jehoshaphat! You're thinking that's more than the number of people who have ever lived. Yeah, so? That leads to only one conclusion: there had to be a lot of incest along the way. OK, not among close relatives, but there had to have been times when a relative from his father's side screwed around with a distant cousin on his mother's side. If he looks around while walking down the street most of the people he sees are probably related.

Had any one of these unions not happened exactly as they did when they did he wouldn't be here—maybe someone else, but not hm. The countless possibilities for something else to have happened is staggering to consider. Say somewhere along this incredibly long line of unions, two people who met hadn't because a horse carrying one came up gimpy and the meeting never took place, or an infection set into a wound and a soldier died on the battlefield before he could get home to see his girl, or a saber-toothed tiger took a different route to a watering hole, or a sliding rock had come loose a second earlier, or a spear had been thrown an inch to the left, or a mosquito had landed on a bare arm instead of a sleeve, or a boat had struck a floating log going a little faster, or rain had made the road impassable, or the plague had come a week earlier, or bad weather had delayed the bus, or the dinner had been burned, or a prince had decided to attack, or the river had flooded, or the road sign had been missed, or a different doctor had been called, or the bridge had been built improperly, or the snake had sunned himself elsewhere, or the suit had fit improperly, or the concert had been canceled, or the sword had been rusty, or the gun had jammed, or the water had been bad, or the electricity hadn't gone out, or the glasses had been broken, or the road had been too muddy, or the sun had been at a different angle, or the floor had been slippery, or the day had been warmer, or the stone had been a little bigger, or the wind had blown the fire west, or the tent had been set on the other side of the field, or the moon had been obscured by clouds, or the tire hadn't blown, or the restaurant had been too full, or the dog hadn't run off, or the ride had been shorter, or the arrow had been fired with greater velocity, or the water hadn't been as deep, or the motor hadn't started, or the bear had been hungry, or the fish had wiggled off the line, or the snow had been deeper, or the shop had been closed, or the bolt had been put on tighter, or the winds had been less, or the herd had been on the other side on the valley, or the wheel hadn't come off, or the rope had held, or the meeting had run longer, or the directions hadn't been lost, or the ice hadn't melted, or the lock had been broken, or the avalanche had begun five minutes later, or the dog had been on a leash, or the window had been open, or the pool hadn't been as deep, or the deer hadn't run onto the road, or the cave had been darker, or the sergeant hadn't been scared, or the horseshoe hadn't come off, or the medicine had been available, or the knife had been longer, or the book had ended differently, or the office had been open, or the warm weather had come earlier, or the pipe hadn't burst, or the winds had been less, or the infection had been caught in time, or … or … or …

What are the odds that he would be him or that he would even have been? That he was ever alive is just pure luck. Luck, like the handle on a piss pot, there but not in it, and as every croupier knows, luck always runs out at some point.

Luck. That's all it's about. He was lucky because most people who could have been, haven't. They won't die because they never were. The stupefying odds against his being that are inherent in the potential of all his relative's DNA are astronomical.

He, like all of us, was born without purpose other than living which carries its own meaning for whatever the hell that's worth and in his case, not a whole lot. Now that he's dead he will be extinguished. From being he will be transformed to non being.

That's it—the whole megillah. Nothing more on the scroll. Running on empty. Neither light nor dark. The illusion that disguised the emptiness within will be history and the world will little know nor long remember that he was ever here.

"I do not fear death," wrote Sammy Langhorne Clemens. "I had been dead for billions and billions of years before I was born, and had not suffered the slightest inconvenience from it."

12

--OK, OK, OK, OK, O fucking K. Look. (followed by a long pause) I was being followed. OK. Something awful. We all see it. We all know what it is. He's big. All I'm saying, you look behind you, he's there ... wait ... wait ...wait he's gaining on you, he's cutting the space.

--Cut the crap.

--But he caught me, ran right up my ass.

--You mean somebody was chasing you?

--Haven't you been listening?

--Babble.

--The Slump Duck got me and he'll get you, too.

--What is that supposed to mean?

--A creature that follows people around causing laziness, complacency—

--A duck?

--and a general disregard for one's well-being.

--You read that in one of your college texts?

--The Slump Duck can only be defeated by pure will power to succeed and wanting it to die.

--And if not?

--It will follow you the rest of your life, however short that may be. "Dude, I don't want to go to class today." Friend, "The Slump Duck strikes again."

--Is that some college—?

--Woman: "I don't really need to shower today, or tomorrow. Wait, DAMN YOU SLUMP DUCK!"

--What exactly are you trying to tell me?

--The duck will get you.

--Boredom, is that what you're telling me? You did it because you were bored.

--Ducking the duck.

--I'm not buying it.

--No?

--That's too easy an out, and besides ...

--What?

--You said so yourself. Said you were angry. Angry I'll buy, bored I won't.

--Well, I'm sure as hell bored now.

13

The world's a hell. What does it matter what happens in it?
— Joseph Cotton, "Shadow of a Doubt."

Personally, I'm convinced that alligators have the right idea. They eat their young.
— Eve Arden, "Mildred Pierce."

Why head to pastures new when I could happily wallow in my manure covered fields of debauchery?

In case you're thinking this was about some kind of revenge, be it nerd or nerdless related … it ain't that simple. Nor was I playing Charlie Bronson playing Paul Kersey playing martinet raining death on curb-to-curb street scum. His rationale for such conduct is that his murderous deeds are done with the greater good in mind: protecting the innocent and victims of crime. Not even Eastwood's dirty Harry Callahan, misspelled as 'Calahan' in "Magnum Force" telling you all you need to know about the film's creators.

"I know what you're thinking: 'Did he fire six shots or only five?' Well, to tell you the truth, in all this excitement I've kinda lost track myself. But being as this is a .44 Magnum, the most powerful handgun in the world, and would blow your head clean off, you've got to ask yourself one question: 'Do I feel lucky?' Well, do ya, punk?"

Ah, yes, Harry was chosen by American Film Institute as the 17th greatest movie hero of all-time, just ahead of Robin Hood and Mahatma Gandhi. Since through Harry's squinty eyes the law is poorly served by an inept bureaucracy, he doesn't hesitate for a single frame to leap across ethical boundaries in pursuit of his own vision of justice to make 45 bad dudes in his films un-alive.

Justice has no soul.

I ain't no sociopathic revenge killer.

Now you can chuck all the horse placenta you like on your neglected-child-turns-into-sociopathic-monster-Dr. Phil theories for bored housewives. I ain't no sociopath. I'm a realist and if the two don't seem

like the same thing to you that's your problem not mine. It's a Dunkin'
Donuts world and I'm a first-class dunker.

Oh, and please don't tell me to stop and smell the roses. I don't need
to smell the goddamned roses. I already know what they smell like. They
smell like roses.

14

--Flashbacks?

--No.

--Nightmares?

--No.

--Trouble sleeping?

--No.

--Impaired concentration. Depression?

--No.

--Self-devaluation?

--Self-hatred, is that what you mean? That deep down, or maybe not
so deep, I really hated myself? That work for you?

--Well, first of all, we don't usually use that term self-hatred.

--You guys have bullshit terms for everything don't you? So at cocktail
parties you guys can talk about dysmorphic disorder or other such crap
so that nobody else knows what the hell you're talking about but they
think you're really smart. Big words.

--Actually the term we use is—

--Big fucking deal.

--persons with low self-esteem.

--Oh, wow.

--Often linked to guilt for something a person did that he or she views
as a wrongful action, and ultimately that's what is at issue here, isn't it?

--My lack of self-esteem?

--Look a man was killed, OK. He was killed because of your action. He was apparently killed because of your actions. Anyway, he's dead. Now the law generally differentiates between levels of criminal culpability based on *mens rea*—

--There you go again.

--or state of mind. Particularly when it comes to homicide, where murder requires either the intent to kill, a state of mind called malice, or malice aforethought or the knowledge that one's actions are likely to result in death. Manslaughter, on the other hand, requires a lack of any prior intention to kill or create a deadly situation. So what I'm getting at here is—

--You want to know if I'm crazy.

--Are you?

--As a loon.

--I'm not so—

--Sure?

--Well, diminished capacity is a defense. Under some circumstances it can serve to negate the mental state of "malice." If the court recognizes that a person can kill without justification, but also without any criminal intent ... that is ... due to a mental defect or mental illness, then the crime can be defined as something less than murder.

--Manslaughter.

--Probably. So we're back to the question of why.

--Why oh why oh why did I ever leave Ohio?

--What? You didn't ever live—

--It's a song. I don't know where from. Some show.

--You threw the switch. You don't deny that. Did you know a train was coming?

--There was no train coming.

--Obviously there was.

--No, there wasn't.

--OK then, what do you want to call it ... a choo choo?

--A work ... I don't know but don't make it sound like some big passenger train or something loaded with people. It was a work carriage or something. One man on it. A work ... I don't know exactly ... a work vehicle.

--Doesn't matter what we call it really.

--But not a passenger train.

--OK.

--One guy on a work ... vehicle.

--Except a passenger train could have been coming.

--I didn't memorize the schedule.

--Unless you, for whatever reason, knew exactly what was coming down the track. Did you know what would be coming next?

--Do you?

--What?

--Know what's coming next. Sort of an existential question isn't it?

--No, it's a question about your state of ... your knowledge of what would be coming down that track and when.

--What does it mean "to know?"

--Oh let's not play games.

--Oh, let's.

15

That's life. Whichever way you turn, Fate sticks out a foot to trip you.
> — Tom Neal, "Detour."

I have a particularly vivid memory of a Rexnor film from right after the war when most American films were about wholesome homecomings and tear-jerking reunions.

"The Best Years of Our Lives" was an apple pie of a flick that outsoaped the soaps. It was about a returning vet—wholesome guy he was—and his teary-eyed family. Of course, it won the Academy Reward race. But the picture from that year that we most liked portrayed a very different version of America. It was called 'Detour" about a man who wandered from a life of little possibility to one of total doom. The rating police wouldn't even rate it. Why? It broke the big rule: the murderer got away seemingly to wander forever the dark streets of the red white and blue.

16

--Maybe I'm just, you know, rotten pure and simple. Viciously rotten for which there is no remedy. A guy's rotten, he's just rotten and there's nothing you or anybody else can do about that.

--Well, first of all I don't believe there is such a thing.

-- Check CNN.

--Not in any—

--Ever hear of a guy named Fritzl?

--Who?

--He locked his daughter in a basement. Kept her there for 24 years. Raped her daily and had something like seven kids with her so he was both their father and grandfather.

--Saves on birthday presents.

--A couple of years ago.

--Vaguely familiar.

--Nasty man. You wouldn't call that evil?

--Actually, no.

--That Danish guy who walked around some island dressed in his police uniform calmly convincing the children huddled there that he meant to save them. When they emerged into the open, he fired again and again.

--It's a matter of how we define—

--Or the Germans turning people into lampshades and bars of soap, or the shooters in Columbine, or that guy in Connecticut who slaughtered the little kids.

--Evil … the concept of evil … is purely a biblical one, said to be the absence of good, or more specifically man's isolation from God, brought about not through God's will but mankind's own doing.

--Which you don't buy?

--Personally, no.

--Good, because everything at some point has been declared the root of all evil.

--And I don't think you do either.

--There you go again, trying to tell me what I think.

--But more to the point, I believe bad people rather than being evil in a theological sense ... see, when you hold up the concept of evil to examine it ... well, it's no explanation at all.

--Does that mean I'm not going to be poked by little red guys in hell?

--I doubt it. Rather than evil, these people suffer from a lack of empathy—

--Yeah, I wondered where I put mine.

...or at least a reduced, ability to empathize. Call it empathy erosion.

--If I call it anything at all.

--Simply the tail end of a bell curve found in every society in the world.

--Oh you mean pretending to care about someone else's problems so they will like and/or trust you?

--If you want to believe that.

--Or sympathy without commitment.

--That's a cynical way of looking—

--A politically correct conversational side-step.

--It's much more than that. We all lie someplace on what you might call an empathy continuum.

--You guys come up with—

--People we call evil are simply at one extreme of that continuum. We're all lined up on it somewhere ... on the continuum ... somewhere based on how much empathy we have. Most people have some, and some people have a lot, and some people, well, they just don't seem to have any at all.

--Yeah, and whose fault is that?

--Ah, that's the question isn't it?

--Didn't I just ask it?

--Most likely it's a product of the way each person's brain is wired.

--So it's not the fault of the individual you mean. He just can't help it.

--Yeah.

--Like a club foot.

--Well—

--Or a hunchback.

--unlike the concept of evil, empathy has explanatory value.

--Which you're now going to do.

--What?

--Explain.

--Do you want me to?

--Do I have a choice?

--You had choice and you decided to ...

He gets up, walks around the table. --Here it comes.

--But there can be lots of reasons for low empathy ...for considering people as objects, for ... devaluing people.

--The ol' empathy erosion bit.

--Destructive emotions such as bitter resentment, or revenge or blind hatred or a desire to protect.

--And me?

--That's what I'm trying to find out. Of course, all of these are transient emotions and they can be reversed ... unless they're the result of more permanent psychological issues.

--Like bad early toilet training.

--Could be.

--Let's go for that.

--On the whole, resentment is usually directed toward those people considered above, maybe higher-status individuals ... authority figures. Anger is usually aimed at people on the same level, and contempt, well that's usually aimed at those considered to be on a lower level.

--So if I say I have utter contempt for you...

--Do you?

--it tells you a lot.

--Yeah.

--Everything you need to know. Let's investigate the possibilities, shall we boys and girls. This will be fun. You'll enjoy it. Let's see, what's first ...? Oh yes, bitter resentment. But resent what you ask? Or is it who? Well, either way it probably has something to do with a wrong, either real or imagined. How am I doing so far?

--Spot on.

--So what was the wrong ... either imagined or real ... that was done to this unrepentant sinner?

   --Was that a rhetorical question?

   --Not necessarily.

   --Well, you're the only one who can answer that, aren't you?

   --That was a rhetorical question, wasn't it?

   --Not necessarily.

   --So what could account for that ... rejection? What could bring it on?

   --A lot of things.

   --Such as...?

   --Emotional denial or rejection by somebody close ...

   --Or ...?

   --I suppose deliberate embarrassment or belittling by another person. Or scorn. Putting down. Something like that. From maybe parents, or siblings. Or for instance, a girlfriend. Am I getting warm?

   --Positively glacial.

   --A girlfriend. You said, Cherry.

   --No, you said Cherry.

   --I'm quite sure ...

   --You're recording this. Go back and fucking listen.

   --OK. It doesn't matter.

   --It sure as hell does—

   --OK.

   --to her.

   --Cherry?

   --Says you.

   --You get defensive every time I bring her up.

   --Who's that?

   --Your girlfriend.

   --Oh, you mean Cherry?

   --Is she your girlfriend?

   --No.

   --You sure?

   --Let's try revenge. Payback.

   --OK.

   --Like shitting on the lawn of the guy who let his dog take a dump in your yard.

   --Well...

   --The Bible tells us it's cool. Vengeance is mine sayeth the Lord.

--I'm not sure about biblical—
--An eye for an eye.
--authority. Anyway that's hardly justification for ...
--Maybe I'm super religious. A super Jew.
--Are you?
--No.

17

I cannot stand these morons any longer
— Clifton Webb, "Laura."

Man with knife tries to rob bank. Guards have guns. Jailarity ensues.

I was invited to be a permanent guest of the government with free room, board and Friday night movies. It was an offer I couldn't refuse.

My pitter-patter lawyer was a Boalt Hall graduate wearing a blonde, going-to-orange rug and Fresh Look color contact lenses, allowing him to choose from a wide range of shades that blend beautifully with the natural color of his eyes. He was also a pedophile, a tidbit of not-so-secret information that would belong in another story altogether were it not for the fact that he was more concerned with his pending arrest than with my post-pending arrest. He would end up visiting me in the big boy school/clink/joint/slammer/ pokey/ big house/pen/calaboose/ hoosegow/graybar hotel/cage (nobody ever sunk to the depths of calling it a prison) from my side of the bars. By the time he got out he was walking like a pregnant girl.

The gratis, scantily furnished, Portland cement-block room smelled like a goulash of piss, shit, feet, ass, nuts, body odor, mildew, and Lysol Disinfectant Spray that kills 99.9 percent of viruses and bacteria on commonly touched, hard, nonporous surfaces in every cell. Most of my meals looked like camel ass fat mixed with burnt baby duck skin.

My uninvited roomie, the imaginatively named "Tootsie Pops," was a real pecker checker but as I have already told you, I'm a big guy and he wasn't, so there was no jailhouse confetti being spewed about in our prodigious parlor.

My eponymous cellie got his nickname because as a kid he apparently lived on the little suckers known and loved by adults and kiddies around the world and available today in more flavors than ever before. The original five-flavor mix—chocolate, cherry, orange, grape and raspberry—has been expanded to include a new sixth flavor that alternates among pomegranate, banana and green apple. He graduated to inhaling anything containing glucose, fructose, sucrose, or lactose as if it were mother's milk. Why he was so spindly remains a mystery akin to the whereabouts of the Higgs Boson.

The hairless Tootsie Pops' face was lean, pitted, scarred and set off by prominent carbon-black eyes above deep grainy brown circles, probably the result of sucking too many lollypops with embedded candy prizes. His reedy body looked as if he had gotten most of his nutrition from meth shakes.

I seldom understood what the hell he was talking about. He would say things like, "Fo shizzle my dizzle, what a bizzo meet me up the gizzo when you get a clizzo," and "yo bro wuz the problemo?"

He moved about as easily and often as an almond in a Hershey bar.

A tattoo of a thorn-crowned bleeding Jesus head in the throes of agony was splayed across his tonsured chest and "AFFA" which he said stood for Angels Forever, Forever Angels covered the side of his scaly head.

Across his scrawny back was "Support your local 81" a number as he explained despite any request for said explanation that was made up of the eighth letter of the alphabet, H and the first, A —a short form for Hells Angels. These guys are oh so creative.

Conversations with the snaggle-toothed Tootsie Pops (I'm guessing he had a real name but I have no idea what it was) were, to say the least, tokenish at best. He didn't know the difference between a gang bang and the Big Bang other than he had been in a lot of the former and none of the latter as far as he could remember.

Tootsie Pops hung with the aptly named Trashcan, a top-heavy milksop with rotten teeth, rotten breath, and a rotten crotch that you didn't have to get up close and personal to smell. Then there's Dopey, whose name derives not from his diminished IQ, but from his close connection to, and affinity for, Snow White. Like the Disney schmuck, he appears stupefied, confused, muddled, befuddled, disorientated, groggy and muzzy. A true incompetenticilicoronic.

Gotta love the self-esteem these guys convey when left to pick their own aliases.

The torpid trio apparently got their white crunch from a clown known as Billy Whizz, who apparently has an inexhaustible amount of the stuff he apparently gets from a guard, who apparently gets it from Billy's old whore-in-Sketchers lady, who apparently gets it from a fuckwit cop, who apparently gets it from a binger he protects.

Tootsie Pops keeps pounding me to get sleeved like most of the inmates. But I don't do tats.

"I've never been inked," I tell him, "and I'll never be inked unless it by the undertaker."

"Then a half sleeve?"

If I thought it would shut him up I'd forever answer him with grunts. As it is, I stick mostly to monosyllables. "Some part of 'no' not clear?"

"You didn't say, 'no,' bro."

I'd tell him it was explicitly implied but I don't want to confuse him. "No, No, Nanette" I whisper just loud enough for him to hear.

"Who's Nanette?"

"A perky young girl who attempts to save the marriage of her uncle and aunt by untangling Uncle Jimmy from several innocent but ensnaring flirtations."

"Whatever, man, but I think if you was sleeved like me things would go better."

"For whom?

"What do you mean?"

"Forget it."

"Guy over in D block will sleeve you on the cheap. I mean gotta show who you're with bro. Jail-ttoo's"

"I am."

"Don't work that way. Protection's where it's at."

"I'd prefer henceforth if, when addressing me, you would avoid ending sentences with prepositions."

For a while that seemed to work. He not only avoided using ungrammatical language with me, he avoided using anything that I even remotely recognized as language, resorting instead to grunts, oinks and other assorted guttural noises.

Apparently the tattouch bag Trashcan, who was tattooed with double sleeves and a tattoo shirt, didn't get the memo designating the right tats. After countless run-ins with the Hispanic gang, T-can crossed the tacit line and his fate to have a jailgina was sealed.

One afternoon while wiling away an afternoon with a boredom hangover, Trashcan was grabbed by three horny pendejo hobbits who dragged him into a conveniently empty shower room. There, with a scalpel-like knife fashioned from a typewriter carriage return they made a small incision inside his armpit. Once the slit healed they had themselves a handy, and always available makeshift vagina. From that day on, Trashcan was very popular.

It was, and remains to this day, my obviously outlandish thought that wardens ought to do something about all the dangerous people running amuck around prisons. A guy could really get hurt in there.

18

--Please don't tell me you're gonna claim you're innocent.
--OK.
--You're not, are you?
--Innocent or claim I'm innocent?
--Either or.
--Pure as a lamb.
--Oh, Christ!
--As a newborn babe.
--How do you sleep at night?
--Usually on my back.

--Because you've got—

--Although sometimes on my side.

--a lot you must be thinking about.

--Yeah.

--Tell me—

--Mostly about where we should go to dinner Friday night.

--Not likely.

--Why? You have some advice? Something not too expensive but, you know ... nice in a bullshitty impressive sort of way.

--Look let's—

--You probably know a lot of places—

--I doubt you'll be—

--that look expensive but aren't.

--going anyplace Friday but if you've got any chance at all you'll start answering my questions more honestly.

--I think I have been.

--No, you don't.

--Whatever.

--You heard the crash ... explosion ... and then ...

--Barely registered.

--People all over town heard it. Heard it ... I don't know ... 10 miles away and you keep insisting—

--There's a difference between hearing and, you know ... registering. Of course, I heard it. I'm not fucking deaf. You think I'm deaf? Maybe you're deaf. I said it didn't register because it didn't. I was numb, OK. So I didn't ... I just walked on like nothing happened.

--Looking for squirrels?

--That's right.

--Bullshit. That's an impossibility. You had to know exactly what you did ... what the consequences of what you did were. I'll buy that maybe you didn't know why maybe but you sure as hell knew what ... and what would ... happen. So you couldn't have ignored it. No way. You didn't just walk away and look for squirrels without ... without feeling ... something.

--You know what "numb" means?

--You tell me. You tell me what it means to you. What does "numb" mean to you? Your word "numb." What?

The boy shifts in his chair. Squints.

--Like when you're a kid and it's almost Christmas and all you want is a bicycle. All you're waiting for is a bicycle because your buddies have them and you don't and you want to go with them, to ... you know, do things with them, but you can't because you can't keep up with them without a bike. See, it's not just the bike, it's a way of connecting with your friends, or at least the guys you want to be your friends. It's important to a kid. You ask your father and he tells you to wait for Christmas and you ask your mother and she says to listen to your father. That's cool because Christmas is ... Christmas, and that's when you get things you really want, so as Christmas gets close you poke around the garage and don't see one hidden behind the workbench where Father usually hides things, but hey that doesn't mean anything. There are places ... I don't know ... maybe at my father's work or in the back of his truck or something, or at a neighbor's. Could be lots of places. Blue would be best and you drop those hints, but any color really. Well, maybe not pink, but just about any other color. Not a weird one, anyway. Not pink or chartreuse or something. Not purple. So you start thinking about it all the time. Riding a blue ... or red bike with cards in the spokes to make sounds like a motor. Mostly though it's you with the other guys. That's what you're thinking about. But then on the night before Christmas ... Christmas Eve you're up in your room and, of course, you can't sleep. First because you're excited but then because you can hear your parents downstairs. Only first they're arguing about something. I don't know what. I can't tell, but that's not unusual, them arguing. That's nothing new. You can tell they've been drinking. Both of them. A lot. A lot, a lot and that's not new either. They start screaming like ... like idiots ... like screaming drunk idiots. Really, really blotto. Calling each other names ... hurtful names that no kid wants to hear coming from parents. You can call guys on the playground those things but you don't want to hear your father call your mother a fucking cunt. Not your father. So you bury your head under the pillow so you don't have to hear but you do anyway. The screaming and then a crash like ... like the tree came down and all the ornaments smashed into little pieces ... like everything downstairs was broken ... like everything was lying all over the place in little pieces. The screaming goes on and then it stops suddenly. But now you really can't go to sleep but you don't want to go downstairs and look. You don't want to see ... to know ... you don't want to ... because ... it's ... it's Christmas, and kids are supposed to be happy on Christmas, and you want a blue bike, and you want to go with your friends, and you want your parents to get along, and your mother can't be called a fucking cunt. So you don't sleep. All night you're awake and you want to know what happened downstairs but you don't want to know what happened. You hope maybe you're really asleep and this is a dream ... a nightmare, but you know it's not because you know you've been awake all night. At first light you finally ... you finally get the ... get the courage I guess to go to the stairs. You go half way down where you can see the living room. There's the tree on the floor, and the ornaments are all over the place, and there's tinsel everywhere, and your mother is asleep ... passed out half on and half off the couch. There are no presents, there's no blue bicycle, there's no father, there's no Christmas. You go back to your room. Numb.

--What did he do, your father? Where did he work?

--Pushed ice cream on kiddies.

--What do you mean?

--I mean he pushed ice cream on kids. A Good Humor pitchman. At least he was then. The funny thing is, he hated kids. Maybe he thought he'd sugar-poison them to death or something. Actually I don't know what the fuck he thought.

--So did you ever get your blue bike?

--Yep. A few weeks later.

--How did you—?

--Stole it. Rode it for years, too. A robin's egg blue Raleigh.

19

I know this drum's full of crackpots. One convict's gonna' buy his way out, another knows the governor's cousin. A third guy's even gonna' float out in a homemade balloon. But I'm not buyin' any pipe dreams. It can be done. It's been done before, and it'll be done again. It can be done here... by us.

— Burt Lancaster, "Brute Force."

Now hold onto your comfort flex Hanes. This was all before I found He-died-for-me-but-I-live-for-Him, Jesus. Yes, I did. I say yes. It was what a hip *Rolling Stone* writer might have called a "Holy shit moment."

One unremarkable night in a long line of unremarkable nights and just when I was beginning to think that the end of my time here was about as far away as the last digit of pi, my Ciceronian silver-tongued cellmate put this eloquent question to me:

"Why you ain't goin' ta Bible readin' meetins' bro?"

After I translated that in my head to English, I said, "Why would anyone ever want to do that?"

"Gets ya out early."

"That so?"

"Even earlier if ya except Jesus as yer savior bro."

"Well, swizzle my whizzle."

"I mean you don't want to marsh your mellows do you?"

"Hadn't planned to."

Tootsie Pops was, if nothing else, (and "nothing else" is accurate), stir wise and canny in the ways of prison survival tactics.

I did some checking and found out that he was right. The if-you-died-tonight-where-would-you-spend-eternity? group were granted all sorts of privileges by a warden who himself had recently seen the glorious light.

That very night I heard the voice of Jesus Christ telling me he popped his clogs, kicked the ol' oaken for the sins of all mankind and that included a wretch like me. (His word, "wretch.") That wasn't even the best part. He said that I could find peace through salvation. "Was I ready to repent?" he asked me.

"The Pope Catholic?" I responded with nary a moment's hesitation.

"Well, I…"

"That's a rhetorical question, Jesus. No answer necessary."

"Are you ready then?"

"Let me think about that for a second. Yes-siree-bob, I'm a-ready."

Oh, Lucky Man! Just when I was about to resign myself to spending the rest of my life in paroxysmal hell forever tormented by thoughts of those nights that I offed my first murderee and his pet rabbit, Jesus said, 'Nah, bro, you're good.' Faster than shit off a greased shovel, all those years I had expected to wallow in suffocating guilt were wiped away. Here's the irony: The last guy I popped was praying like a Mantis religioso during the whole gory event.

So if it weren't for the blessed Savior, I'd still be living with a Dante-esque horribly tormented conscience like some bedeviled booby asshole. Once upon a time I thought that just maybe if I were to devote myself to a lifetime of good works and contrition that some of my guilt could be eased. Not that I was about to do that, just that I thought it. But once God's grace washed over me—and that happened presto on the spot—I knew I was in the clear. Halleluiah, shazam, alakazam, instant salvation.

Why live in the past when the present is oh, so much better now that I walk in the ever-loving light of the Lord. This animal whose most recent foray into the world of thuggism took seemingly innocent lives in a beastly manner and then mixed himself a glass of Tang with 1/2 the sugar of 100 percent juice might just as well be another person.

Goodbye guilt/regret/remorse/self-condemnation/self-reproach. Hello blissful peace. Sorrow is no longer my constant companion. How great is that!

And I sleep a helluvah lot better. Oh, yeah sure, I'm sometimes awakened by visions of that clown with the broken neck pointing at me, but that's why I keep ol' Johnny 1:9 taped to my ceiling in plain view of the warden: "If we confess our sins, he is faithful and just and will forgive us our sins and purify us from all unrighteousness." There it is in black and white and who would dare argue with the Good Book because the Bible is the true and accurate word of God claimeth the prison chaplain, Padre Dick, and you can't argue with the Dick because, praise the Lord, he is always right. How do I know that? I know it because he said so, and since he is always right about the Bible, he must also be right about being right. Can't argue with logic like that.

He may have learned the art of inefficacious sincerity from Jean-Jacques Rousseau, its putative inventor.

And it's not like the dead bozos aren't in heaven right now, bathing in His loving light and everything.

See, God's looking out for all of us.

It would be wonderful if the family of the murderees forgave me, too but hey, that's between them and God. The best I can offer is forgiveness for them having judged me.

Jesus has shown me a road I never knew existed. I can't say for sure what's down that bumpy toll road with the FasTrak lane but I'm a happy camper these days. I'm thinking of taking up quoits.

No matter how long I had to stay behind bars I knew my soul had been set free by the Lord and by the sacrifice of His only son

Had that happened earlier, I would have killed way more people.

20

--It's written all over you. The mock bravado-bullshit. The stoicism—more bullshit. You're hurting. It's OK to hurt. It's natural to hurt after what you've been through ... what you've done.

--You don't ... know.

--I know.

--You haven't ... you don't ... can't—

--I've seen it enough to ... I can empathize ... Put myself in your position. Well, not literally, but ... emotionally. I can easily understand what you're going through.

--Because you're special, it that it?

--Normal. Because I'm normal.

--You don't have a fucking clue what I'm going through and you never will. We live in two different worlds you and me.

--Tell me about yours.

--I'm an artist.

--Are you?

--The world is full of us—starving artists. Kick any garbage can and a starving artist comes out.

--OK.

--We look at the world differently from ... guys in suits and ties. We're not locked in like you are to see everything in neat little boxes that tell you how everything is ... behaves ... how everything behaves. It ain't a lock-step world despite what you might think ... or want to think. All your neat little labels are nothing but ... neat little labels. They're not insightful. They're limiters ... put fences around everything ... borders ... walls. We take them down. That what artists do. We ignore the walls. Walk right through them. Blow the fuckers up. Show things in juxtaposition, not neat and clean but in ways that make us look at things ... differently and so bring if not meaning, then at least understanding. It's a sloppy world and oh, there's no right or wrong here. No neat little boxes. Fuck your little boxes. Fuck your neat and nifty answers. And while you're at it, you might as well fuck yourself, too.

--You done?

--Nope.

--You can't control life. Art you can.

--Well, I imagine—

--Live with it.

21

"Always bothers me when those hoodlums get religion."
— Humphrey Bogart, "The Enforcer" aka "Murder, Inc."

After my miraculous conversion I regularly attended Bible study classes with Tootsie Pops, Dopey and the perpetually sore Trashcan.

You may have heard of the Bible—an ancient novel full of murder, corruption, bestiality, incest and cruelty. It's often read to children on Sundays.

The meetings were led by Padre Dick, an avuncular self-proclaimed Trumpet of the Lord who blew his own while dispensing the word of God, indulgence, and hand tossed pizza with so many toppings and crust options that everyone could have his favorite! From these meetings I gained insight, 5 pounds, and the promise of an early release. Praise Jesus!

The good Padre read to us from the goodie book with an Ambien like sing-songy Terfel-ish baritone voice without either the top or the bottom notes. Sometimes, in pathetic but failed attempts to show that he was "one of the boys, he would play tapes of religious songs that he assumed would appeal to his truly captive audience. Songs such as "Are You Drinkin With Me Jesus?" with the truly touching lyrics:

Does your head pound Jesus as hung over you do rise

How does paradise look Jesus, through holy bloodshot eyes

Should we take a cab home Jesus...aw man we can hoof it from here

Other Padre Dick favorites included "Would Jesus Wear A Rolex On His Television Show?" "Are You on the Top 40 of the Lord?," "Drop Kick Me Jesus (Through The Goal Posts Of Life.)," "I Don't Care if it Rains or Freezes 'Long as I Have My Plastic Jesus Sittin' on the Dashboard of my Car," and "Jesus Loves Me But He Can't Stand You."

The forever shambolic Padre called himself a Biblicist which he said meant he took as literal gospel such stories as the Genesis account of creation, the deluge and Noah's ark as well as the strict historicity of the narrative accounts of Ancient Israel, the supernatural interventions of God in history, and of course, the many miracles of J.C. himself.

"Gee, Padre Dick, do you think those accounts are really true?" I asked during one session when I was feeling particularly obstreperous.

"They are true and I can prove it."

"Gee, Padre Dick, they sound so unbelievable."

"Only to the unbeliever," he said with unassailable logic.

"Gee Padre Dick, why would all those atheistic scientists insist the universe is 13.75 billion years old-give or take a measly 0.17 billion years?

"The truth is the earth is 5,491 years old.

"Gee, Padre Dick, are you sure about that?"

"We must learn to trust what the Bible tells us, or else ..."

"Yes?"

"Or else we won't know the truth."

"Which is?"

"Five-four-nine-one. And I can prove it."

"I am all ears."

"Well, you see, in the beginning God created the heavens and the earth. God called the light 'day' and the darkness 'night.' There was evening, and there was morning, marking the first day. On the sixth day, God created humankind in his own image, in the image of God he created them, male and female he created them. Therefore we can assume that the age of earth is just five days older than that of Adam. Now we can use the Bible to calculate from there. When Adam had lived 130 years he fathered a son in his own likeness, according to his image, and he named him Seth. So, the age of earth while Seth was born would be 130 years. When Seth had lived 105 years, he became the father of Enosh. When Enosh had lived 90 years, he became the father of Kenan. When Kenan had lived 70 years, he became the father of Mahalalel. When Mahalalel had lived 65 years, he became the father of Jared. When Jared had lived 162 years, he became the father of Enoch. When Enoch had lived 65 years, he became the father of Methuselah. When Methuselah had lived 187 years, he became the father of Lamech. When Lamech had lived 182 years, he had a son. He named him Noah. When Noah was 500, he had his first son …"

Who knew Noah was still a horny boat-builder at 500? Kinda gives a guy hope. Maybe in another 450 years I'll have a kid. I'll have to start shopping for a present.

"Now his son…"

The basso profondo Padre rattled on with his "proof," and in so doing implied a definition of that word with which I was completely unfamiliar.

"So when Noah is 601, his ark comes to rest and …"

By this time, with little interest in keeping up with the arithmetic that lead to 5,491, I had tuned him out, pushed the delete button in my mind, went on a virtual cruise to Hernando's hideaway.

"…and there you have it--absolute proof. The Bible has all the answers for those willing to carefully look."

Split infinitive aside, I was about to erupt into a paroxysm of protest when Tootsie Pops leaned over, grabbed my arm and whispered, "That's a no go, bro."

I am loath to admit Tootsie Pops had the upper hand in this situation, but he was right. Questioning the Bible was tantamount to admitting to child rape when it came to prolonging one's stay as a guest of the state, so I nodded like a Michael Jordan bobblehead with a stenciled puerile grin.

Forget that any cruel, inhuman, and degrading treatment of prisoners in which severe pain or suffering, whether physical or mental, is intentionally inflicted, has been prohibited by the United Nations

Convention Against Torture and has been ratified by 147 countries.

Had we the option of waterboarding or Bible class for our illegal torture, I might have opted for the former. "As it was …

"Oh, now I understand," I said still bobbleheading like Mike.

"That's why it's called the Bible."

I stopped nodding.

Was he trying to be existential? Could he be summonsing up Delphic wisdom? Nah.

As the Prince of Denmark tells us, "I have of late, but wherefore I know not, lost all my mirth." And me being such a mirthy guy and all.

22

Not that you mind the killings, God. Your book is full of killings.
— Robert Mitchum, "The Night of the Hunter."

Under Padre Dick's benevolent tutelage I learned a lot from reading the Bible, much of which I found most encouraging and spiritually uplifting. For example, I discovered, much to my everlasting surprise that God is not only cool with murder, but under certain circumstances, he actually demands it. No, not suggests, recommends, or ecclesiastically hints but outright demands it as in "kill these or pay the consequences forever." For example, here, with chapter and verse (courtesy of the good Padre) is but a small sampling of some of those on the big guy's hit list:

    People who don't listen to priests--Deuteronomy 17:12.
    Witches—Exodus 22:17.0
    Homosexuals--Leviticus 20:13
    Fortunetellers--Leviticus 20:27
    Adulterers--Leviticus 20:10
    False Prophets--Zechariah 13:3
    Fornicators--Leviticus 21:9

DUCKRABBIT

Daddy and mommy hitters--Exodus 21:1
Women who are not virgins on their wedding--Deuteronomy 22:20-21

And the beat goes on, including but not limited to, people who work on the Sabbath, anyone who approaches the tabernacle, blasphemers, people who follow other religions, false prophets, sons of sinners, and children who make fun of bald people. (Which perhaps is why God sent us Rogaine, the only topical brand Food and Drug Administration-approved to regrow hair.)

If you think I'm exaggerating, look it up. It's all there in black, white and blood. Well, not the Rogaine part. That's my interpolation.

The Lord does seem to go a little overboard at times such as when he commands his followers to kill an entire town because one person worships another God.

But remember, God loves all his children.

Of course, he doesn't do a lot of this personally, (He is after all, above it all.) rather he sends his personal hit man, his angel of death.

The angel of the Lord went forth and struck down one hundred and 85 thousand men in the Assyrian camp. Early the next morning, there they were, all the corpuses of the dead--2 Kings 19:35.

OK then, according to the Bible, how many people does God murder? Since I had lots of time on my otherwise idle virtual hands, I added them up and came up with 2,476,633 without counting the victims of Noah's flood, Sodom and Gomorrah, or the many God-sent plagues, famines, fiery serpents and other assorted grisly extinctions. God is clearly a world class serial killer, far surpassing the measly totals of Hitler, Stalin, Pol Pot, Ghengis Khan, Idi Amin, Benito Mussolini, Harry Truman, Mao Ze-Dong and Slobodan Milosevic put together. Padre Dick did promise the Bible is awe-inspiring. By comparison, the devil is but a puny dilettante, slaughtering a measly 10. Not even enough to make America's Most Wanted or a between-Plavix-commercials appearance on "America's Most Wanted." I don't know what Daniel Webster was so worried about.

Then there's this: Jesus kills a fig tree for not coughing up figs on request. I guess he needed to teach that tree a lesson it would never forget. Now you might think the son of God would know that figs don't bear fruit in the dry season. Apparently his father forgot to tell him.

As far as I could determine, God is a guy who talked to some Jewish guys, some Christian guys and some Islam guys, and accidentally (or not) caused more people to die than anyone else in human history. So be it.

I became a master at sitting in the Bible study class with a look of beatific attentiveness splayed across my frozen face while my mind was as far away as galaxy MACS0647-JD, which sits some 13.3 billion light years away from my private pokey. Every once in a while Padre Dick's endless drone would make its way across the murky void and I would become vaguely aware of his interloping biblical fairytales.

One example. The Padre is reading a part in the Bible from some guy name Ezra, who says that some guy named Cyrus, along with some guy named Mithredath brings out a bunch of pots of loot which he counts out: 30 of gold, 1000 of silver, then 29 censers, 30 more of gold, 410 more of silver, and then 1000 other vessels. Then he totals them and comes up with 5,469.

"Hold on there Pythagoras, 30 plus 1,000 plus 29 plus 30 plus 410 plus 1000 does not add up to 5,400,"

"No?"

"Not in the base-10 positional system of numbers."

"The what?"

"What we use—"

"Well maybe they used another system back then."

"Actually they didn't."

"Well, if it's in the Bible—

"That's right, I forgot. I'll just have to learn Bible math. Damn and I was just getting to learn my numbers all the way up to 100."

Oh, and just to make sure the Padre wasn't making up stories about the made up stories in the Bible, I checked out the Ezra bit. Padre Dick gave it to us straight.

I also read in Kings that Bible math says pi equals three. And all along I thought it was 3.1459. Some guys never learn. I was going to discuss this with the good Padre but I figured if I mentioned pi he would ask me whether it was apple or lemon meringue, so in the interest of self-preservation I let it slide.

23

Why are you looking at me like that?
— Jack Palance, "Sudden Fear."

This might be a good time to get something muy straight. I can imagine you're thinking, now this guy's around the proverbial bend. T'aint so. OK, I'll admit to being a little on the different side but I'm not gaga. I don't hear voices, not even from that demonic black Labrador retriever owned by Sam's son's neighbor. (All right, I did hear Jesus but that's a voice of a very different timbre and it was also heard by every other guy in that Bible class.) I don't hallucinate. I do know right from wrong. I know that I did wrong but now that I have been forgiven, well frankly I don't give a rat's ass. Praise the Lord!

Oh, and while I'm at it, you should know I don't do drugs. Not P-dope, soap dope or road dope. Not black rock, coco rock, double rock, G rock, garbage rock, hard rock or moonrock. So don't blame chemicals other than chocolate containing alkaloids such as theobromine and phenethylamine, which have physiological effects on the body; coffee with two types of diterpenes-kahweol and cafestol-which have physiological effects on the body; and beer containing malted barley and hops which have psychological effects on the mind.

24

--What about conscience?

--Oh yeah, you mean like washing your hands in the men's room even if nobody is watching?

--I suppose that's one way of—

--What a burden—conscience.

--Guilt. You know what that is.

--Yeah, wing frost.

--What are you—?

--Stuff that weighs you down so much you can't even walk around anymore, let alone fly.

--Is that you?

--No, it's stupid, it's useless. It can make you go nutzoid.

--How do you figure?

--Because after you've done the deed, the deed is done and there's no changing it, so there's absofuckinglutely no reason to feel—

--Guilty?

--Yeah.

--Are you really that cold?

--What am I going to get, 10 to life for lack of emotion?

25

Did I ask to be born? Did I?
— John Derek, "Knock on Any Door."

When they said I was delusional I almost fell off my unicorn. I can tell you this though, no man is happy without delusions of some kind. Delusions are as necessary to our happiness as realities.

Maybe I'll carry on, maybe I won't.

Maybe I will be held accountable for my actions, maybe not.

Maybe it doesn't matter.

Maybe that's my delusion.

26

"Those gates only open three times. When you come in, when you've served your time, or when you're dead."
— Charles Bickford, "Brute Force."

When the magic Jesus can opener worked and I was released, I went to see the brothers grim—Cletus and Roscoe—but my old job as their security adviser/doorman had been given to a sheep-faced midget with a lisp. The brothers think this is not only amusing but it will bring in customers. I miss the logic in this, but who am I to argue with their superior deductive qualities?

What, I ask you, is the world coming to? Where was the gratitude for all those selfless nights spent in defense of their dark dank dump? I briefly considered several retaliatory scenarios, but then dismissed them as requiring more effort than I was willing to expend on revenge since I am not by nature a vengeful individual, and besides, I was filled with the Spirit if not the spirits.

I wasn't feewing wery wucky.

27

Everybody is somebody's fool.
— Orson Wells, "The Lady From Shanghai."

As a condition of my early release I was required to meet with my probation officer, a pasty man whose droopy belly was a perfect accompaniment to his droopy stash and even droopier personality and whose name was apparently "Call me Chip."

Actually, what he said was "Call me Chip, and call me often." His attempt at wit.

I can clearly picture him as a guy desperate to wear his mousy gray hair in a ponytail a la Genghis Khan with a piglet's tail hanging from his gaping bald spot like a Minotaur's entrails. However, due to folic reverses Mongolian style excess would not be his.

Although my body language emphatically states that I am of the non-embraceable persuasion, Call me Chip heads straight toward me and gives me a I'm-always-here-for-you-buddy hug.

He asked if I understood all the rules about probation.

"You bet," I said. "Can't leave the state, gotta call you regularly, and can't kill anybody."

Call me Chip actually smiled at that. Who would have thought?

"I understand you've seen the light."

"Positively blinded by it. Praise the Lord."

"Screw up and you're headed back just as surely as God made little green apples. You understand that, don't you?"

"Hold on here a country minute. Glen Campbell said God didn't make little green apples and it don't rain in Indianapolis in the summertime."

"What are you talking about?"

"He also says there's no such thing as Mother Goose or Doctor Seuss. So who the hell wrote the "Cat in the Hat?"

"What hat?"

"Because I'm going to be traumatized if you tell me it wasn't Doc S."

"What does this have to do with—?

"In the last book Ted ever wrote, Yook and Zook are standing on a wall that divides their two countries, each poised to drop a Seussian nuclear bomb, at which point Yook's grandson asks:

'Who is going to drop it? Will you …? Or will he?'

'Be patient said Grandpa. We'll see. We will see."

"Have you heard anything I've said?"

"What?"

"Listen wise guy…"

If I had to pick evil over stupid I'd do it any day of the week and twice on Sundays.

It didn't take long to put Call me Chip in the rearview with no plans for a reunion with the happy huggist any time soon.

28

--Let's talk about you.

--We're not here to—

--About how your—

--look into my—

--lousy childhood turned you into a … what are you exactly?

--What am I?

--Exactly.

--I'm a professor of practical ethics.

--What is that? Morality with loopholes?

--Well, it's a linking discipline, linking theory and practice.

--And someone pays you for that?

--Harvard

--Couldn't get a real job?

--Nah.

--So they send you out to interview the wackos.

--Among others.

--And do what, file a report that goes into a file of reports so that someone can report on the file of reports?

--Something like that.

--That must be pretty satisfying.

--It can be.

--Lordy, lordy.

--My field is the neuroscience of morality … what brain networks are involved in moral decisions that might account for people's individual differences in judgments. It's a field that's waiting for a big revolution sometime soon.

--Maybe this afternoon.

--Maybe.

--Sounds like unadulterated bullshit.

--Well, we've determined that three brain structures—the medial prefrontal cortex, the posterior cingulate and angular gyrus on the left and right sides—play a central role in the emotional processes that influence personal moral decision-making.

--You don't say.

--A moral feeling which seems to be related to these areas is what takes the recognition that an act is immoral and translates that recognition into behavioral inhibition. It is this engine that functions less well in anti-social, violent and psychopathic individuals.

--Which is supposed to get you what?

--Recently we compared the functional magnetic imaging on 22 criminal men and 22 men who were not offenders. We found that most participants gave similar responses to moral dilemmas. But their brains told different stories. The criminals tended to show less activation in the medial frontal and posterior cingulate cortices in responses to moral dilemmas.

--So you want my brain, is that what you're saying?

--I wouldn't mind.

--But I would.

--Yeah.

--So what now?

--You tell me.

--You're left with … guesses.

--I guess.

29

One way or another, we all work for our vice.
> — Sam Jaffe, "The Asphalt Jungle."

We just are, said Tyler Durden who wasn't Tyler Durden but maybe was. We just are and what happens happens.

One of the great inconveniences of life in the 21st century U.S. of A. is that it takes mucho stacks of dead presidents to enjoy all that this wonderful country has to offer, but being an ex-con isn't the greatest reference for one seeking a job to earn the aforementioned said dead, so …

My first choice would have been Supreme Court Justice since the job comes with life tenure irrespective of medical or psychological deterioration and you get to sit down a lot. However, just my lousy luck they had no openings. I briefly considered becoming a hay and forage merchant but I was advised the market for said merchandise was in steady decline. Then I began asking myself, what profession offers unlimited respect, little (bordering on no) physical labor, free room and board, and maybe a neat silver mesh chapeau with rubies, sapphires and other precious jewels. Unfortunately Darth Benedict (aka Emperor Palpatine) had dibs on that job after apparently throwing Darth John Paul down a mine shaft or so goes the story.

Then I thought: Even without an army maybe I could go into the salvation business.

I'm in a wooden chair in a storefront room in a crappy area in a dirty downtown in a dying city in a dead state. It's raining.

But business is good. Mine is no Edsel-Betamax-Woolworth-Polaroid-Pan Am-Enron-Schwinn-Napster-Lionel-TWA-Sharper Image kind of business. No siree, bob. (Now that I think of it, I'm still angry with Sharper Image, because now I'm forced to buy my overpriced, Japanese made, brushed steel, throwaway executive nose hair trimmers elsewhere and that's inconvenient as hell. And Betamax, just because the machine was bulky, complicated, ugly, expensive, publicly ridiculed, horribly marketed, and disdained by the media is no excuse for its premature departure from this mortal coil. What in the world can I now do with my beta tapes? A question perhaps best left unanswered.)

Ah, mine is a business with unlimited growth potential, offering a product with never-ending need, comes with an endorsement from an unimpeachable spokesperson, and a life back guarantee.

I offer for sale (albeit not cheaply) a fate worse than death—immortality--but I keep that part a secret.

Sometimes I have sales. Two for the price of one in which a loved one can be included as a freebie, or 30 percent off if purchased after midnight.

The rain never stops.

A man in a spiffy salvation Armani pin-striped suit and silvered imitation Ray Bans comes barging through the front door, a look of grim determination on his face, a Mossberg 835 multimag pump action 12 gauge (designed to stay the course) pulled tight to his shoulder.

"You lyin' bastard," he says just before he opens up spraying me and the room with deadly tungsten polymer pellets.

Bam, bam, bam. Pieces of the room and me flying everywhere. Bam. Smoke, noise, total destruction.

Then I wake up.

What a cheaper-than-cheap cheap shot. I hate it when they do that in movies--make you think something is real, and then faster than a film editor's scissors (I'm thinking old film noir here) and a cheesy Elmer Bernstein key shift ... oh that wasn't a dream after all, the director just wanted to amp up the conflict the lazy way.

30

I don't pray. Kneeling bags my nylons.
> — Jan Sterling, "Ace in the Hole."

Reality check: I ended up settling for a slightly less prestigious job arranged for me by Padre Dick. I became a sorter, pricer, and tagger at Sister Sarah's Nifty Thrifty, an emporium of pre-owned gems, a veritable treasure trove cove for every cheapopotomus with either a buffalo nickel to burn or a pocket deep enough in which to slip riches untold. It was a place for those who were either looking for those hard-to-find 'Occupied Japan' figurines or pre-owned underpants. The thrift wiff of old shoes, old clothes, old books, and old people seeking same was unmistakable— noxious vapors that might rival Chernobyl.

Those with limited funds can make their money go further by shopping at the Nifty Thrifty. An emporium of semi-abused goods for the discriminating shopper. Everything from plastic chachkas to life's essentials. No appointment needed.

The joint was run by the eponymous Sister Sarah who was attended by two obsequious assistant sisters who took bowing and scraping to a higher art form.

As she explained to me, Sister Sarah was a member of the Sisters of St. Francis of "Third Order Regular Franciscans."

"A religious sister, not a nun," she said.

"What should I call you?'

"Sister Sarah."

She wore neither a penguin suit nor even a visible cross. You'll have to ask someone else whether she wore one under her clothes.

After careful training by Sister Sarah, the Nifty Thrifty doyenne herself, I was finally able to sort the plastic flower pots, plastic rosaries, plastic vases, and plastic Santas into their appropriate piles. Although it took some time, I was eventually granted the shop's highest honor. I was in charge of our biggest seller—the George Foreman Grills, many brand new still in their boxes, some even with removable plates. Cleaning up has never been so easy with detachable grill plates you can soak in the sink or simply pop in the dishwasher. Where this big stash of grills came from I don't know. I never asked and she never said.

I got so good at my job that when somebody came in and said "I do Steiff," I actually knew what they meant even if, as unfortunately so often was the case, we were Steiffless.

"May I suggest a George Foreman Grill instead?"

I got so I could tell a Clarice Cliff Crocus Pattern Bowl from a Pier One Small Buttons Bowl and a Moorcroft Lapland Vase from a Cost Plus World Market Square Branch Vase and those are very important things to know.

"May I suggest instead a George Foreman Grill?"

Behind her beatific back, we called Sister S. "Attila the Nun," in deference to her unmitigated mean streak.

"What devil or what witch was ever so great as Attila, whose blood is in these veins?" wailed Dracula."

A mercurial enigma, she could be as sweet as Doris Day in "Pillow Talk" one moment and as nasty as Faye Dunaway in "Mommy Dearest" the next. A big horsey-faced, muckle-mouthed woman with sharp cut lines and a heart of iron pyrite, she looked as if she might have been the result of a quickie-in-the-closet liaison between Henry Kissinger and Tallulah Bankhead. As far as I could tell she was, to quote Roosevelt on Taft, "a real puzzlewit."

Mother Theresa she was not, but then again, neither was Mother Theresa. She seemed to be on a power cruise through life, a monster to humanity who lurked to feed off men's souls for her own pleasure, said souls belonging to "my people" as she called us serfs, most of whom were on release programs from one form of custody or other.

Were she a character in a play the stage directions would read, "Enter stage right snapping."

We began each day with an obligatory prayer followed by assorted acts of control freakery. She was hell and Jesus with a whip of contempt which she unleashed mercilessly on anyone who dared question anything she did, said, implied, suggested or thought, and she could pass judgment faster than a Nuremberg judge with a dinner date.

Once when I made the unmitigated and apparently unforgivable mistake of pairing one men's light black/gray/charcoal Burlington Original Cotton Mix Argyle Sock with one men's black/charcoal/beige Burlington Original Cotton Mix Argyle Sock, Sister Sarah went semi-postal. How could I have been so foolish? Apparently I didn't know there was an eighth cardinal sin on a par with lust, gluttony, envy, sloth, pride, wrath and greed—missorting.

"What is wrong with you?"

"Bad early toilet training."

"Are you stupid or something?"

"Something."

"Go clean the men's room."

I had no interest in jousting with an unarmed, cortically sub-illuminated dimweed.

All of us indentured sock-sorting servants who worked at the Nifty Thrifty owed our "salvation" to her goodness without which we would assuredly hit the slippery slide to hell. Through her, the salvation dance was not only possible, it was inevitable.

We were all, according to her oft-repeated threat, on semi-permanent "praycation," a state of being that could and would be revoked by any egregious action not to her liking and would result in our immediate return to the state's rent free accommodations.

"I'm sure you understand that."

"You betcha!"

"Because God wants you to succeed. And so do I."

We had a steady stream of homeless folk stop by our cheapo depot to pick up the day old bagels that Sister Sarah collected each morning from Abe's Bagelry, although the homeless ones had to come around to the back so the sight of disheveled beggars for whom jail would be a step up on the social ladder wouldn't upset the sheveled freema donnas as they searched for bargain ashtrays. She handed out these little rings of yeasted wheat dough as if they were Christ Crispy communion wafers.

In time I learned my lines:

"This flogger is made entirely from upcycled and repurposed bicycle tubes that have been discarded and have found a new life in these creations! Each flogger shows subtle signs of these rough-and-tumble past lives- whether slight raised numbers on the rubber or white manufacturers' marks. These floggers are made without the use of glues or tape, so there's nothing to crack or get sticky with time."

31

Conjugate me a verb. For instance, "to promise."
— Burt Lancaster, "Sweet Smell of Success."

You're an amusing boy, but you haven't got a drop of respect for anything in human life.
— Edith Atwater, "Sweet Smell of Success."

It was at the Nifty Thrifty that I met Smudge, a crackhead with a keyboard, who used his moonlighting piano tuning appointments to pluck whatever he could find around an out-of-tune house, some of which he would fence for go money to buy crack.

Smudge is about as bright as a bag of hammers but he knows it which is a mark to his credit.

We shared a pied-à-terre two seedy blocks away from the schlocktorium. Smudge was a bony-thin guy with a scrubby moustache that made him look like an imbecile impersonating a toothbrush, but thanks to his quick hands, our place was chock-a-block with such gems as the finest Buccellati Lucrezia sterling gravy ladle for our ungravyed meals, a Baccarat Byzance Gold Rim Wine Decanter, useful should we ever decide to decant our beer, and two lovely Philippe Deshoulieres Athos Red and Platinum 5-piece place settings which looked positively smashing with pizza and pretzels.

"Took me four trips to get them place settings."

"The piano must have really been out of tune."

"Awful."

Among his possessions was a Thomas the Tank Engine duvet, (aka Tommy the Choo Choo) given to him, he said, by this mother the fence. He said he couldn't sleep without it.

There may have been a slate or two loose on Smudge's roof but he provided a welcome hiatus from the dominatrix. He was a joke teller which was OK with me because without a joke buddy, you're just an ass laughing at something nobody else finds funny. In keeping with his personality, most of his jokes were tasteless and rather stupid. Viz: "An elephant and a camel meet on a road. The elephant asks, 'why is it you camels have your breasts on your back?' The camel answers, 'that's a stupid question coming from someone who has a dick on his face.'"

"Really."

"What is the definition of innocence?"

"I give up."

"A nun working in a condom factory thinking she's making sleeping bags for mice."

"What would you call Sister Sarah if she had a sex change operation?"

"What?"

"A tran-sister."

"How could you get Sister Sarah pregnant?"

"Immaculate conception?"

"Dress her up as an altar boy."

"Sister Sarah goes to confession. She tells the priest that she has a terrible secret. The priest then tells her that her secret is safe in the sanctity of the confessional. She says, 'Father I never wear panties.' The priest says, 'That's not so serious, Sister Sarah. Say five Hail Marys, five Our Fathers, and do five cartwheels on your way to the altar.'"

Smudge offered a seemingly endless supply of Sister Sarah pleasantries.

Smudge laughed at his own jokes even if no one else did. Nevertheless, as lame as his witlessisms were, they mitigated the sisterly drudgery of each day's assorted sortings.

The piano tuner wears a hearing aid and turns up to tune up with his mother. That doesn't matter much because Smudge the tuner ain't no crooner so he wouldn't know the difference. Diamonds-are-forever, Smudge. An-allotrope-of-carbon-for-life, Smudge. Create-a-moment-that-lasts-forever, Smudge.

I don't like Smudge, and I tell him so, but just so long as I didn't turn my back on him, he was my best friend.

Diamonds are a girl's best.

Don't tell nobody.

Who am I going to tell?

The wind.

Mariah.

Away out here they got a name for rain and wind and fire. The rain is Tess, the fire Joe…

Celebrate the special moment with a sparkling diamond or perfect ring.

How much for the ring?

Smudge's mother shows up occasionally saying she needs to keep an eye on the "reprobate conduct of her worthless son." Smudge only understands five of the words in that phrase, but he never asks for clarification of the sixth and she never tells.

When he asks me I tell him, "It's someone who believes truth is subjective. Someone who does not know the difference between moral and amoral or right and wrong."

"I know the difference."

"And what is that."

"Wrong is when you get caught. Right is when you get away with it."

There's something to be said for the simple-minded.

Mrs. Smudge, is a hatchet-faced, liver-lipped woman with a dolichocephalic head and a kiwi-sized mouth out of which hangs a perpetually ash-tipped Vogue Menthol Super Slim cigarette, which for no apparent reason stays put even when she is speaking. She appears to survive only because of Smudge's alternative-to-buying lifestyle. I have no idea where she lives but Smudge makes it clear that it won't be with us, to which his incessantly surly mother responds with "woe-is-me-ing" mews and pleas for "pity on a poor mother" and assurances that Smudge will sure as hell end up there. She had taken to insisting that she be called "Portia," presumably after the long-suffering virtuous wife of the Roman statesman, Brutus. The fact that the reference was lost on her only son was a source of considerable joy. She had, although one would not know it to look at her, a college degree, proving that either she was smart or the college wasn't.

When I asked her what she studied, she said it was "ethical circumnavigation" which she went on to describe as "morality with loopholes" and self referentially often referred to herself as a skilled "loopholer."

Her obfuscating ways notwithstanding, she was surprisingly perceptive. Once she said I was inclined to "emotional incontinence," an observation with which I have no quarrels.

Her contribution to her son's chosen occupation was to suggest that, when the tuning business turns flat, good home burglaries could be had by checking the obits in the newspapers and then targeting the homes while the funerals were under way.

"Nobody's going to stay home when one of the family is being buried," she opined once again proving the incontrovertible value of a college education. Smudge picked up some nice jewelry this way not to mention scores of delightful floral displays.

Although duplicity was her default state, with me she was uncommonly blunt.

"I don't like you," she told me on more than one occasion.

"I know," I would respond matching her blunt for blunt.

"You're a bad influence."

"Implying something or someone that causes a person to degenerate or become a worse person?"

"What?"

"It's all relative, isn't it?"

"I don't know what you're talking about," she said shooting me a grumpy look.

"And therein lies the joy."

32

--Right and wrong?

--You've heard of them?

--Can't recall.

--Surely your parents must have—

--Vaguely.

--You know the difference, right?

--No.

--You don't?

--I know that what one culture considers wrong might be right in another, and vice versa. No such thing as a universal standard of morality so no one has the right to judge another person's customs … actions. Anyway not another society's customs. What is right or wrong is determined solely by the society … or the individual.

--The individual?

--Sure.

--What about truth?

--Take Genghis Khan. Immoral? By our standards, sure; by the standards of the 13th century steppe culture, anything but. Not revenging the murder of your father was immoral; killing the murderer was not. Torturing your enemy was immoral; killing him quickly was not. Adultery brought the death penalty. The fact is. Ol' Genghis was one helluvah progressive ruler who not only established a strict code of international law but subordinated his own power to it. He demanded social tolerance and humanitarian values. He abolished the then standard sale of women. In fact it was said that a virgin riding a horse loaded with sacks of gold could ride thousands of miles across Mongol territory without being touched because men knew what the consequences would be. When one of his ambassadors was killed by a foreign ruler, Genghis sent his army to exact revenge. To not do so would have been fundamentally wrong. Oh, and while he was at it, he granted diplomatic immunity, established free trade, built schools and championed literacy. An immoral man? Depends on whom you ask. The Mongols thought he was a paradigm of virtue.

His undeserved bad rap is owed to 18th century anti-Asian sentiment.

--A real hero?

--To some people.

--But not most.

--I'll have to check the Pew poll on that. Oh, and once upon a time almost everyone was gung-ho for the witch theory of causality, and burning women at the stake was considered to be a moral good in the name of improving the community.

--Look, we need to get—

--Try this. The ancient Mayan practice of self-mutilation and human sacrifice. Good or bad? Neither. They're simply cultural distinctives … like our shooting fireworks on the 4th. Human sacrifice and fireworks, simply different products of separate socialization.

--Look, let's—

--There are Amazonian tribes … the Siriono … I think, that will abandon the man without a family to die alone in the jungle. Right or wrong? It's essential for the survival of the tribe. They think it's right, do you?

--You're very impressed with yourself, aren't you?

--I have my moments. Some tribes in Africa believe cannibalism is morally permissible just so long as you're not dining on someone from your own tribe. That may sound horrific,

--And it does.

--but if we look at it with less horror and with a dash of critical inquiry … it's important when looking for that ever illusive truth you seem to always be chasing.

--Chasing, yeah.

--Like when President Bush referred to some terrorist nations as an "axis of evil." What bullshit. How can anybody in one society call another evil? Bullshit!

--So you don't think suicide bombing of civilians is evil—read "wrong?"

--No, do you?

--As a matter of fact.

--Look, Bush, the Islamic belief in the necessity of jihad is every bit as valid as any belief in Western civilization, and don't kid yourself we're as much to blame for the 9/11 attacks as the terrorists.

--I don't know that's true.

--No, you don't.

--OK.

--There is nothing either good or bad, but thinking makes it so.

--Says who?

--Hamlet.

--That so?

--It is.

--How do you figure?

--Because something can only be bad for something else ... or to something else.

--I don't—

--Like rain is bad for staying dry but good for slowing forest fire.

--OK, I'll buy that.

33

One who follows his nature keeps his original nature in the end.
—Michael O'Hara, "The Lady From Shanghai."

Now it came to pass that various priests stopped by the Sister Sarah's pre-owned and pre-pre-owned emporium to pick up ... whatever priests needed. Some became regulars apparently needing a lot of whatevers.

We, Smudge and I, got to know a few of them.

Introducing Father Joe, kiddie fiddler extraordinaire.

Father Jo (or Father Jo-Jo as the boys called him) was a little roly-poly butterball of a man/priest, a cherry-cheeked cupcake with collar.

"What do you give the pedophile priest who has everything?" asks Smudge.

"What's that?"

"Another parish."

"Three strikes and you're transferred."

"Actually the church is finally cracking down. Now if a priest is transferred to another parish, he can't take his live-in boyfriend. They have a new policy: Don't ask, don't confess."

Father Jo would regularly come into our shop of trinkety horrors looking for little baubles, bangles, or beads of appreciation that he would hand out to boys at the deaf school where he worked. Every favor deserves a favor. Right Father Jo?

"The boys need attention."

"They like little things, do they?"

He was a walking advertisement for AT&T Reach out and touch someone. I hope he had shares.

There was no 'can't tellya' about him. His pedophilactical ways were about as secret as Liberace's sexuality. I suspect Sister Sarah knew but, of course, she never talked to us galley slaves about such matters.

I know for a fact that at least one employee went to the Bishop informing him of Father Jo-Jo's ... indiscretions. Perhaps the Bishop was a graduate of their deaf school because nothing happened. Father Jo went on his merry molesting way.

The employee, who shall go nameless on account of I can't remember it, told us that one kid said it began when Father Jo-Jo called him into his office and then pulled down the kid's pants and touched his penis. Then reprised his touch-a-thon in his car, his mother's country house, on class excursions and fundraising trips, and in his dormitory bed at night. After that, Father Jo got down to serious buggery.

The nameless one said the kid came to him because he had seen him in church and he wanted somebody to do something.

"Somebody oughtta," said Smudge.

"Yeah, somebody."

34

The biblical injunction "Thou shalt not kill" is one that requires qualification.
— Edward G. Robinson, "The Woman in the Window."

I'm feewing wucky. Again.

No weather report here. No "it was a dark and stormy...," even if it was.

A time to be born, and a time to die; a time to plant, a time to reap that which is planted.

A time to kill, and a time to heal; a time to break down, and a time to build up.

A time to murdelize.

Be werry werry quiet. I'm hunting wabbits.

What is that I see yonder?

Wabbit twacks!

Cue the *Ride of the Valkyrie*: Kill da waaabit, kill da waaabit, kill da waaabit.

I follow the twacks.

Oh, those little sugary zero grams trans fat crumbs of evidence. No doubt about it, he was coming from a Krispy Kreme, a leading branded specialty retailer of premium quality sweet treats, including its signature Hot Original Glazed doughnut that delivers the one-of-a-kind Krispy Kreme taste that people have loved for generations.

A busy, street jammed with pedestrian pedestrians. I can see him a few yards in front of me. He has on one of the Nifty Thrity's balloggans knit headgear resembling a cross between a ball cap and toboggan. And, yes, unbelievably he is wearing the standard uniform of the highly accomplished pedophile—a Burburry's Bonded Fine Stretch Wool Gabardine trenchcoat, presumably with deep pockets known in the trade as pedophile pockets leading directly to the crotch. A handy dandy place in which to stash things such as candy or doughnut holes.

"Hi, little guy. Like to find the candy in my pocket? Dig deep now. And don't be afraid to rummage around down there?"

"Father, you said candy, I don't want a god damn banana!"

"Don't swear. God doesn't like it."

I hang back for several blocks. No need to rush. The status is going to remain quo.

For a second I find myself walking between two men as big as cement trucks. Paranoid? Not me

They walk on. My best guess is that they're going in search of necks.

Meanwhile, Father Bad Touch stops at a 7-Eleven where since 1927 they've been bringing convenience to so many neighborhoods near us.

Oh, thank heaven for 7-Eleven. The only place where you can buy a gallon of Dr Pepper in a single cup or any other unhealthy impulse purchasable item that is legal: beer, tobacco, lottery tickets, tabloids, and high sugar content foods and beverages.

I wait outside the store hoping that he gets out before they get held up. I figure it at a 50-50 proposition.

Oh, my, what is he buying? Yes indeedy, a bite-sized assortment of Tootsie Pop Drops in all five great Tootsie Pop flavors--the totable Tootsie Pop treat without the stick, an implement he will supply later on his own.

Not that it matters a whit, but when he comes out I turn the other way doing my best Sam Spade impression. It seems like the thing to do.

He meandered, I meandered. He stopped, I stopped. He turned the corner. We ended up face to face.

"Hi, I thought that was you," he said.

Apparently my cloak-and-dagger methods were more dagger than cloak.

"Tis I."

"Going my way?"

"Apparently."

So we moseyed past the downtownies and scores of old men looking derelictish in their tattered raincoats.

"If you don't mind my saying," he said, "but you seem ... well, you seem rather more highly educated than most of the ... the ..."

"Sorters?"

"Yes."

"Not really."

"I've heard you talking to ... your friend ..."

"Smudge."

"about ... oh I don't know, things like cosmology and ...

"Actually, cosmogeny."

"What is that? I don't know—"

"The branch of astrophysics that studies the origin, evolution and structure of the universe."

"Really? Does Smudge—?"

"He nods a lot."

"So where did you ... learn all of this."

"I'm a rogue learner."

"Meaning what may I ask?"

"You may."

The long pause that followed needs no explanation. So, for the sake of sanity I eventually jumped into the lacunae unprompted. "Autodidacts who rely on alternate sources for learning, for example online, mentors, self-directed research, school of hard knocks, people who believe that traditional educational institutions do not have a monopoly on education, persons who rely on their own assessment of what is important to learn and source their own education ..."

"Then how did you end up in ... what sent you to prison?"

"A judge."

"No, I mean what did you do that got you jail time?"

"Father Jo, let me ask you a question. Do you think evil is a dark force outside of us that we are all vulnerable to that we must all work to resist?"

"Well ..."

"Or is it inside of us? A stain on what you would consider a soul?"

"Well, what the church teaches—"

"Or is a dysfunction of the brain?"

"is that there are three kinds—physical, moral and metaphysical."

"Or is it just a word we use to distance ourselves from inherently human behavior?"

"I wouldn't say that."

"Do you think religion causes more harm than good?"

"What do you mean?"

"When I hear from people that religion doesn't hurt anything, I say, really? Well besides wars, the Crusades, the Inquisitions, 9-11, ethnic cleansing, the suppression of women, the suppression of homosexuals, fatwas, honor killings, suicide bombings, arranged marriages to minors, human sacrifice, burning witches and systematic sex with children, I have a few little quibbles. And I forgot blowing up girl schools in Afghanistan and shooting cartoonists in Paris. Yeah, I know it isn't the only cause of world violence, but it does rank high on the list. Don't you think?"

"I've really got to go."

"Yeah."

35

--Where do you think our sense of right and wrong comes from?

--A Cracker Jacks box?

--I know you know what you did was wrong.

--Whatever.

--So where did that knowledge come from? Something inside of you. Inherently—

--More bullshit.

--part of all of us.

--That's your bag, not mine.

--My bag?

--A piss poor attitude people put on when they think they're the—

--Here's what I think. I think the human mind has an infinite capacity to make us kind or cruel, caring or indifferent, selfish or generous, and to make some of us villains and to make some of us heroes.

--And I'm the villain?

--Do you think you are?

--Is it either or?

--Villain or hero?

--Yeah.

--Well, I suppose—

--I'm neither.

--there's more to it really.
--Most of us aren't, you know.
--Yeah.
--We just go about our crappy little lives in our crappy little towns in our crappy big country.
--Is that what you really think? Is that all there is—
--I told you, didn't I?
--Is that all there is to it?

36

Did you ever want to forget anything? Did you ever want to cut away a piece of your memory or blot it out? You can't, you know.

— Tom Neal, "Detour."

If that's all there is my friends, then let's keep dancing.
Let's break out the booze and have a ball.
If that's all there is."
"Shuddup, Smudge." Smudge the tuner still ain't no crooner.
"Why? Are you asleep or something?"
"Or something."
"Peggy Lee."
"Except she could sing."
"Must have had your day in mind."
"Except she's dead."
"So?"
"She couldn't have had my day in mind."
"You never know. Maybe she's looking down on you or something."
"Don't bet on it."
"Maybe he is, too."
"Who?"

"Father Jo."

"Go to sleep."

"Can't. Can't stop thinking about it. About what you done."

37

--You think that you're exempt? I'm talking to you. Do you think that you're exempt?

--Do I think that I'm exempt? Exempt from what?

--Mistakes.

--No, I don't think that I'm exempt.

--You know, I think you're hiding something. Lying. I think you're lying. I think you're a liar. You're a liar, aren't you?

--I am.

--Are you lying now?

--I am. I lie to myself all the time. The deal is, though, I never believe me.

38

Don't be too sure I'm as crooked as I'm supposed to be.
— Humphrey Bogart, "The Maltese Falcon."

Meanwhile, back at the ranch I was wrestling with a mind-numbing dilemma: do I put the Tupperware Quick Shake Red Container with other red Tupperware pieces or with other Tupperware container pieces, when the Catholic, crypto-fascist sister came gliding across the floor like an ecclesiastical air hockey puck on a goal-seeking mission.

"It's a goddamned miracle," mumbles Smudge.

"You seen Father Jo?" she asks/demands.

"Many times," I said.

"Recently?"

"Day before yesterday."

"Where was that?"

"Coming out of the Donut dump over on—"

"Talk to him?"

"For a while."

"Did he say anything about not coming in this morning? Because he always comes in Thursday mornings."

"Didn't say."

"Any idea where he might be?"

"Not an idea, no."

(Didn't I say I wasn't a liar?)

"If he comes in, tell him I want to see him."

"If he comes in, I sure will."

"And put the red with the red. Don't you know anything about how we do things here?"

"The light red with the dark red? Or its own category?"

"Don't be an ass."

"OK."

With that she floated back to her lair.

When Father Jo didn't show up at all that week, Detective Edd did. (Full name: Edd Ott. His parents were apparently saving vowels or maybe just letters.)

"Can I talk to you for a minute?" he said adjusting his Genuine Police Sunglasses with gunmetal frames and silvered lenses. (Henceforth and forever he was known as "Shades" to those of us graced by his polarized presence. His parents apparently had them permanently attached to his face since nobody seems to have ever seen him without them.) Said glasses protected his eyes from debris while undoubtedly giving him a sense of peace designed to intimidate others, project detachment and hide emotion. Like a good old friend, a good pair of silvered sunglasses is hard to forget.

"Probably."

He had a face to send shivers down the spine of a 50s casting director--squinty James Dean eyes, dimpled Kirk Douglas chin, ski-jump Bob Hope nose, gap-toothed Ernest Borgnine teeth.

"You know Father Jo, right?"

"Who's asking?"

Without disguising his irritation at the cheeky question, he contemptuously flipped open his id case and stuck it about an inch from my nose.

"In the office."

Honoring his polite invitation, I followed him into the holding cell cum office, where to the grating voice of Nancy Grace, the CNN/HLN carnival barker providing the background audio…

"Father Jo?"

"The priest from the deaf kids' place."

"The same."

Long pause. Then, "He seems to have gone missing.".

As a dedicated peevologist that phrase, "gone missing," pisses me off.

"Gone missing, you say."

"No one has seen him for more than a week."

"What happened to words like 'disappeared,' 'vanished,' 'misplaced,' 'stolen,' 'lost,' 'deserted,' 'absconded?'"

"What?"

"See 'gone missing' has less meaning, or less exact meaning, than any of them. People have become so afraid of expressing meaning. Why is that?"

"Look pal—"

"What's more, 'gone missing' sounds willful or deliberate, and, indeed, sometimes that connotation is accurate, but the person who has been kidnapped is hardly agreeable to having been so."

"Who said anything about kidnapped?"

"I just did."

"I'm talking about Father Jo."

"He's not here."

"I know. That's why I'm here."

"To work with the kids?"

"To find him."

"Oh."

"Do you want to do this downtown?"

"Not particularly."

"Father Jo. I understand you have shown a particular ... interest in him."

Long pause.

"Well?"

"I didn't hear a question."

"How well do you know Father Jo?"

"I know he likes his boys."

"From the deaf school."

"Yes."

"What else?"

"He's partial to trench coats."

"Coats?"

"Burburys. Any time we get one in his size, Sister Sarah makes sure we save it for him. Forty-eight chubby if I recall correctly."

"What else?"

"What else what?"

"Can you tell me about him?" he asks while leaning against a small table not realizing that it's on wheels. The result is a Daffy Duckish moment with Shades going comically sprawling across the cluttered room bringing down an oversized vase of artificial flowers including the splendid and colorful tropical bird of paradise which always looks great mixed in with bouquets, or used as an individual. Neither Nancy nor I laughs. I, for one, hate slapstick. I'd rather have an appendectomy with a rusty spoon than watch the Three Stooges or Charlie Chaplin.

"Where were you?" asks Nancy gracelessly and right on cue as if she were picking up for Shades. "Why aren't you telling us where you were that day?"

I am immediately reminded of a "Sherman's Lagoon" cartoon in which Sherman encounters deep sea vent worms who, when encouraged to act "dumb and scary," do so by doing a Nancy Grace impression.

Meanwhile, Shades seemingly oblivious to his locum tenens relief questioner, does his best to extricate himself from the tangle of stems, bracts, bright yellow and orange elongated petals, and the long extension of the blue tongues that reach well away from the stamens.

Since extraction with dignity is out of the question, he ends up falling back again like a bad party clown.

"You need to explain yourself," demands Nancy with all the intensity Her Naselness can muster.

I suppose I might have helped him up but why spoil the Kodak moment with an act of unsolicited intervention? So I stand there as stone faced as Old Four Eyes on Rushmore while Shades attempts to regain the gravitas he has assigned to this grilling.

Finally: "They ought to put a warning sign on those things."

"Are you hiding something?" asks Nancy.

"Something you're not telling me?" asks Shades brushing the non-existent pollen from his jacket.

"Well, let's see. My life story for one."

"About Father Jo."

"I had a discussion with him maybe a week ago about evil."

"That so?"

"It is."

"Why ... what... what did he have to say about it?"

"He was against it."

"Evil."

"Would a priest lie?"

"I wouldn't think."

"No, you wouldn't."

"Sister Mary tells me—"

"Sarah."

"What?"

"I don't know any Sister Mary."

"Your boss—"

"Sister Sarah."

--tells me you have a record."

Another long pause. "I can look it up you know."

"I'm sure."

"Want to tell me about it now?"

"Not particularly."

"Well, do it anyway."

"An unauthorized bank withdrawal."

"A note job?"

"Had it gotten that far."

"Armed?"

"Knife. But it wasn't very sharp."

"And you got what?"

"Woolworthed."

"Five to 10."

"Early release because I found Christ."

"Did you now?"

"Ask Sister Mary."

"I thought you said her name was Sarah."

"I did, didn't I?"

The stimulating Q & A session continued in a similar if unproductive manner until interrupted by a diminutive swooshing force of dotage, determination, and hair gel known to the sister's peonage as the Bic Bitty who, even though she didn't then and never had smoked, collected cigarette lighters of any and every description and, even though she didn't then and never had gone fishing, collected antique fishing lures.

"Do you mind?" snapped Shades.

"Sometimes," said the Bic Bitty with what appeared to be a non sequitur but maybe wasn't.

"This is a private conversation."

"Oh, I won't tell. I never do."

"A police matter."

"Like on television."

Shades, apparently having met his match adjusted his Ray Bans that didn't need any adjusting and declared in his best Jack Webb meets the Duke voice "OK that will do it for today, but if I have reason to ... think ... I'll be back."

"We close early on Saturdays," I remind him in case he hadn't seen the notice on the door.

"Smart ass," as he left.

"I've got a new lighter. Been saving it for you," I tell the Bic Bitty.

"Oh, goody."

I think I made her day. Goody gumdrops.

"Who was that?" asked Smudge who arrived on the scene as Shades was making his exit.

"A devilishly handsome individual who investigates and ruthlessly abolishes mysteries of all kinds."

"What does that mean?"

"He's a dick. A veritable gumshoe, a hawkshaw."

"What's a hawkshaw?"

"A dick."

"What was he doing here?"

"Detectifying, gathering information necessary to determine the best course of action. From 'detegere,' meaning to uncover and 'fy,' from 'ficere' meaning to do or make."

"Looking for Father Jo?"

"He's gone missing."

"That's a bit careless don't you think?"

"I do, yes."

"The church should be more careful with its property."

39

--What do you feel about the man who died?

--You think I'm a psychopath? (Long pause before resuming.) Jeffrey Dahmer? Ted Bundy? Maybe even Hannibal Lecter?

--Could be.

--Or was Lecter totally schizoid?

--If you mean schizophrenic—

--Yeah.

--that's not the same thing as schizoid. The similarity in name is because they basically mean 'split from society' and 'split up mind' respectively.

--Call somebody something and that's what they are forever. How neat and how ... lazy. You guys all want to do that and I'm fucking sick of it. Oh, he's a psychotic and therefore he will ... go ahead and fill in the blank.

--Look, I don't want to—

--A psychotic will ... what? Tell me. What will a fucking psychotic do? You know. You've got dandy answers. What will a psychotic always do?

--Their hallmark is a stunning lack of conscience.

--So they will always ...?

--Seek self-gratification at the other person's expense.

--Bingo, you've won the day. Now you can go home.

--That's not what I'm—

--You found the label. Congratulations, now you can go ask for a raise. Goodbye, and oh, have a nice day.

--I think I've hit a nerve here. You've been diagnosed before as ...

--Labeled before. You mean labeled.

--You've been labeled with psychopathic ... tendencies. Is that right?

--Or maybe I'm a sociopath.

--You know the difference?

--Yeah, do you?

--Then you've been down this road before.

--Is that a question or an accusation?

--Call it an observation.

--What's the difference?

--Does it matter?

--What's the difference? Let's at least get the labels right.

--Well, off the top of my head, I'd have to say that psychopaths are born with temperamental differences, so they don't internalize social norms. Sociopaths generally have relatively normal temperaments with their personality disorder being more an effect of negative sociological factors like parental neglect, delinquent peers, poverty, and extremely low or extremely high intelligence.

--Nature or nurture then.

--Genetic predispositions or environmental factors. Is that what you're asking?

--I'm not asking anything.

--Well yes, psychopathy leans toward the hereditary whereas sociopathy tends toward the environmental. Happy now?

--Delirious. So which label do you want to pull out of your spiffy detection kit?

--What do you think?

--Oh, please, don't pull that crap on me. What do I think? Who the fuck cares? Because it doesn't matter. Not one bit. We both know that. What matters is what you think and only what you think. So?

--It's not that simple because—

--Psychopath?

--...psychopathy is a syndrome, or more accurately a cluster of related symptoms.

--How about socio-psycho-wackopath?

--Well, that might be accurate in some cases.

--Like mine?

--You tell—

--No, goddamit, you tell me.

--Sociopaths and psychopaths share many traits.

--Try me.

--Disregard for the rights of others—moral or legal.

--And if the laws stink?

--Well, some people would argue for civil disobedience.

--Like Gandhi.

--Martin Luther King, Thoreau—

--I'm a big supporter of animal rights ... except when I'm hungry.

--Another common trait is a failure to feel remorse or guilt.

--I missed the Rauschenberg show and I'm sure as hell guilty about that.

--A disregard for laws and social mores.

--I almost never stop for stop signs on my bike.

--A tendency to display violent behavior and emotional outbursts.

--Goddamn it! Fuck! You've got me there.

--But there are differences. Sociopaths tend to be nervous and easily agitated. Often they're not highly educated and maybe live on the fringes of society unable to hold down a steady job, wandering around a lot. They may have an attachment to a specific group—

--I was thinking of joining the Hell's Angels—

--but usually not much of a regard for society in general.

--or maybe the Black Panthers.

--In the eyes of most people, they're disturbed ... crazy.

--Did I mention I'm a pencil?

--When they commit a crime it's usually spontaneous ... disorganized.

--Psychopaths on the other hand are ...?

--Usually charming. They're manipulative. They gain people's trust easily because they've learned to mimic emotion and to appear "normal" to others. They're often highly educated, hold regular jobs, appear steady enough that most people never notice. When they commit crimes they're carefully planned. Usually anyway. According to some researchers, the etiology of the disorders is different.

--The what?

--Causes.

--I guess I got a lousy education. I'll have to look that one up.

40

Now, do you wanna talk business, or do you wanna play house ...?
— Robert Mitchem, "Out of the Dark."

Cherry came into the schlockatorium looking for ... love in all the wrong places? Nah. She says she was looking for ... drum roll, please ... a grill, a framework of metal bars on which to ... grill things. How prophetic was that? Positively Delphian I tell you.

"May I suggest a George Foreman Grill? We've a special going on at the moment."

"Really."

"But it will only last until our sun goes red giant, so you'll need to get on it soon."

"Soon being ...?"

"Five billion years."

"Or as few as four?"

"Some think, yeah."

"Whoa, I hate that kind of pressure."

Now the thing that immediately impressed me is that Cherry, all 5' of her in Antique Tan Vintage Tony Lama cowboy boots, a Larry Mahan

Milano Cowboy hat and looking as if she just came off the range, seemed to know what a red giant was.

"You know a lot about red giants?"

"I know they're red and they're big," she said but as I was to learn she knew a lot more than that about them.

"Leave your horse tied up outside?" I asked.

With just the hint of a nod she tugged on the bill of her hat Junior Boner like. "Bucephalus."

"Alexander's horse," I said matching her one-for-one in the department of useless ancient history knowledge.

"My motorcycle."

"Ah."

"Never rode a horse in my life. Other than on the Carousel at Central Park."

"New York?"

"Born and bred."

"Doesn't your hat blow off riding a motorcycle?"

"Nope."

"How do you manage that?"

"Don't wear it when I'm riding."

"That could explain it."

"That does explain it."

"Where do you ...?"

"Strap it on the back. Bucephalus is careful with it."

Cherry's hair was cut short, but snaking out from under her hat I could see that it was red ... ish. Simmering red, not flaming.

"In 'The Catcher in the Rye,' Holden Caulfield says that people with red hair are supposed to get mad very easily. Do you think that's so?"

"I know it's so."

"Personal experience?"

"I know that's what Holden says. But he also says his brother Allie had very red hair and he never got angry."

"But he was dead."

"Not because of his hair color. Leukemia."

"In the Middle Ages red hair was thought to be a mark of a beastly sexual desire and moral degeneration."

"One out of two isn't bad."

"Which one is that?"

"I'll never tell. About the grill ..."

"The George Foreman, lean, mean fat reducing grilling machine, in silver. Features grooves sloped to drain away grease and fat, floating hinge to cook varying thicknesses of food, drip tray included, nonstick coated cooking plate, all to ensure your food is ... lean and mean."

"Which is how I like it."

"Except if you bought it, you couldn't possibly carry it on a motorcycle."

"Except if I bought it you could deliver it."

"What if I also rode a motorcycle?"

"You don't."

I took a long look at this little sprightly duelist with her rambling green mesmeric eyes and dangling smile that had to be a skillful proposition. "Your address?"

41

She was playing me with a deck of marked cards and the stakes weren't any blue and yellow chips. They were dynamite.
— Fred MacMurray, "Double Indemnity."

Cherry wasn't really Cherry. She was Belinda. Cherry who was Belinda wasn't from the range. She was, as advertised, from New York. The city. Cherry now lived in an apartment that didn't allow grilling on the deck. Cherry owned a new grill.

"And you wanted a grill because ...?"

"I want to grill things."

"Even though it's against the law or something."

"I'm an outlaw."

"Your hat is white."

"I'm a white-hatted outlaw."

"Are you now?"

Cherry unleashed her tight-lipped crooked Holly Hunter-ish semi-grin that suggested more, but I didn't know what—sort of an enigmatic expression of 'I know but can you guess?'

Her apartment looked far too big, far too well appointed, and far too neat to house someone who shopped at the Nifty Thrifty. Maybe someone who would stoop as low as Crate and Barrel (but certainly not Ikea low).

Would Smudge ever have a field day in here!

No plants.

"I couldn't grow a fern in a swamp," she confesses.

On her marble, or marble-like or marble-ish coffee table was a neat stack of 'New Yorker' Magazines. Now, I'd be willing to wager a week of my meager combat pay that no one who has ever shopped at the Nifty has ever read a single word of the 'New Yorker.' Peeked at a cartoon while waiting at the dentist's office perhaps. ("Peek at" in this context should not be confused with "understood.")

Among a stack of books was Stephen Hawking's "On the Shoulders of Giants," which might have explained the earlier red giant acknowledgement.

Standing in front of a painting of a black X on a white background, Cherry looked absolutely sophisticazzo, as sophisti-sexy as Audrey Hepburn in Tiffanys, even in jeans.

Seldom at a loss for words, the best I can come up with is, "I like your painting."

"Why?"

"It's a ... a ..."

"Black X."

"Very black."

"Turned on by Xs are you?"

"They're very X ... like."

"They are, yes."

"And black."

I was beginning to feel like a babbling idiot failing miserably to untangle the ... tangle. And it was obvious she would neither throw me an instruction sheet nor move on to another subject. I would wallow in the miasma of minimalism until I could come up with a self-extricating explanation or surrender to her superior position. But why would she bother? I'm a minimum wage charity case parolee in a junk shop and she's ... what?

"And very minimalist," I said somewhat recklessly while trying to remember what I could dredge up in my limited memory bank of art terms. Something about fictive in favor of the literal or lack of self-expression but I'm not sure enough to proffer an opinion.

"Very."

"Who's it by?"

"Hobsbawm."

"Ah."

"Know him?"

She's testing me. Why? Maybe she enjoys embarrassing people.

"We've never met."

"But you know of him?"

Trapped. Do I know a Hobsbawm artist? Maybe I should but I don't, so I opt for my seldom-used honest-answer-with-women card.

"Not that I recall," I say while wondering why I'm even caring about this. She's why.

"He's such a jerk."

"Really?"

"Why I threw him out."

"Some particular significance for him...the X? Some symbolism?"

"I asked him that once but like all artists ... most anyway, he was hesitant to say anything. After a little ... enticement, though, he said x was a letter that teaches us to find."

"Find what?"

"The value of x in any equation. Want to stay for lunch? I could grill us some sausages. English Cumberlands. The sausages."

"Well, I should be—"

"The good sister won't mind if you're late will she?"

"Yes."

"Do you care?"

"No."

This little red-haired, minimalist-loving, cosmology-wise horseless New York cowgirl is acting like a clerk flirt, which doesn't make sense, which makes me ...

"Thirsty?"

... curious.

"Help yourself to a beer. There's some in the fridge."

When I open her Bosch Exxcel Undercounter Fridge the perfect choice for anyone looking to declutter their kitchen I find Homer J. Simpson's "cause of and solution to all life's problems!" Beer, but not any beer. A handy six-pack of Duck Rabbit Wee Heavy Scotch Ale Beer.

I'm guessing this is a setup. What else could it possibly be other than that or a compartmentalized serendipity formed by an underlying synchronicity--i.e., a coincidence. $2.65? Wow, what a coincidence. That's exactly what I have in my pocket!

"That's an interesting beer," she calls from the other room. "Ever try it?"

OK, I'll bite. "I have."

"Wow, what a coincidence."

"You're right, it's good."

If I didn't already suspect it, I knew then I would have to be <u>sehr</u> careful with her. But despite the obvious peril there was something alluring about confronting an opponent worthy of the contest, and by all indications, she was just that. After all, watching me fight Muhammad Ali wouldn't sell many tickets, but watching Ali fight Sonny Liston would be worth the price of admission. A contest between equals is always more interesting. It was looking as if her ticket price might be worth it.

"Not too many people know it out here. I think it's from back east someplace."

"Want one?"

"Sure."

I return with two bottles of the rabbits which we clink together in a toast to ...

"What Jesus made when the wine ran out," she says.

"I didn't know that."

"And Jesus touched 12 more vessels of water and behold, they turned into clear, golden beer."

"Proof that God loves us and wants us to be happy?"

"Helping white people dance since the 1600s."

"I don't dance."

"Neither do I"

She's got a decided hitch in her giddyup which she notices me noticing.

"Afghanistan," she says.

"What?" I say, pretending not to notice that she noticed me noticing.

"The leg. A wound from Afghanistan."

"What in the world were you ...?"

"The Marine Corps."

"I didn't realize—"

"Since 1918." She'd obviously been down this chauvinistic road before.

"Land of the free, home of the brave. The few, the proud."

"What did you do in the Corps?"

"Looked for bad guys."

"Find any?"

"Oh, yeah. I'm real good at that."

"What is it you do now exactly?"

"I'm not that precise."

"What?"

"I look for people."

"Do you?"

"Often."

"What do you mean?"

"I'm a private detective."

You're not!"

"And all this time I thought I was."

"A private detective? Not exactly Miss Marple ... or Angela Fletcher ... or Nancy Drew," I say quickly exhausting my memory stack of private chick dicks.

"I'm good at it, too."

"I bet."

"How much?"

"What?"

"Do you want to bet that I'm good?"

"It's just an expression of—"

"Ten bucks says I've found the guy I'm looking for right now."

"Who's that?"

"You."

42

when they tolded me i could join the guys in iraq i was a happy camper cos this jarhead didnt want no part of gitmo no way and then when i got in iraq and they throwed me on that truck to go out to bombaconda i was finally a real marine. semper fi the few the proud. i couldnt wait to go full battle rattle against them ragheads.

43

She was worth a stare. She was trouble.
— Humphrey Bogart, "The Big Sleep."

The situation was surreal, and I don't mean as in a surreal arithmetic continuum containing the real numbers as well as infinite and infinitesimal numbers, but rather a surreal comedy based on violations of causal reasoning with events and behaviors that are logically incongruent.

Maybe we're really in a virtual Monty Pythonish sketch involving bizarre juxtapositions, irrational situations, and other weird displays and scenes of nonsense. A Lewis Carrollinian world where Magritte meets Bunuel meets Dali meets Artaud meets Cherry.

Why did the elephant sit on the marshmallow? Because he didn't want to fall into the cup of hot chocolate.

"About my brother."

"Your brother?"

"Father Jo."

"I didn't know he had ... has a family?"

"Imagine that."

"Who wouldda thunk?"

"I know that you know where he is."

"No, you don't. You think I know where he is. Thinking and knowing—not the same things."

"Am I wrong?"

"About thinking that you know? I don't know."

This cunning bucket of contradictions urban cowgirl/private dick/marine was testing me, challenging me to a duel, an *affaire d'honneur* to see if I would pick up my noetic sword.

I imagine a slap with glove.

What? I demand satisfaction, sir!

Let us duel. What shall be your weapon of choice?

Nerves.

Strap-on!

Ok ...

I involuntarily grinned.

She grinned back, albeit crookedly. I'm still not exactly sure what that grin signifies but I damn well know it was still a loaded grin ready for ... something.

"Maybe you could set up the grill while I get the sausages ready," she says leaving the grin hanging in existential space. A tease with a promise of more to come.

If she's expecting me to fold like an origami bird ... But she isn't, of course. She knows I'm battle rattle ready. She must.

I am inextricably drawn to her for reasons that are inextricable.

Lunch proceeds like a scene from a civilized-to-the-edge-of a mind-numbing Merchant Ivory movie with a pre-Hannibal Lechter Tony Hopkins and a post Nanny McPhee Em Thompson mixed with pregnant Pinter pauses.

"There's a lot of skullduggery in the world these days. Am I right?"

Pause.

"Indeed."

Pause.

"Not like in the old days."

Pause.

"Perhaps not."
Pause.
"I'd say definitely not."
Pause.
"You're probably right."
Pause.
"Would you like another sausage?"
Nary another mention of her detectification quest but her Pinteresque jousts probed loudly and often in the unspoken dialogue. I, however, could and did match her pause, for pause, subtext for subtext, enigmatical gaze for enigmatical gaze. Steve McQueen playing chess with Faye Dunaway.
"Working at the thrift store must have its benefits."
"Such as?"
Pause probably pregnant.
"Meeting lots of new people. Interesting people."
"Some are."
"And some aren't. I know what you mean. It's not exactly in the best of neighborhoods. Probably lots of disreputable people down there. Druggies, rapists, murderers."
"But you could find those anyplace now, couldn't you?
Pause definitely pregnant.
"I could make some coffee. Would you like some coffee?"
"I'll have to get back to the Nifty, so I don't think I can—"
"Got you on a short leash, does she?"
"You know the good sister."
"I don't actually."
"You're missing a great treat."
"I'll pass."
"I can assure you."
"Y'all come back and see me now won't ya? I'll leave the light on for you."

44

I don't go soft for nobody.
— Alan Ladd, "This Gun for Hire."

I was more than an hour late returning to the bench where I was the incumbent sortermeister, an entrance not missed by the straw boss herself.

Like Bugs Bunny with smoke steaming from pointy ears, she bellowed, "Where the hell have you been?"

"Helping a customer set up a grill she bought here."

"Do you think we're the Geek Squad?"

"Maybe just a little geeky."

"I know what you've been up to. Don't think I don't." Sister Sarah's eyes were getting beadier and beadier. "Having a relationship with Jesus does not make you perfect because you will still sin, but believing will bring you the truth. Trusting in God is the only real answer to freedom from condemnation and from being controlled by guilty feelings."

"Guilty feelings?"

"You can't expect to take two hours for lunch and not face the consequences. I'll have to report this to your parole officer."

"Check the dive bars."

"And clean the rest rooms good."

She had obviously seen "Platoon."

"Today and every day."

"Do you have a toothbrush I could borrow?"

"Toothbrush? What are you talking about?"

"So I can get into those little cracks in the tiles. Those suckers are hard to get—"

Sister Sarah stormed away like she was auditioning for "The Wicked Nun," meets "The Vengeance of Achilles" on a bad hair day.

"clean."

45

--Let's talk about guilt.

--Yours or mine?

--In general.

--Like corporate CEOs?

--What do you mean?

--Assholes who don't give a shit about anybody or anything other than their own power, money, prestige. Everybody else is a victim to them. I'm right, aren't I?

--It's hard to argue the point.

--Most really successful CEOs are psychopaths.

--I don't know about most.

--How about this: A factory in a southern town makes ... I don't know, toasters or ashtrays or some widget essential for civilized life and everybody in the town is dependent on the factory for their lives, as shitty as they may be. I mean they nine to five it there for years sweating it out for the gold watch. Then this asshole CEO comes in and closes the factory because he can get his widgets made for less in some fourth world warlord-controlled Asian shithole. He doesn't give a damn about the people in the southern town. Doesn't lose a second of sleep. Loves himself all the more because he can do this without remorse. Where do you put him on your handy-dandy empathy scale?

--Probably near the end ... the bottom part.

--And he's a ...

--Psychopath? Is that what you're saying?

--You tell me.

--I guess he could be.

--Explain that. Tell me how ... why that happens.

--Well, they're social predators who charm ... manipulate their way through life, usually leaving a broad trail of broken hearts, shattered expectations ...

--No conscience.

--And empty empathy wallets. No ... no feelings for others. They take whatever the hell they want and do as they please.

--You mean I could be a CEO? Make a few million, or billion?

--The man you killed, do you feel bad for him ... or maybe for his family?

--Nope.

--Not even a little?

--Nope.

--No remorse ... regret?

--Not a widget's worth.

--I don't believe you.

--So you really want to know if I'm a psychopath or a sociopath or even a psychotic.

--How are you so up on these things? Why do you...?

--I pay attention in class. You want to know if I understand the difference between right and wrong.

--Do you?

--Yeah, I'm right and you're wrong.

--About what?

--Oh, I don't know. Everything. Who should be president. The nature of existence. McDonalds or Burger King? Does she or doesn't she?

--I mean in the moral sense. Right and wrong.

--Like from religious instruction?

--Could be.

--Or parental teaching.

--But not necessarily.

--Is that so?

--It's a hypothesis.

--You mean a guess by someone with a Ph.D.

--I was thinking more along the lines of a prediction based on current evidence that is yet to be tested.

--That's what I said—a guess.

--An educated guess.

--A guess is a guess is a guess. Gertrude Stein.

--It's my belief ... my hypothesis ... my educated guess ... that people possess a moral grammar wired into their neural circuits by evolution.

--Psychobable.

--Well, the roots of human morality are clearly evident in certain social animals like apes and monkeys where the animals' feelings of empathy and expectations of reciprocity are essential to their group living. So we might consider that a counterpart of human morality and with that comes the idea that parents and teachers don't teach us the rules of correct behavior from scratch but are, at best, giving shape to...well, to natural behavior ... to innate behavior. And it suggests that religions are not the source of moral codes but, rather, social enforcers of instinctive moral behavior. Look, both atheists and people belonging to a wide range of faiths make the same moral judgments—

--Yeah?

--implying that the system that unconsciously generates moral judgments is immune to religious doctrine.

--And you come up with this because...?

--The quick decisions that must be made in life-or-death decisions are inaccessible to the conscious mind. They're generated subconsciously.

--Oh, you mean decisions like throwing a railroad switch.

--For one.

--Or not.

--Yeah.

--So what's up Doc? My grammar go missing someplace?

--I'm not—

--Neurons got scrambled or something?

--The grammar, it's a system for generating moral behavior, not a list of specific rules. It limits human behavior so tightly that many rules are in fact the same ... or at least very similar in every society. Do onto others—

--Or screw others as they screw you.

--avoid adultery, incest and pedophilia—

--Unless you're a man of the cloth.

--don't cheat, steal or lie.

--Unless you're a politician or banker.

--Don't kill.

--Unless your government or religion OKs it.

46

In the heat of action men are likely to forget where their best interests lie and let their emotions carry them away.
— Sidney Greenstreet, "The Maltese Falcon."

Back at the apartment I found Smudge sitting on Tommy the Tank. "How'd it go with the cowgirl? he asked. Get any ... ?"

"Sausage."

"Her or you?"

"Me."

"A drag, man. She's foxy."

"You don't know the half of it."

"Should I?"

"I don't know about 'shoulds.'"

"A thought just crossed my mind."

"It must've been a long and lonely journey."

Without hesitation Smudge continues, he being sarcasm proof. "She have a piano?"

"Not in her apartment anyway."

"Some nice things, though? In her apartment."

"Minimalist art."

"That worth anything?"

"Depends who you ask."

"You for instance."

"How does a black X on a white background strike you?"

"Stupid."

"Then you probably wouldn't pay much for it."

"But somebody else would?"

"Could be."

"Really stupid. Is that supposed to be art or something?"

"It's not supposed to be anything. It is what it is."

"What is it?"

"Modern art."

"Stupid art."

"If you can hang it on a wall it's a painting. If you can walk around it, it's a sculpture."

"How much do you think I could get for it?"

"Probably 10 years."

I couldn't get the thought of cheeky Cherry out of my mind. I didn't know if that was because I was concerned or intrigued, with intrigued getting most of my attention. She was, to further abuse a much abused and helpless term, "charismatic" in the gift of grace sense that inspires the devotion of others but stops far short of theological "charism" or the miraculous power of healing, speaking foreign languages without instruction, or similar miracles attributed to many early Christians.

Was I a moth flying too close to the fire? The thought did arise, but oh, was I ever up for the challenge. My life had become duller than a Sandra Bullock self-produced comedy and I was wallowing in a slump duck like numbness that needed to be attacked head on by a ... challenge.

Bring it on, Cherry. Scare the crap out of me if you can. Shake me out of my ennui, deliver me from my butt-clinching boredom, strike at the heart of the Nifty's tedium, send the ol' slump duck simpering.

With the insight of hindsight I realize that I was prone, as the French say, "to that awful yawn which sleep cannot abate," although not yet ready to off myself as that archetypal cad, the actor Georgie Sanders did, leaving a note saying, "Dear World, I am leaving because I am bored."

Actually I was bored enough that in my extensive free time I was memorizing pi, about as useless an undertaking as exists short of watching Fox News.

I didn't know what game Cherry was playing, what the rules were, how a winner would be chosen, but I knew it was closer to Clue than Parcheesi. And I really didn't know what the winner gets, but I was betting it was not an Amana Frost Freeze. The bigger question, though, was what the consequences would be for the loser. Perhaps a place where you get poked with pitchforks by horn-topped goatlegged red men and listen to the Village People sing for the rest of eternity. Or maybe Neil Diamond.

> *She got the way to move me, Cherry*
> *She got the way to groove me*
> *She got the way to move me*
> *She got the way to groove me.*

47

You tell me the story of your life and maybe I can suggest a happy ending.
— John Garfield, "Force of Evil."

So when Cherry came into the Nifty again ostensibly looking for a set of barbecue tools ...

"We just happen to have a nice set of stainless steel tools including a '3-In-1' spatula, tongs, fork, knife, basting brush, grill brush, four skewers, and eight corn holders in a durable plastic case."

"I want to make sure the basting brush is good."

"Only the best."

"Because I'm a wicked baster."

"I'm a son of a baster myself."

"Come for dinner tonight. We can baste away."

I did both the dinner and the basting.

All evening she danced on and around the subject of my brother the father like Martha Graham on speed.

"We grew up in a posh upper east side New York apartment," she says, "complete with door man, elevator, part-time maid/cook, and stuffy neighbors."

"What does your father do?"

"He's a professional thief."

"Really?"

"Euphemistically an 'investment adviser.' Mostly he advises rich people to make investments, most of which ends up in his pockets. My mother stays home and counts the money."

"I guess someone has to."

"If not, you wouldn't know how much money you had, now would you?

"Not likely."

"He reveled in the junk bond mess like a pig in a mud hole, took bond mail to the level of fine art. His specialty was going into the market, buying a bunch of distressed bonds and then telling the issuer to pay up or he'd force them into bankruptcy after which they'd lose the company. A tough and mean guy."

"Or psychopathic."

"Could be."

She says that when they "played in the yard," it meant Central Park.

She says they sometimes hocked candy bars from the nearby Gristede's Market but that's the worst thing they ever did.

She says they went to private schools in Manhattan.

The "they" in all this apparently was Cherry and her brother, Joe.

He went to the Browning School, St. John's University, and a Jesuit School of Theology; she to the Chapin School, The City University of New York's John Jay College of Criminal Justice, and Parris Island.

"Parris Island!"

"I always wanted to go to Paris. Spelling was never my strong point."

"Ah, but for an 'r.'"

"How did you ... what made you go into the Corps?"

"We were rebels, me and my brother. We weren't Catholic and we weren't military, but we saw ... opportunities. He in the church, me in the service."

"Ever kill anybody?"

"Except we never called it that."

"In Afghanistan you never had to ..."

"No."

"Don't you?"

"We don't do those sorts of things."

"The Marines?"

"Wasted a couple. Eliminated, removed, dispatched, disposed of a few, but kill? Never."

"And the bombings?"

"Clean surgical strikes"

"Civilian deaths?"

"Collateral damage."

"Label it and it becomes so."

"Absolutely."

"I didn't know women actually carried weapons and actually got involved in the actual fighting."

"You think we did the washing—

"No I—

"and cooking for the men?"

"I guess I ... didn't know what you did."

"I carried an M249 Squad Automatic Weapon that everyone just called the SAW. But that wasn't why we were there. Most of us were sent over because they were having to body search a lot of the local women because the Taliban were using the women to move around ammunition and weapons underneath their burqas. They couldn't go to school but they could carry weapons, and sometimes suicide bombs. You figure that one out. Anyway, it would have been Armageddon if the men body-searched Muslim women. They were no-look, no-touch, so it was our job to do the searches. But with no clear front lines we were in harm's way much of the time anyway and it isn't only men who can pull a trigger. Know what I mean?

"Yeah."

"Doesn't take a man."

"Yeah."

"Ever do that?"

"Pull a trigger?"

"Feel that power."

"I used to hunt. As a kid. Rabbits mostly."

"Take a life."

"Just rabbits."

"That's all?"

"That's worth talking about."

"Then you've missed out on one of life's great pleasures."

"Poor me."

"You know, men and women go to war for all sorts of reasons, but they only admit to one. Oh, they find different ways of wording it: they want to do something for their country, they want to give something back, they want to make a difference. That's unadulterated crap and we all know it. Some go because they don't fit in back at home, some because they're bored, some because they come from military families so they're expected to go and they don't want to disappoint their families— usually their father. Some are running away from something. A broken relationship maybe. Some can't find another job. Some are drawn to the comradery of a military group. Some because of peer group pressure; some because they've seen too many old war movies where the soldiers are treated as real heroes. Some because their testosterone level is off the charts, and some, well, they get their jollies by killing. Know what I mean?"

"Jollies. Yeah."

"They love the smell of blood just so long as it's somebody else's. I saw a lot of it. In Afghanistan you could shoot ragheads all day and not only wouldn't you get in trouble, you'd get prizes for it, high fives, respect, maybe a medal to take home. Kill a camel jockey booger-eater, win a kewpie doll. And it's cool because following orders takes the responsibility of killing off the killer's shoulders and places it on a higher authority.

"And you? You like the smell of blood?"

"I do. Don't you? Doesn't everybody?"

"I don't know."

"Sure you do."

"Think so?"

"Well, here's the real skinny. Every combat soldier knows it but they seldom talk about it: kicking ass and wasting the bad guys can be a lot of fun, and I mean real fun, kickass fun. Like a narcotic high, a liberating feeling. The context of battle, brothers and sisters in arms. There's something positively basic about it. Elemental, pure from within our natures. We are, and always have been a violent species. Why do you think "news" programs love battle footage? So people vegging out on their sofas can share the joy by proxy. There is a thrill to the kill. Know what I mean?"

"I suppose."

"Sure you do."

"Because you know."

"Survival of the fittest isn't it? Our ancestors, going way the hell back, survived only because they killed off threats to them, human and otherwise. They killed to eat. They killed to survive. And if they didn't? Well, they ... didn't survive, and we wouldn't be here today. Our ancestors were the good killers. The lousy ones didn't make it. Killing is in our genes. Deny it and we aren't being true to our nature. We're killing machines."

"You enjoyed it then, the ... wasting?"

"Yeah, I enjoyed it. It's good fun. Let's you know you're alive. Oh, and I wouldn't be afraid of doing it again ... for good cause, of course."

"Of course."

"Say revenge. Or should it be 'avenge.' I sometimes get the two mixed up. Let's see, as I recall, both avenge and revenge can be used as transitive verbs with reflexive pronouns. That's right, isn't it?"

"Well, I don't—"

"But I guess revenge is the more common—"

"Yeah."

"usage. Not only repaying a wrong but getting justice on somebody else's behalf to repay that wrong. That would be like getting even with an adversary by, you know, inflicting punishment or harm. Something like that. Avenge maybe is more like not only repaying a wrong but getting justice on somebody else's behalf as a remedy for that wrong. What do you think?"

"I hadn't really given it a lot ... considered the—"

"It's kind of a fine distinction though, isn't it? Probably doesn't amount to much."

"You obviously have given this some thought."

"Too much free time I suppose. You know how it is. The mind wanders a bit."

"Boredom, yeah."

"Avenge, revenge, retaliate ... all in the name of ... some cause we say is better than their cause," says Cherry between swigs. "I saw my share. Did my share."

"In Afghanistan?"

"Yeah."

"Nasty place I hear."

"The Afghanis seem to like it well enough."

"But not a Manhattan cowgirl."

"It was a screwed up time made worse by some screwed up brass. FUBAR—all fucked up beyond repair ... reason, recognition. A lot of times at a higher ... maybe even, you know, higher than battalion. They set these timelines and we all felt we had to stick to these timelines cos ... well, because that's the military way of doing things even if there's no ... there's no intel driving it. There's no ... you know, there's no events driving it. It's just a damned timeline, and we felt we had to stick with it, and that's what drives that kind of stuff."

"A bureaucratic fixation on meeting arbitrary deadlines."

"We called it 'bullshit.'

"Only fools and horses ..."

"Missions just had to be checked off a list so they could be tallied as 'accomplished,' because the idiot Secretary of Defense, Rumsfeld, was obsessed with achieving positive 'metrics,' that could be trotted out to show that his private war on global terrorism was making progress."

"Was it?"

"Who the fuck knows?"

"But you had to give that illusion."

"Illusions are everything ... in the military. They're everything."

"Illusions, yeah."

"Tell me at least you were afraid ...had moments when you were afraid."

"You know what they say about Marines—that if you try to kill us, we'll just go to hell and regroup."

"Who says that?"

"I heard it in some movie."

"I suppose we could test it."

"Here's a bedtime story."

"I'm not very tired."

"Once upon a time I was in a Humvee driving through some narrows," says Cherry who was Belinda, her voice tightening with increasing anger, "on the way to a village called ... called ... I don't remember, but we were going to check out a report that some of the women there were moving weapons for the Haji under their long dresses. Anyway, we were just about to exit the narrows when we ran into one hell of a firefight. The first thing we noticed was a Humvee in front of us shooting up the hillside and someone shouting, 'Those are friendlies up there! Those are friendlies!' I look up and I see dudes waving on the high ground. And I'm sorry, but they were pretty obvious. It was getting dark, yeah, but it wasn't *that* dark. They were ours, but the guys in the Humvee were going nutzoid on the dudes up on the hill. Firing like they were possessed or something. Lighting up the hill. And let me tell you, there were no Taliban around. None."

"The guy manning the SAW was a little Oakie named Roscoe. I can't say I knew him but I'd seen him around some. Not the brightest bulb in the pack. He was always talking big but as far as I could tell not doing anything to prove it. An insecure twerp who had a twin brother who was if anything, even twerpier. Anyway, he was firing nonstop up the hill."

"Twin twerps?"

"Double trouble."

Now she really has my attention. Coincidence, or trap? Either way, I'm in too deep to stop playing now. I do my best to appear as unruffled as Cary Grant on a first date.

"I tried to stop the little shithead. I'm shouting at him. I mean I'm really shouting and you may have noticed, I've got a voice. I'm yelling at him to put his gun down. Finally I scream, 'Put the goddamned gun down or I'll blow your fuckin' head off.' But he doesn't stop, so I fire a couple of rounds over his head and I mean barely over his head. If he had thicker soles on his shoes, I would have nailed him good. But he doesn't stop. So I fired another two rounds. The Okie wheels around and fires at me. Hits me in the leg and I go down on the spot like a sack of … something. What everybody else in our truck was doing was … I don't know what. My leg was bleeding but with all the chaos going on nobody, including me, gave it much attention. We could hear screaming, 'Oh my fucking god! Oh my fucking god! Oh my fucking god!' I didn't know who it was but guys were rushing up to where the screaming was coming from. I followed as best as I could. There was a Marine there kneeling next to one of the guys who got hit. He was in a state of utter terror … crying, drenched in blood and spattered with splinters of bone and bits of brain matter. It was our guys who did it! They fucking killed him. The pain in my leg began to register and I hit the dirt again. After a while somebody helped me down the hill and drove me back to camp."

"Jesus."

"Later I heard the last words the guy who was killed spoke were to a nearby soldier who was lying on the ground crying out to God for help. 'Would you shut your fucking mouth?' the guy yelled. 'God's not going to help you. You need to do something for yourself, you sniveling moron.' I guess he wasn't real popular with some in his unit."

"Maybe none of them."

"He had a close friend up in the rocks next to him. I don't know about—"

"Friends of a feather."

"Could be. Then when they were lowering the body down the hillside on a stretcher, he became unpackaged and the body with most of the head missing slid down on top of a soldier who became unglued. I mean really freaked out big time. Wouldn't have happened to you though, would it?"

"Being hit by a semi-decapitated body?"

"Or ever seeing one."

"Not likely."

"Because you've seen a lot of bodies in your time?"

"A few."

"With their brains blown out?"

"Not that I can recall."

"Which you would certainly have remembered had you seen one."

"You would think."

"I certainly would."

"And that's the story of my lame left leg."

"And I'm all the better for it … for knowing it."

"Really, why is that?"

"I don't know. I just sort of … said it."

Cherry settled into her couch like—and I don't know a better way to say it—like she was coming on to me. Like she was ready to play that ever popular party game, comeoniwannalayya. Me. I wouldn't exactly say I'm as ugly as a sack full of assholes, but neither is anyone going to mistake me for any of the Ryans— Phillippe, Goslin or Reynolds or the Hughs— Jackman, Grant or Dancy. Could she really be that obvious?

"What if I killed the guy who killed the guy?" she asks without losing her pixie-ish position. "I could have. I was in position."

"But you didn't … did you?"

"Nah."

"What happened to the…?"

"Brushed under the carpet probably. The military way. I don't know for sure but I wouldn't be surprised."

"No, I wouldn't either."

"But do you think I would have been justified in taking him out?"

"Do you mean do I think murder is ever justified?"

"Do you?"

"What are you really asking?"

"I think you know."

"Just a question: which gives the hound greater pleasure, the chase or the kill?"

"Oh, I'd say the kill. Definitely the kill."

"I think I should leave now."

"Past you bedtime?"

"Past something anyway."

48

i seen a lot over there in the sandbox. i seen things nobody should see on account of i was there. i seen lots of ragheads killed and some of them small kids to and lots of women. there aint a day go by i dont think of them days and the greef we caused. i even seen jarheads killing jarheads. see they said we was fighting against the bad guys but that's not really how it was. i dont like this at all but i got to say that this world is filled with bad ass people. anyways thats what i think. fubar.

49

--Let me tell you a story.

--I'm all ears.

--A true story. Once upon a once, with a crew of four on board, a British yacht set sail for a journey to Australia. However, before they could round the cape the yacht capsized, sank, and the crew was left floating in a small lifeboat. So for something like 18 days they drifted around the ocean a thousand miles or so from any land. Their food and water ran out. They were, to say the least, in lousy shape and …well, desperate. The worst of them, though, was a 17-year-old cabin boy who was drifting in and out of consciousness. So the captain of the ship comes up with a plan that if no vessel was sighted by the next morning, they would draw lots to select one of them to be killed so that they could use the body for food and the blood for liquid. One of the crew objected and the boy, well, he wasn't consulted. Wasn't able to be consulted. On the next morning there was no rescue vessel in sight and the boy was then lying at the bottom of the boat quite helpless, and extremely weakened by famine and by drinking sea water, and unable to offer any resistance. One of the crew offered a prayer asking forgiveness for them all and then went to the boy, and told him that his time had come, put a knife into his throat and killed him then and there. The three men then fed on the boy's body and blood. Four days later they were rescued by a passing ship. They were alive—barely. They genuinely believed that the boy would likely have died regardless of what happened, and that all of them would have died if he was not sacrificed.

--And the question is were they were morally justified in killing him?

--Lots of killing is justified. I mean we justify it anyway—capital punishment, euthanasia, abortion, war. A surgeon separating conjoined twins killing the weaker to save the other. To protect one's life and limb, or the national interest, or if somebody says God commands it. Murder is justified if we say it's justified.

--Was yours?

--I say it was.

--Do you think anyone else would?

--If they knew.

50

--I'm a postmodernist.

--That so? --It is so.

--I thought you didn't like labels. OK, I'll bite, what is it?

--Postmodernism?

--Yeah.

--A cow.

--Really?

--Because everything you say about postmodernism is encompassed by it.

--In other words artsy-fartsy stuff.

-- It is my ardent belief that the postmodern contemporary quasi-political agenda of corrupt governmental authority has positively altered the postmodern macroeconomic state of affairs postmodernly.

--Is that supposed to mean something?

--Beats me.

--In other words, artsy-fartsy—

--The idea that there is no objective meaning, only subjective meaning, the meaning one brings to a thing, irrespective of the intent of the author, artist or of reality.

--That's the kind of art you do?

--Art that is aware of the fact that it is in fact art.

--Can we get back to the … the issue we're talking about?

--I'm sure we can.

51

You can't just go round killing people whenever the notion strikes you. It's not feasible.
— Elisha Cook, Jr., "Born to Kill."

Here's the skinny, Minnie. Something is wrong only if we decide it is wrong. Eating your enemies for example. The bible is full of lines like, "You will eat the flesh of your sons and the flesh of your daughters." I don't know how many times the Bible says that or something very like that, but it's a bunch. That, courtesy of Padre Dick. OK, these verses do not exactly say. "Eat your sons and daughters. Here are some recipes." Still there is a commandment that says thou shall not covet thy neighbor's donkey, but not one that says thou shall not eat him.

In some societies cannibalism is the cultural norm. Eat someone else before they eat you. The Asmat for example. The guys who ate the Rockefeller kid. Michael. He of one of the most obscenely powerful families in the history of the universe begun by his great-grandfather, once the wealthiest man on the planet, or so it was claimed by money list people. He was related to the John D. Rockefellers I, II, III, IV, V and VI, the family having more money than imagination. His father had bought the governorship of New York when, in 1961, Michael disappeared. He had been on an expedition to the Asmat region of southwestern Netherlands New Guinea looking for tribal art when he found a bunch of hungry natives instead.

The goryless details. He was trying to swim ashore when his boat capsized. Oh look, there are friendly natives waiting for me on the shore. Oh, look again, they're hungry natives and their golden arches just ran out of Big Macs, the two all-beef patties, special sauce, lettuce, cheese, pickles, onions on a sesame bun.

The Asmat knew what they were doing, had done it dozens of times before, were following sacred rules that prescribed every step, rules that defined them, made them men, made them whole. They took Mikey's power, became him, restored balance to the world.

Directions for preparing oysters Rockefeller: Insert spear into chest, push head back until vertebrae cracks, make deep cut from anus to neck through one side of collarbone to throat and down other side, twist arms and legs and cut them off, pull out entrails, place pieces of meat in fire to roast. When fully charred, pull legs and arms out of fire, tear meat off bones and mix with sago. Hold head over fire long enough to scorch hair and then mix with saved blood. Smear mixture over bodies of celebrants. Shake brains into leaf of palm, scrape inside skull with knife to get every last morsel, mix it with sago, wrap leaf up and roast on fire.

Pairs well with cheap Chianti.

Sacred violence.

Ask any of the Asmats if they'd done anything wrong. No siree bob. Not if the meat comes from another tribe. We wouldn't munch on someone from our own tribe, of course, but anyone else is fair game. Isn't that what's done everywhere? OK, maybe the recipe changes from time to time, but it's always what we've done.

52

She had warmth, vitality. She had authentic magnetism.
— Clifton Webb, "Laura."

You need to get the fuck out of here," says Smudge looking up from the un-hallmarked silver salver he was polishing before dispatching it to My Mother the Fence. "You need to skirt out before ..."

"Why, because you've got somebody coming over?"

"I mean for good. That titless phony cowgirl, she knows man, knows what you done."

"She doesn't know."

"You're not falling for her act are you?"

"No, no, hell no."

"Because she's—"

"I know what she is."

"Sure don't seem like it."

"Vixious."

"Say what?"

"Part vixen part vicious."

"She's got you on a string."

"And what am I?"

"An asshole?"

"Other than that?"

"I don't know. What?"

"A puppet master. I can play her, too."

"She scares me."

"So does your mother."

"That's different."

Sure, I could Richard Kimble it and go search for a one-armed man but that's too much like work. Too many sweaty runs across rickety trestles. I could play Buttons the Clown and hide in the greatest show on earth but I'm allergic to grease paint.

If my brothers could disappear with nary a trace why couldn't I? A rhetorical question if ever there was one. After all, it's not like it hasn't been done large. In 119 the Ninth Roman Legion composed of six thousand men marched off to subdue a confederacy of tribes in northern Britain and disappeared without a proverbial trace although had Steve McQueen's Papa Thorson been on the case, traces, (not to mention bodies) might have been found.

Add that to the list of useless information at my beck if not call.

And this: During the Gallipoli campaign in World War I, the British First-Fifth Norfolk Regiment under Col. Sir Horace Beauchamp pursued the enemy through forest territory and disappeared as traceless as the Roman guys. The regiment was composed of 250 soldiers and 16 officers. Their strange story was reported in an eyewitness account by General Ian somebody in a dispatch to War Secretary Kitchener claiming that the men marched into a huge cloud but when the cloud lifted the men had disappeared. And generals are by dint of authority, eminently trustable fellows proclaimeth the army.

Nah, what's the fun in running? You've always got your back to what's chasing and as Satch said, don't look back, something may be gaining on you and you'll never get away with it.

53

--Did you think you could get away with it--

--Furthest thing from my mind.

--that nobody would—?

--Or should that be "farthest?"

--I don't...look, who cares?

--Well, my English prof for one.

--You didn't think people would be looking for you? The police...

--It's like "less," and "fewer. So many people use "less" when they mean "fewer."

--That so?

--In my experience.

--When you left the scene ... what were you ... what did you think would happen? That you'd just walk into the sunset and nobody would be the wiser?

--They do in the movies.

--Which, as you damn well know, isn't life.

--Now you tell me.

--Not real life.

--I suspected as much when I realized it didn't come with popcorn.

--OK, so I can understand what you're doing with your smart-aleky, defensive, I-don't-really-give-a shit attitude. I understand that. I can see that, but sooner or later you're going to have to come to grips with reality. At some point you're going to have to face it whether it's here with me now, or with me later, or, I don't know, with someone else you're going to have to, and let me rest assure you—

--That you're the guy? My priest in the confessional. That somehow if I tell you everything, I'll have my sorry ass saved.

--It's not like that.

--Please Father, forgive me. There, I'm all better now.

--There's value in genuinely understanding what you did was wrong and being sorry that it happened.

--And if I do, what does it get me?

--A start. But I said "genuinely" and that means no remorse or regret just because you were caught, and it means no feigned remorse just to avoid punishment.

--So you want me to say what I did was wrong, I know it was wrong, and I'm sorry?

--Sometimes it's tough to tell genuine remorse from talented pretending.

--Except you're the professional, so you can?

--Let's just say I have experience. I know the pattern ... the signs.

--A body language expert.

--It's much more than that, it's ... well, you tell me. Tell me you regret your actions. That's the first step.

--Yeah? What's the second?

--Repentance.

--Like, self-flagellation?

--Like apologizing to the person wronged.

--Except in this case ... he's doornail dead.

--Obviously. I think it is a very real question whether forgiveness can be given in such cases, even by ... I don't know, some Almighty—

--You're kidding, right?

--Do I look like I'm kidding?"

--Actually I wouldn't know what you look like when you're kidding, never having seen you kid.

--I'm very serious.

--Let's just keep your imaginary buddies out of this.

--Look, if there's any forgiveness to be had in this case the regret has to be genuine.

--Like the priest who immediately says he forgives his killer as the killer is plunging the knife into him with no hesitation about doing it?

--No. He's ignoring the crime, not forgiving it. The priest can say he is forgiving but that's like saying you will call every loss in baseball a real victory.

--Calling something something else does not make it so.

--Think about it.

--'Forgiveness,' now that's a rather elastic word, isn't it?

--Depends on how you—

--But sometimes it's justified.

--What's justified?

--Taking someone's life.

--Like in war, or the death penalty, or ...?

--Think Bronson and Eastwood here. "Death Wish," Dirty Harry." They off the bad guys because they really are bad. These guys enjoy it, they register zilch on the regret meter and they're about as far away from an apology as ... say me from you, and half the time they're even trying to ply their evil on Charlie and Clint themselves. See, the bad guys show no reasons why they should be forgiven ... or shown, you know, mercy or ... like clemency. And here's the thing: nobody's doing squat about it. Not the cops, not the legal system, not the bad guys' mothers, not imaginary guys in the sky, not—

--If you're saying there are tons of unanswered questions about clemency or mercy, or about punishment—

--You think?

--about responsibility, about what constitutes legitimate excuses for doing wrong, about criminal intent versus negligence, well then I'll have to say I agree with you.

--That's a first.

--You're not trying to suggest that what you did had some ... had some ... justification are you? That's not what you're trying to say, is it?

--Can I have something else to drink? A beer or something?

--No you can't have a beer.

--What kind of joint are you running here?

54

Okay wise guy, you found me. Now what?
—Jack Elam, "Kansas City Confidential."

I was cleaning a pair of Bodum three Cup Shin Bistro Coffee makers known to all Bodum cognoscenti as the crème de la crème of second-rate coffee makers when I see Attila charging across the floor like she was out to pillage Gallipoli. She was closely followed by Shades doing Steve McQueen doing Frank Bullitt sans the turtle neck but not the sunglasses.

"You," she shrieked while pushing her holy finger at me. "I took you in, I trusted you, I gave you a new life, and this!"

I didn't know what she was referring to but then I seldom had either the patience or the interest to follow her eruptions theological or otherwise. Religiotards can have that effect on me.

Shades, making no effort to throttle his gotcha-suckka grin, grabs me, spins me around, pins me face first into a table full of used athletic shoes that smell like used athletic shoes, and after fumbling with his cuffs finally manages to shackle me like a common criminal ignoring the fact that I am anything but.

"OK asshole," says the cuffer to the cuffee, "you're under arrest."

He pulls me up by my collar at which point I match him shitty grin for shitty grin.

"You have the right to keep quiet," he says with groping, albeit ostentatious authority.

"Remain," I remind him.

"What?"

"You have the right to 'remain' silent."

"Shut up. Anything you say or anything you do will be held against you in court."

"Which court?"

"Shut up."

"You mean a court of law."

"Any court, asshole."

"I just wanted to be sure because there are squash courts and Margaret Court, and kangaroo courts, and—"

"For the last time, shut the fuck up. You have the right to speak to a lawyer and if you can't afford one, they'll find one for you. Do you understand these rights that I have just read to you?"

"Spoken to me."

"Do you understand them?"

"Would you mind repeating them?"

"After all I did for you," says Her Sancitude in an off-with-his-head accusatory tone.

"As sinnocent as Badin, the demon with the mind of an angel. Although in his case he kept her mind in a little glass jar, but at least he had a pure mind, even if it wasn't his own."

"You have been Mirandalized," says Shades.

"You might be interested to know that they were created when a guy named Miranda was arrested," I said in an effort to impart an educational component to these proceedings.

"That so?"

"He pleaded that he didn't know he didn't have to talk to the police so he was found innocent."

"Well, you won't be," says Shades resurrecting the smile.

"This name means admirable in Latin. Miranda."

"And yours means shit outta luck in English."

Smudge is watching, one hand steadying the stack of silver thimbles, always a delightful collection when arranged neatly together, there being many decorative styles including filigree work, scenes, plant and animal depictions, cherubs, borders, fleur-de-lys and sewing-related themes. Some thimbles even have tiny Bibles attached to them, or doors that open to reveal a little scene.

Smudge looks as if he doesn't know whether to shit or go blind, stay with his thimbles or run, speak up or meld into the tacky second hand surround. But then again he was about as decisive as Zsa Zsa Gabor.

"What are you doing with him?" demands the Bic Bitty. Apparently the only true paladin amongst the otherwise dithery onlookers. "He didn't do anything."

"You're not his attorney, are you?" asks Shades playing to the crowd.

"Maybe I am."

"Oh yeah, Gloria—"

"We sing that in church."

"Sorry I didn't recognize you. Ms. Allred isn't it?"

"He promised to find me a new—"

"He's going to need Clarence Darrow."

"I don't remember ... something."

"OK," says Shades pushing me forward, "Time to say bye bye."

"Bye bye."

"The only way you're ever going to see this place again is if you're reincarnated as a cockroach."

"What is it the Good Book says? 'That he who sheddeth another man's blood by man shall his blood be shed!' That's as fair as a man could ask who lives by the gun and knife."

"Leave him alone, you goon," says the Bic Bitty indomitable in her defense of the otherwise defenseless charity case bound before her. "He didn't do anything."

"Seven murdered nuns over at the convent that's all."

Shades drags me outside, shoves me in the back seat of his car with a flourish worthy of Toscanini and acknowledges his audience with a look of mock modesty worthy of Elton John, in a state of gin-soaked self-loathing.

As we drive off bidding a fond and final adieu to the palace of schlock he unleashes an unimaginative barrage of intended insults most of which included the words "asshole," "mother," and "fucker," none of which included either wit or invention.

Speeding across town we are in a film noir world where they never drive into the daylight, where it is impossible to imagine motoring off to a happy sunlit ending.

Of course it starts to rain and all the color drains from the world.

"Why don't you put on the sireen?" I say.

"Shut up," he explains.

"You peel back the layers. There are maggots underneath and they're writhing."

"What are you—?"

"Dashiel Hammett."

"Shut the fuck up," he says apparently thinking the modifier will strengthen his demand.

We sidle around corners slightly too fast as befitting an ace detective bringing in one of America's Most Wanted with voice-over commentary by John Walsh the man whose groundbreaking television program has helped take down over 1,050 dangerous fugitives and bring home more than 50 missing children in the past 20-something years.

We zip past pedestrians and other cars drawing as much attention to us as Shades can attract. Make way. Part the masses, unwashed or not. Bow down you plebeians. Here comes the hero. Shades acknowledges his audience by not acknowledging them. As cool as Bullitt, as tough as Spade, as clever as Columbo, he is far above such demeaning recognition.

Shades is likely rehearsing his press conference speech trying to determine the level of humilosity to portray. I could tell him that the definition of humility probably came from the root word "futility," but I'm guessing he probably doesn't want my input.

Had my hands not been cuffed I would have offered the royal wave. I did, however adopt a royally vacant gaze.

After a few dizzy moments I notice that the buildings whizzing by have been replaced by trees whizzing by and I immediately deduce that we have left the treeless town for a buildingless countryside. Shades shoots a wickedly self-serving grin ricocheting off the rearview mirror but I won't give him the satisfaction of even the slightest response. I can out cool him any day of the week. I've seen the films.

With calcified grin firmly entrenched, he slows the car down and pulls off the road coming to a jolting halt under a leafy tree which is a blessing because, I am without my SPF 30+ non-oily sunscreen lotion to provide high broad spectrum protection against sunburn. I know it's an overcast day, but one can never be too careful with that sneaky ol' sun.

"Time to go for a walk," Shades says with more joy than I think the occasion merits.

"No thanks, I get poison ivy easily," I say. "I think I'll stay here, but please feel free to amble off without me."

Getting out of the car: "No such luck, buttwipe."

"Or if you don't like to amble you could—"

Without finishing the invitation he yanks me out of the back seat and onto the wet ground next to the car. I look up at the sunglassed face of Shades before a sunless sky covered with brooding inky clouds. Cue the mournful sax.

As befitting the situation it was getting darker by the moment. A genuine noirish world where goodness is as rare as natural sunlight.

"You touch me and you won't live to see morning," I say.

"Says who?"

"Lucille Fay LeSueur."

"Who's she?"

"Joan Crawford."

"You sick mother. Did you think in that warped brain of yours that you could get away with it?" He says delivering a firm kick intended for my stomach that gets more dirt than flesh.

"Dirty cop abuses suspect. News at 11."

"News, yes, but it won't be just abuse. Serial murderer tries to escape. Turns on officer. Said officer shoots murderer in self-defense."

"Maybe you didn't get the innocent until proven guilty memo."

"Maybe you didn't get the one that says scumbags to be treated like scum," he says while fumbling with his keys in an attempt to unlock my cuffs.

"Cheap cuffs. How are you going to explain the fact that I wasn't cuffed?"

"Must of dropped the keys in the back seat." Finally he gets the shackles off. "OK, asshole, make a run for it."

"I never run without my Adidas ClimaCool running shoes."

"Try.

"Made with strategic climacool ventilation, they cool your feet on those days when the heat is trying to hold you back."

"Here's the deal. I don't trust those, you know, lefty juries these days. They do more to protect the guilty than the innocent, so I'm just going to serve as your jury and give you the sentence you deserve and the hell with the liberal bastards."

"Liberals?"

"Yeah, you know, anti-American hypocritical lying atheistic bleeding-heart self-righteous guilt motivated freedom-haters. In other words, streaming piles of shit."

This did not seem like a very good time to enter into a discussion about philosophies either reasoned or idiotic, an observation apparently not shared by Shades.

"The vile person shall be no more called liberal, nor the churl said to be bountiful. For the vile person will speak villainy, and his heart will work iniquity, to practice hypocrisy, and to utter error against the Lord, to make empty the soul of the hungry, and he will cause the drink of the thirsty to fail. The instruments also of the churl are evil: he deviseth wicked devices to destroy the poor with lying words, even when the needy speaketh right."

"Oh that you can memorize."

"If you think you're gonna get a cushy cell with cable TV and an Internet connection, forget it."

"Only if it's wireless."

He pulls out his trusty six-shooter. "You'll be a worm buffet before ... no, wait. Not even the worms will want shit like you."

True to the noir genre, the lawyers are all crooked, the DAs are all bent and the cops, you wouldn't trust them to tell you the time.

"What time is it?"

"Time to go."

See what I mean? That's not what my watch says.

"You're whimpering."

"I'm not whimpering."

"Your last sound."

"I've never been on the whimper wagon. Never will."

"Quick and easy is too good for a piece of shit like you. I want this to hurt. A shot in each knee, then ..."

"Do you really think you can get away with this?"

"Why not? Nobody cares about you. And murdering nuns! Who hates nuns?"

"Oh, you mean all those short fat woman who don't have sex, dress like penguins and beat the shit out of little girls and also beat themselves when they have impure thoughts, not to be confused with the male version who only beats and molests boys?"

"How did you get to be so fucked up?"

"Inbreeding."

I'm not exactly crazy about the idea of dying at the moment but there's no way I'm going to give him the satisfaction of begging or even showing fear although I had more than an ample supply that I could show.

"Kiss your ass goodbye."

DUCKRABBIT

I promised no "dark and stormy"... . However, it is another dark and stormy ...

On average, about 200 people are killed by lightning in the United States every year.

The chance to be killed by lightning is 1 in 2,000,000, about the same as dying from falling out of bed.

Shades is.

> *To stand against the deep dread-bolted thunder?*
> *In the most terrible and nimble stroke*
> *Of quick, cross lightning?*
> — Shakespeare, "King Lear," Act 4, Scene 7.

The energy contained in a single lightning strike can power a 100 Watt light bulb for 90 days. Or it can turn a crooked cop into a crispy critter.

Zappo! Out of the sky comes a bolt from ... the sky. Probably about 300 kilovolts. Instant external flashover, shutdown of brainstem respiratory centers, french fried cerebellum, myocardial explosion like a dropped watermelon. The lightning flashes over Shades blowing off his shirt.

Oops that looks really painful.

When a man is hit by lightning Tyler Durden insists, his head burns down to a smoldering baseball and his zipper welds itself shut. That didn't exactly happen but his metal-rimmed sunglasses look as if they've been welded to his face, and I wonder if they're what attracted the lightening in the first place.

The only sound he makes is a guttural gurgle as he drops to the ground.

Glory hallelujah. Praise God. A miracle.

Littlewood's Law writ large.

Oddly enough Littlewood's law was formulated by a guy named Littlewood, a Cambridge math whiz. He defined a miracle as an exceptional event of special significance occurring at a frequency of one in a million. He estimated that during the hours in which a person is awake and alert, he will experience one event per second, which may be either exceptional or unexceptional (for instance, seeing a page of a book or a computer screen). Assuming that a person is alert for about eight hours per day, he will in 35 days have experienced about 1 million events.

Therefore one can be expected to observe one miraculous occurrence within the passing of every 35 consecutive days. So seemingly miraculous events are actually commonplace.

Ding dong the witch is dead.

Still, timing is everything. Shades' time is up; mine isn't. Momento mori. So it goes. And I went.

55

I didn't really have any kind of plan. Just figured if you deal enough cards sooner or later you'll have a poker game."
— Bill Pullman, "Fallen Angels: Tomorrow I Die."

I am on to other fast-cut scenes in the film of my fast-cut life subtitled My Life on the Lam (from the Old English meaning to get the hell out of Dodge) or How I Scarper Into the Unknown.

Hit the road Jack and don't you come back no more, no more, no more, no more.
Hit the road Jack and don't you come back no more.
What you say?
Hit the road Jack and don't you come back no more, no more, no more, no more.
Hit the road Jack and don't you come back no more.

Going back is the furthest thing from my mind. Unless there is something about the arrow of time unknown to us all, life has to be lived in only one direction. I suppose you could run a film backward but that would make life a comedy, although as we all know, it's really a tragedy.

So I leave the wonderful world of schlock, dreck, and grills with nary a nod toward Chip, Attilla or even Smudge who, when the French Fried Shades is discovered sans his prisoner, will likely piece together a reasonably accurate scenario. However, at least for the time being, I want to remain as invisible as Casper the Friendly Ghost, as quiet as Helen Keller, as enigmatic as Clark Rockefeller.

I check my pockets--$12.22. I check Shades' charred pockets—$442. Thank you Shades, the cop who keeps on giving. He also has a wad of credit cards but since they are easily traceable I leave them, take the cash, his Russian CZ Gem Quality Cubic Zirconia fake diamond ring, and just for sentimental sake, help myself to the sunglasses. A shadeless Shades ain't Shades.

First things first. I'm no fulminologist, but I know damn well lightning can strike twice in the same place, something I learned from King Vidor's minor noir film of the same name starring the stunningly bland Richard Todd. In said film, Todd sits on death row, awaiting execution for murder. However, he gets out and disappears into the West Texas desert.

Lesson learned.

Jump on the bus, Gus, don't be coy, Roy, you know what I mean, Jean.

56

--What if the guy had a family?

--Did he?

--Did you think—

--A family?

--about that? I'm guessing no.

--What do you know?

--He was some kind of a drifter. They don't know.

--Who he was or anything? What do you think you know?

--A complete zero. Would it have made a difference to you?

--No.

--And you think I will do what?

--That's what I'm trying—

--Do it again?

--That's something only you—

--Wreck another train? Fly a plane into a building? Shoot up a school? Mass murder some nuns?

--Why would you say that? About the nuns.

--OK forget the nuns. Assassinate, I don't know, maybe—

--You said nuns.

--some politician. The president, maybe.

--Strange choice, the nuns.

--What difference does it make? I was just trying to ... list the possibilities, for you know ... dastardly deeds.

--Are you going to do something like what you've already done? Are you planning another ...?

--If I was, do you think I would tell you?

--Would you?

--Or take out a billboard with—

--No.

--Then why the hell did you—

--Forget it.

--ask?

--OK.

--You could at least say you're not?

--Not what?

--Going on a killing spree.

--And that would mean something? Saying it would mean something?

--Yes.

--You're an idiot.

--So go ahead. Say "I'm not going on a killing spree."

--No.

--Because?

--I'm planning on blowing up every choo choo in the country including the Atcheson, Topeka and the Santa Fe, Thomas the Train, and The Little Engine that Could. Why? Because I have a train fixation stemming from being abused as a kid by a priest on the trans-Siberian Railroad someplace just outside of Lake Baikal which they tell me is very pretty but since I was bent over most of the time I didn't get much of a view.

57

Conscience. What a thing. If you believe you got a conscience it'll pester you to death. But if you don't believe you got one, what could it do t'ya? Makes me sick, all this talking and fussing about nonsense.
— Humphrey Bogart, "Treasure of the Sierra Madre."

My filmography has a limited spectrum.

Life on the lam is exactly what you'd think it should be—every corner dark, every voice pregnant with threat, every day on the brink of nevermore, and everything gooey with cynicism. Nothing sheepish here. Even if I'd had a choice I wouldn't have had it any other way. I was born to live in the slowly fading shadows.

What did you expect, a vivid commingling of lost innocence and doomed romanticism? Not in this lifetime.

This I know to be true: Everyone owns his own storyline even if the final chapter is unknown. So while waiting for that chapter I'll continue to wander as an expression of the psychic shadow of society.

58

What a place. I can feel the rats in the wall.
— Franchot Tone, "Phantom Lady."

The Chihuahuan Desert—a sandy, hot-as-hell ecoregion, bordered on the west by the extensive Sierra Madre Occidental range, and overlaying northern portions of the east range, the Sierra Madre Oriental.

Bogart may be buried nearby since he was killed by Gold Hat in them thar mountains.

Ah, yes, the conscience bit. The little voice in the back of your head that tells you somebody is watching. But nobody is watching here other than the buzzards, and buzzards are notorious for lacking the aptitude, faculty, intuition, or judgment of intellect that distinguishes right from wrong. Ever see a buzzard helping an old lady cross the street? Point made.

I figure this is as good a place as any to hang out while they lionize Shades as a heroic public servant, characterize Sister Sarah as a caring mentor, portray Smudge as a naïve roommate, and stamp the Bic Bitty as the sage of shoppers.

Now, Cherry, I can picture on Trigger galloping across the gravelly range waving a Colt 1873 silver-plated, engraved Peacemaker revolver, the sidearm of choice for intrepid cowboys and cowgirls alike. I can picture this clearly enough that I find myself frequently squint-scanning the ubiquitous and dusty horizon. Still it is rather farfetched to think she could really find me out here, but then again she is cut from rather farfetched cloth anyway so I keep my paranoid guard up.

Isn't it out in the desert that the mahatmas of the mountains say one can go to find oneself? Well, all I can say to that is, that is bullshit. Our irreducible and undefinable existence is something that we have to encounter and engage through actually living it, not through any acts of intellectual posturing or by putting together abstract theories or systems to describe existence. As I see it, life is a rough-and-tumble affair, it is higgledy-piggledy jumbled. It is a dreary mess. Just like this dreary desert.

Anyway, Emerson claimed that few men find themselves before they die, and who wants to argue with a guy named Ralph Waldo?

Anyway, I'm not trying to find myself out here, I'm trying to make sure nobody else finds me. To this end I come across an old, abandoned cabin on the top of a rocky rise giving me a pretty good 180 degree view of a lot of other rocky rises. The place comes nicely appointed with a cot and stove. However, much to my dismay I have looked high and low but cannot find the Gideon Bible. I'll have to get on room service about this when they come to put the little mint on my pillowless cot.

Something else is also missing: water. I have brought a few bottles of Evian Natural Mineral Water. Bottled right at the source in the French Alps, the water remains completely untouched by man throughout the process, so I can enjoy its naturally pure and refreshing taste anywhere, any time. I have enough for maybe a week.

Still, thanks to the tutelage of Tootsie Pops I learned how to hot wire a car's ignition, remove the ignition cover, identify the battery and starter wires, strip and connect the power wires, connect the power wires to the starter wires, and I have an old VJ-3 Willys Jeepster with a 134 cubic inch Go-Devil flathead four-cylinder engine and a three-speed Borg-Warner T-90 manual transmission. So when the time was either right or necessary, I could ditch the dirty desert.

I remember Padre Dick assuring us that Jesus spent 40 days and nights in the desert during which time the devil appeared and tempted him. Then angels came bringing food. I'm assuming tacos, although the Padre was not clear about this. It must have been a different desert, however, because I see neither the devil unless he is disguised as one of the many nocturnal predatory arthropods cohabitating my cabin, nor any taco-bearing angels.

This place is about as boringo as Cameron Diaz in a film of a James Patterson novel, only it lasts longer and there are few, if any, opportunities for what were once called Kodak moments before Kodak died at the hands of the digital devils. Watching a banana sleep would be more exciting than whiling away the days out here. Boredom is so boring, a very severe and widespread epidemic, it is not fatal, although attempts to get rid of the disease have been known to be fatal at times. Offing myself, however, is the last item on my bucket list.

Smoking cigarettes and watchin' Captain Kangaroo would be an exciting upgrade.

I have nothing to do but muse.

Why are we here? We don't know. We never knew. We never will know because there is nothing to know except that we will die and our actions count for nothing so I pursue my course because that is what I have chosen to do. This life is all I have so it's nonsense to ask its purpose. What purpose does a Siafu African ant have?

You've got me there, you reply.

Twenty million ants strong, one single colony can ravage the African countryside obliterating everything in their path including humans where a single bite can cause asphyxiation and a slow painful death.

To steal the cosmic question from the old song and movie, *"What's it all about Alfie?"*

The words "human existence," "meaning," and "purpose," don't belong in the same sentence.

How do I know? you ask.

Because human existence occurred out of a random chance in nature, and anything that exists by chance has no intended purpose.

Or maybe as Dougie Adams says, the answer is 42.

Once upon a once in a land far away, Genghis Khan was no longer getting his jollies by winter hunts over the prairies. One day in the pavilion at Karakorum he asked an officer of the Mongol guard what, in all the world, could bring the greatest happiness.

"The open steppe, a clear day, and a swift horse under you," responded the officer after a little thought, "and a falcon on your wrist to start up hares."

"No," responded the Khan, "to crush your enemies, to see them fall at your feet, to take their horses and goods and hear the lamentation of their women. That is best."

Genghis didn't become the Khan by kissing little Mongol babies and winning an election.

Survival, that's all it's about. We don't make a choice whether to live or die. We survive. End of story. We don't choose between nonexistence and awareness. Rather we slog on bleary-eyed in a muzzy cognitive middle-ground. A foggy place we call sane. A place where we don't acknowledge the haze.

One night I have a dream about a dream I had some time ago. Another in a long list of "holy shit" moments. The one where I'm running a storefront immortality salesroom. Then I remember it had a Shades-like Ray Banned guy blasting me to pieces. This is either precognition (from the Latin præ-, "before," + "cognito", acquiring knowledge), sometimes called future sight, a type of perception involving the effect of future information that cannot be deduced from presently available and normally acquired sense-based information or laws of physics and/or nature. Either that or it is mere coincidence. I'm betting on the latter.

The dream keeps coming back, each time with increasing violence. If I didn't know better I'd think I was catching a conscience. I acknowledge that our sense of right and wrong comes directly from our Darwinian past, but can easily be turned off by Xanax or any of several other post-Darwinian marvels of modern chemistry.

I'm actually a bigger fan of proscience, that dandy part of your brain that tells your conscience to go to hell so that you enjoy yourself. A good proscience not only opens doors of exciting, dangerous thrills, but actually convinces you it's safe.

Living as I am in dullsville, I find my normally slow meandering mind meandering in overdrive. I think about my little sister, Candy Darling, a thought that hadn't come to me in years. Where would she be today had she not lost the battle with that ice cream truck? She had a hobby that very well might have turned into a profitable career. A veritable pint-sized prodigy, she was a shoplifter supreme. Crave a Snickers Bar packed with roasted peanuts, nougat, caramel and milk chocolate, so it can handle your hunger so you can handle, well ... anything? Call Sis. Because things go better with Coke, thanks to her a lot of our things went better. Where other kids were caught Winona Rydering, she skipped her merry way home bearing goodies for her ever-thankful brothers. Passionate about providing great food and service, she was dedicated to catering our summer afternoons in what passed for the Levittown woods thereby making our anti-social events memorable. I haven't had a Snickers Bar since. Call me sentimental. I miss her.

59

What are you gonna do? Kill me? Everybody dies.
— John Garfield, "Body and Soul."

Random conversations with my uninvited Gila monster houseguest I named Herman:

We're like what, the 21st attempt at getting it right? Let's count. Nineteen hominids came before us and then there were the Neanderthals who stuck around long enough to interbreed with modern man. There were a shitload of different dinosaurs whether ridden by the Flintstones or not, and when they didn't work out, the big guy in the sky completely gave up on the idea and scrapped them altogether. Then there were lots of mammals that didn't work out and when he finally came up with an acceptable version of man he killed off a number of those.

God apparently needed some time to come up with all of his convoluted, absurd, and cruel tricks to play on his creations. Not being very bright, he thought he could blame everything on Adam, Eve and mankind, failing to consider that since he made everything the way it is and also knows how everything turns out, he is either the devil, or the most inept criminal in the universe.

And Herman nods as if to say, I'm 25 years old and I don't give a shit.

How old is man? That depends on what we call "man." Seven million years is as about as good an educated guess as any, since there isn't a sharp line that separates early apes from early men. Not even a dull line. Instead, it's a continuum whose nature is deciphered from sparse fossil remains, a slow process leading from amorphous sludge to our present two-legged, opposable-thumbed, essentially sludgeless form.

Here's the deal. Hominids began walking the earth late on a Thursday afternoon several million years ago. Then, interestingly enough, also on a Thursday afternoon 50,000 years ago *Homo sapiens*—that be us—made our grand entrance and we've been beating the crap out of all the other species ever since. King of the jungle, desert, mountains, seas, rat holes and every place on, under and in between.

So, how many people have there been? One hundred and 8 billion, give or take three or four.

How do we know? Let me count the ways.

At the dawn of agriculture 10 thousand years ago, the population has been put at about 5 million. Growth was slow for a long time, if for no other reason, life expectancy was pretty short—about 10 years for most of human history with infant mortality about 500 per 1000 births. Among the hunter-gatherers, children were one hell of a liability. Infanticide anyone?

At the time of the Roman Empire the population was some 300 million but by 1650 it had only increased to about 500 million. Ah, yes, the old Black Death was largely responsible. The dreaded plague erased about 100 million people in pretty short order.

But things babywise picked up after that. By 1800 a billion people were running about the earth.

So, figuring the number of people ever born means selecting population sizes for different points from antiquity to the present, starting with the ever popular duo of Adam and Eve, or Ben and Jerry, or Jack and Jill, or whoever, and we come up with the aforementioned 108 billion, meaning that about 6.5 percent of all the people who ever lived are alive today and 93.5 percent aren't. That's more than 100 billion who were once, aren't now.

People die. It happens.

Yeah, I'm not sure I want to live on this planet either, yet here we are.

Every man for those 7 million years is now dead save for a relative handful who now muck about the planet. In geologic time we're all here for a mere flick of an instant and then we're gone and the world goes on. How many of those dead were murdered? Surely billions. And for what? Greed, anger, jealousy, fear, religion, power? Let me count the ways. No, I can't count that high and it doesn't matter. Know what I mean, Herman?

Our experiential time frames are framed by lifetimes. We may think of a lifetime as something short of or around 100 years, Noah and his biblical buddies notwithstanding.

When scientists smash into electrons with light and measure how fast those little suckers move after being bombarded they come up with the shortest interval of time ever measured—20 attoseconds. One attosecond is one quintillionth of a second. An attosecond is to a second what a second is to 31.71 billion years. So, on the cosmic scale, a human life comes into existence and then disappears in the equivalent of attoseconds. A barely perceptible flash of light in the cosmos that comes and goes in attoseconds. And if a life is shortened by an attosecond or two more than it would naturally have been, what possible difference could that make in the big picture?

The universe, having been created by a Big Bang on a Thursday afternoon 13.78 billion years ago, went along just fine for 9.24 billion years without what we call earth. Then 4.54 billion years ago earth coalesced (coincidentally also on a Thursday) and it got along fine without simple cells for more than another billion years. Then 3.5 billion years ago simple cells arose and then in another billion years some of them began to join symbiotically into primitive multicellular organisms. After a couple of zillion mutations and blind explorations of evolution some creatures emerged with the ability to remember and to wonder what the hell it's all about.

Here's the kicker: It was all happenstance—flukes upon flukes upon flukes.

The chance that we would be here today to screw up our little home in the big dark-mattered space in the universe is like taking your change from a microwaved burrito at a 7-11 and picking 12, 87, 42, 3, 55, and 66 to win the Powerball lottery, which the Powerball pundits predict would give you a 175 million to one chance to win the big jackpot, and then pick six more random numbers for something like another thousand times and win each time.

Now if that weren't chancy enough, throughout human history, scores of weird things had to happen exactly as they did or we would have been wiped out.

As Stephen Jay Gould wrote, if we replay the history tape it would be extremely unlikely that Homo sapiens would ever evolve again.

We're related, Herman, you and I, and we're related to every other being including the four-legged bird people, burrowing and swimming animals, insects, plant and fungi people, and the star people. And not just in Mr. Rogers' neighborhood, but on every one of the billions upon billions of celestial bodies at least in this universe, and who knows, maybe billions of other universes as well. We're all stardust anyway and to stardust we'll return.

Most species go missing within 10 million years, so 99.9 percent of all species that have ever existed are now extinct. We won't last anywhere near that long. Maybe another 100 years. When the population increases to 8 or 9 billion, people will fight over food. Add to that ecological destruction and over consumption and we're doomed. Look what happened on Easter Island.

Of course, after humans go extinct, the earth will bounce back. And the bacteria shall inherit the earth. Anyway, it is their planet and we're here only because they permit it. Theirs is the great success story of the planet. These little guys were here long before us and they will be here long after we are gone. They had a dandy time for billions of years before we showed up, but we couldn't last a day without them. They are as essential for our survival as we are irrelevant to theirs.

They also can live for a very, very long time. Like at least 250 million years. Or at least some did that were released from deposits thousands of feet underground in New Mexico which, if you have to be in this Land of Enchantment, is a very good place to be. Bacteria ain't stupid or they wouldn't have hung around so long.

It's your world, bacteria. Thanks for letting us visit here for a little while.

Herman, like all other Gilas in his clan, is capable of dispatching a venomous neurotoxin. Its bite supposedly hurts like holy hell, but unlike snakes, which inject venom, Gilas latch onto victims and chaw away and allow neurotoxins to move through grooves in their teeth and into the open wound. They have been known to swallow whole birds and lizards.

Herman ain't no small fry. I judge him to check in at about 4 pounds and just under 2 feet long. He's got a big head, powerful-looking jaws, short legs with big feet, large toes and long, strong claws.

Has Herman or his kin ever killed anyone? I'm guessing no but I don't know for sure and my reference material here is limited to a couple of Heinz Baked Beans labels informing me that they are packed with fiber, low in sugar and virtually fat free. They offer no hints about Gila venom.

As Daddy said, "If you are attacked by a circus, go for the juggler."

So my question then becomes, should I kill Herman before he bites me or go kumbaya and let all the earth's creatures live in blissful harmony?

You slap a mosquito on your arm. So what? You don't give it a nanosecond of thought. Squished mosquito. Dead. There's no remorse, regret. You're smarter than the mosquito. You're bigger and stronger than the mosquito. Smart and big win. Always.

I know I'm bigger than Herman and I'm assuming I'm smarter although I have no empirical proof of that.

Chimps, monkeys, dolphins, and elephants are considered smart so they usually get a pass on the killing list.

Cute (most often used to describe little kids doing funny things) also wins. Who wants to shoot pandas? They're too cute. So are dolphins, puppies, kittens and bunnies. Gila monsters are ugly. So are vultures, alligator snapping turtles, naked mole rats, blobfish and sea cucumbers, and you could probably add spiders and cockroaches for many people.

Kill ugly, spare cute. Kill stupid, spare smart. It's the way of the world to steal a title from Willy Congreve.

Or as Kipling observed, the wildest dreams of Kew are the facts of Katmandu, and the crimes of Clapham chaste in Martaban.

Herman, you're exceptionally ugly, a fact which you must face, so you've got to go, and since I have scant few tools at my disposal here, the best I can do is to bash in your repulsive head with a rusty nail-studded board.

Look big guy, this is how it is: When you're dead you're dead. Just like all of us—you, me, Genghis Khan, Methuselah. No Gila heaven, no seven Gila virgins, no harps, no free beer and tacos.

Herman, you're on your way to becoming stardust via Gila dust. Granted it will take a few hundred thousand years but that's nothing in the total schema of things. A mere instant, my grotesque groveling companion.

Herman does not go gently into that good night. Rather, he puts up a fight worthy of Genghis v. Sultan Muhammad. Gila blood spurts on otherwise all-brown walls turning them into proto Jackson Pollocks.

Observation: When fighting a Gila, you don't stop fighting when you're tired, you stop fighting when the Gila is tired. Herman doesn't tire easily but eventually my rusty Excalibur sword/board brings him to his knobby knees.

The stench of rotting Gila meat tells me it's time to say adios and mosey on. (Moseying is about as fast as it gets out here in the desert.)

I suppose patience should be the order of the day. Wait it out until ... what? Anyway, patience is for those who die waiting for something to happen and that isn't on my to-do list.

60

When a man stops caring what happens to him, all the strain is lifted off of him.
— Jason Patric, "After Dark, My Sweet."

In the movies bad guys always die.—almost always die. If movies still had reels, maybe I was in the last one. I figured my past would eventually catch up with me. I just didn't know who the catcher would be, although I did have some ideas.

Live a life of violence; die a life of violence. Poetic justice. Why not?

In all those good guy v. bad guy movies, I always had the feeling that, of course, the bad guys had to know that eventually they could be/would be shot down in a hail of self-righteous bullets. Sonny Corleone had to know that, even if he didn't suspect a toll taker with an attitude. (In my experience toll takers tend to be pacifists.) I mean what the hell did all those Mafioso clowns think? They would die in a hospice looked after by sanctimonious, honey-voiced women posing as sotto voce angels of mercy? The wise guys created their lifestyle and had to live and die with it.

With my what-the-hell attitude I could tackle anything sans the *sturm und drang* that normally accompany a life less nonchalantly lived. Assume you're already dead and not a whole lot bothers you. It's the first man up the hill to attack the bunker stuff, the Roman front line Hastati stuff. Dead man walking a la Sean Penn as Mathew Poncelet.

But as we all know some serial murderers get away with … murder. To wit, anyone knowing the whereabouts of any or all of the following, please contact your local FBI or Interpol: Jack the Ripper, Jack the Stripper, the Atlanta Ripper, the Lisbon Ripper, the Axeman of New Orleans. The Phantom Killer of Texarkana, the Zodiac Killer, Bible John, the Monster of Florence, the Freeway Phantom, various Alphabet Murderers, Charlie-Chop-off, The Doodler, the original Night Stalker, the Gypsy Hill Killer, the Monster of Udine, the Chicago Tylenol Murderer, Stoneman, Beerman, the Smiley Face Murderer, the Eastbound Strangler, the West Mesa Murderer, the B1 Butcher, the Daytona Beach Killer, the February 9 Killer, the Frankford Slasher, the Colonial Parkway Killer, the New Bedford Highway Killer and … and … and. And I've barely scratched the surface. It's a long list.

Then, too, there was a time in our history, and a long time ago it was, when it was considered cool, even *de rigeur* to murder. Like in some places it was cool to sacrifice virgins in order to appease any number of appeasable gods and there were ever so many of those waiting in the wings for their offerings. The Aztecs, for example, believed that for every 52 years that passed, the world would end unless the gods were strong enough. And, as is common knowledge, the best way to toughen up a pissed off god is with a steady stream of constant human sacrifice (throw in a dash of cannibalism, just for good measure). If that doesn't qualify as serial murdering, I'm not sure what does.

Well, actually, I do, because the world's foremost authority on authority, the Wickedpedia, says that in order to qualify as a serial killer, one must have murdered three or more people over a period of more than a month with a cooling off period between the murders. This clearly sets the serial murderer apart from the mass murderer, or spree killer who commit murders in two or more locations with virtually no break in between. However, some categorists suggest a hybrid category of spree-serial killer for cases in which there are extended bouts of sequential murders over a period of weeks or months without the ever popular cooling off period.

At any rate, I wasn't exactly in select company.

61

--So you were ... depressed because ...?

--Because ... let's see. The state of the world ... war ... poverty ... hunger—

--If you want to play this game—

--the banks ... the stock exchange—

--None of this is—

--You're the expert—

--what really—

--on bullshit. Maybe even wrote the book on it. The bullshit bible.

--OK you admitted you were pissed at yourself. You volunteered that. So I'm thinking you consciously or unconsciously want me to know why. OK, you were angry at yourself because you flunked a test? Lost money in a poker game? Couldn't get it up? Had a fight with your girlfriend? Let me know if I get close. Bet on the wrong horse? Forgot your mother's birthday? Screwed up some—

--Diddled around.

--Diddled?

--Took forever when I knew better. Didn't have the guts to ... to follow through ... to ...

--You knew the driver didn't you? You knew the engineer. This wasn't a random act at all. You planned it. You murdered him.

--Wow!

62

I probably shan't return before dawn. How I detest the dawn.
The grass looks like it's been left out all night.
— Clifton Webb, "The Dark Corner."

Oh, how I hate to get up in the morning, moaned Irv Berlin. He must have known about the desert. So, after too many identical mornings in the sandbox I decided it was time to mosey on.

After a browse and a ponder and driving more than a few pulverulent miles from my blood-splattered cabin I came across a packed-dirt airstrip with a corrugated metal hanger in front of which sat an Aeronca Model 7 Champion single seater fixed conventional gear plane more commonly known as the Champ. Sitting on a beach chair next to it was a paunch-bellied Harvey Hyphenation who by his own introduction was an Irish-Argentinean-French-Australian-Chinese-Paraguayan ace pilot. A regular thoroughbred mongrel. His T-shirt read "SPQR RULES!"

"I was a pilot before Pontius," he announces with accompanying chuckle.

"What is that supposed to mean?"

"I'm experienced."

"Yeah, but are you any good?"

"Let's find out, shall we."

So we head off yonderly more gray than blue but whether wild or not remains to be seen.

Wasn't that wowely?

63

Cue the Hans Zimmer music.

PART TWO

Rabbit

I came to understand that when all else fails, there is always the delusion of truth.

64

Fade in on Cherry. Close up.

65

I rode Bucephalus up the winding road. The sun was sliding down beyond the horizon like it knew what was coming. I sure as hell didn't.

The road, dropping steeply away on the left side, didn't invite strangers. At the top of the hill a pair of phallic-thin evergreens stood sentinel on both sides of the massive weathered wood gates. I edged past them into the cloistered garth and parked next to a chicken pen with nary a chicken in sight. The rectangular open space was surrounded by covered walks with open arches on the inner side running along the walls of an ecru stone building. Not surprisingly, everything looked faultless, planned, undefiled. In the center of the yard, a large iron cross.

I got out of the car, not bothering to lock it. Directly across from me were double oak doors with round iron handles. I walked to the doors, pulled the handles and the heavy doors swung smoothly open. There wasn't much light coming through the leaded windows. Just enough to see seven bodies hanging from ropes looped over massive beams. Seven nuns.

For a moment I couldn't catch my breath.

Christ almighty!

I looked in several small rooms off the main space. Nobody.

In one of the rooms I found a phone, picked it up and dialed 9-1-1.

"I'm up in the convent. Up on the hill. I just found the nuns ... all hanged ... six or seven ... yeah that's what I said ... from the rafters ... no

... no, I'm not fucking putting you on ... yeah."

I hung up and went back into the main room and after lighting a few candles, sat quietly in a pew looking up at the grotesque scene, what was left of the late afternoon sun coming through the leaded windows throwing Caligari-esque film noir-like shadows against the stone walls.

I'd seen death, I'd seen dead bodies, I'd seen grotesquely mangled bodies. I'd never seen anything like this.

66

Lieutenant Traxler was the first to arrive. A cement truck of a man, he bellowed more than spoke, a real gum-bumper.

"Jesus H. Fucking Christ," he says.

"Not likely.

What the hell?" He walks under the bodies, looking up at each habit-clothed nun. "You find this?"

"Yeah."

"Just like this?"

"Except the candles."

"You lit the candles?"

"Yeah."

"Why'd you do that?"

"It was dark."

He whips off his sunglasses as if he hadn't noticed. "Who are you? You work here?"

"No."

"What are you doing here?"

"Looking for someone else."

"One of these—"

"No. Nothing to do with ... I just happened to come in and find them like this. Maybe 20 minutes or so ago.

"Twenty minutes?"

"I didn't check the time exactly."

"OK, just wait over there. We'll need to get ... we'll need to talk to you."

Within minutes the place was swarming with police, medical people, and I didn't know who all else but I'm reasonably sure there was more activity than that normally serene cloister had seen in a long time ... if ever.

High on the list of things that didn't add up was this: Presumably you'd have to hang the nuns one at a time. What were the others doing during this? And don't tell me praying. It would seem to suggest that there was more than one assailant. That's what the police are saying. But I'm not so sure. There was something more ...

Anyway, as far as I can figure, the Lieutenant Traxlers of this world are about as likely to find him as they are to find Jimmy Hoffa and he's been missing for more than 30 years.

Someone has to go and dig up a ladder so they can cut the bodies down.

When Traxler returns: "You sure you didn't move anything or—"

"Look, I know better than that. I didn't touch anything. I didn't contaminate the crime scene, OK?"

"And you didn't see nobody?"

"Not a living soul."

"Coming up the hill?"

"Nobody."

"Leaving. Somebody leaving?"

"No."

"So what are you doing here?"

"Talking to you."

"Why'd you come here in the first place? And don't tell me to talk to me."

"I'm looking into the disappearance of my brother and I thought the nuns might have ... I don't know ... some information I might use. A fishing trip I suppose."

"What made you think they'd—"

"He's a Jesuit priest."

"Oh, the one that went missing."

"That's why I'm looking for him, yeah. He's missing."

"A Jesuit you say."

"Yeah, you know, guys who find colleges with good basketball teams."

"He was a basketball coach?"

"He was a priest."

"Kompany is on that case. Lieutenant Kompany with a 'K.' There was another detective, but ... it's Kompany now."

"We've spoken.

"What'd he say?"

"He didn't know where my brother was. He's missing."

"OK, you found them just like that—the nuns."

"Well, I sure as hell didn't put them up there."

"I wasn't suggesting you did. Any ideas?"

"In general or about the murders?"

"Well, we can't say for sure yet that it was murder."

"What, mass suicide?"

"It wouldn't be the first."

"They would all have to have stood on something and then jumped ... stepped off. There's nothing like that around and I told you I didn't touch anything. Besides, their faces hardly look beatific."

"What?"

"Angelic."

"Yeah."

"No, somebody had a grievance against ... what? Nuns, the church, religion?"

"Or an absolute crazy maybe."

"Maybe."

"Was your brother ... did he have some connection with this place? With any of the nuns?"

"Definitely not."

"As a priest he must have—"

"No."

As they untie the rope from around the neck of the last sister, another detective asks me the same questions again, takes down my particulars, and tells me I can go but that they'd get back to me later. Among the questions not asked is if I have any idea who might be responsible for such a horrendous act. I do.

67

The next day I looked in the paper for the story. Nothing. I checked the TV news. Nada. Blogs? Nary a byte. The secret world of the secret religious Reich. Somebody higher up didn't want the story to go public. Why exactly? Curious.

Anyway, I was more interested in getting to the bottom of my brother's disappearance, than solving the riddle of the flying nuns.

Then for several months, to keep myself afloat I took a series of jobs tracking down deadbeat husbands, cheating wives and derelict … derelicts.

I had forgotten neither my brother nor the nuns but they were for the nonce taking second place to my selfish need for food and rent.

Then quite by accident I heard about a strange film from a cousin, whose ex-boyfriend with whom she still stayed in touch said he saw it last year on the wall of a skating rink in Montreal where he was taking classes at McGill University while working nights as a barrista at the Bar St-Suplice.

I was skeptical because my cousin is about as reliable as a Wikipedia article on dark energy.

She claimed that Alain the barrister cum medical student was passing a skating rink late at night having come from a club. Although she thought otherwise, this implied that he may have been high, drunk, tired or all of the above and so may have been hallucinating or vividly imagining moving images on a wall.

"I don't think so," she said. "He's pretty … straightforward about … he's not much of a—"

"He doesn't drink or do drugs?"

"I didn't say that."

"So he might be full of shit."

"No 'might' about it."

"You believe him anyway?"

"About this I do."

"If he's so damn reliable, why aren't you still with him?"

"Long story."

"When was this supposed to be? The showing."

"A little while ago. I don't know. Two weeks maybe."

"At a skating rink?"

"The wall."

"And it was called *Duckrabbit?*"

"What he said."

"About the murder of seven nuns?"

"I don't know about seven, but it was a bunch. Maybe it wasn't all of it, but it was in it. A part of it."

According to cuz, it was so stunning that Alain can't get it out of his mind, but when pressed for more details she said I'd have to ask Alain directly because she didn't remember a lot of what he said.

68

On my cellphone: "Hello, is this Alain?"

"Make it fast, I'm at work."

Busy bars are incredibly noisy places especially when coffee grinders are grinding, frothers are frothing, and espresso portafilters are being slammed clean.

"I talked to my cousin Emily about your seeing that film."

"The film?"

"The one you saw on the wall. I'd like to ask you about—"

"The film?"

"Emily told me you—"

"Sorry, who is this?"

"Emily's cousin."

"Can't hear you."

"I'm Emily's cousin."

"It's too noisy here."

I heard him talking to a customer before he got back to me. "You'll have to call back … later. It's too noisy here and not enough bars in the bar anyway."

"I'll call back."

"Call back."

"No, I think I'll come up to see you."

"Why?"

"The film you told Em about."

"Don't bother."

"I just want to ask you about—"

"Gotta go."

69

The Bar St. Suplice was immense, crowded and, as previously noted, noisy. It was four floors of febrile activity housed in an old building with brick walls, open beams and metal tables. Very industrial like.

It took some time to track down Alain the barrister in this sprawling complex. It looked as if you could drink in a different bar each day of the week and save a couple for Sunday. I finally found him in the bar they called La Place de l'Ange at the top of a magnificent staircase that looked as if it came from a different era, which it probably did. The room was dominated by a huge sculpture in the shape of an angel and big floor-to-ceiling, wall-to-wall windows.

Alain was sitting at a table drinking from a bottle of Labatt Blue. Alain looked as if he should be drinking from a bottle of Labatt Blue in a busy Montreal bar. Presumably he was on a break. Like he was right out of a *GQ* piece on French Canadian hip. He was casually elegant in his black blazer with turned-up collar, gray T-shirt, appropriately pre-ripped jeans and leather sandals sans socks.

My cuz must have been crazy to break up with this guy. I introduced myself and told him why I was there.

"The movie you saw."

"On the wall."

"Yeah."

"Tell me about it. How did it come … how did you know it was going to be shown?"

"Didn't. Nobody does I guess. That's the thing. It just shows up. You want a beer?"

"Uh, sure," I said. I didn't really but I assumed that he was more likely to spend time with me if we were drinking together. He waved his hand like an imperious monarch and the foamy brewski appeared within seconds.

"I only saw part of it," he continued, "but that part … well let's just say it, you know, caught my attention big time."

"You just happened to be walking by?"

"Yeah, well who the hell expects to see a movie on a skating rink wall? And without popcorn to boot."

"It's always too expensive anyway—the popcorn."

"The only way to see it. Nobody knows when or where it's going to show up or even who the filmmaker is other than the credits say Hobwarm, something like that."

"Hobshawn maybe?"

"Could be. It went by fast. I don't know. Hob something anyway."

"What kind of a film was … how would you describe it?"

"I wouldn't."

But not a documentary."

"I don't know what you'd call it. A lot of dark and shadowy scenes."

"Was there a scene … scenes where a man … someone kills a priest?"

"That's not clear."

"And a bunch of nuns hanging."

"It's a little more complicated than that."

"But the nuns—"

"I shouldn't really."

"That's what I'm looking into … investigating."

"Some murders?"

"Tell me what you remember about it. Scenes, characters, anything you can recall."

"I remember the film ends with the camera moving in toward a stone wall with writing on it. It's hard to make out at first, but then as it comes into focus it's very clear. It says in big capital letters DON'T TELL ANYBODY."

"Meaning what?

"The film, I guess. Don't tell anybody about the film."

"Why is that, do you suppose?"

"Why are you so interested in this?"

"I think there might be some personal, you know … connection."

"Why, your mother a nun?"

"Not exactly."

"You a reporter or critic or something?"

"Or something."

"Well, I'll tell you there's something cool about that film, the whole idea of it. The wall and everything and, you know, I feel like I should honor what that guy wants and not tell anybody."

"Why in the world—?"

"I don't know exactly. Just seems like the cool thing to do."

I can't figure out what's so cool about not talking about a homemade film shown on a public wall, but the more I pressed, the more entrenched Alain became and the less he was willing to share. His conversation ran out at the same time as his beer and it was back to making lattes.

I hung around for another day and intercepted him on several occasions but learned nothing more. He was, as I came to learn, one of many people who saw the film and felt as if they were somehow privileged to have been let into a cabal of the select few and decided to honor the film's final request. But still, there are always rebels who will go against the group. Finding one, though, proved difficult.

It seemed as if there were those randomly chosen few who had seen *Duckrabbit* and the rest of us who hadn't and never the two should meet.

Then stories about it began popping up everyplace—online, in print, even "60 Minutes" and I always trust Leslie Stahl even when she doesn't get her lipstick on straight. In popular parlance, the story went and remained viral.

"Duckrabbit the Reel Deal" read an article in "Variety" quoting an unnamed source.

I called the "Variety" office but they said they couldn't reveal their source as if they were connected to the inner circle of a national security scandal.

It had apparently spread across the United States and who knows how much of the rest of the world, with viral unstoppability. "A specimen of cinematic hubris," wrote one journalist who claimed to have seen it. "A monumental montage of music and mystical moments."

That doesn't sound like a formula for a blockbuster.

"An experience both wildly exhilarating and supremely dislocating," read another report.

Someone described it as a drama that is also a comedy that is also an existential cry for help that is finally a testament to human endurance—whatever the hell that's supposed to mean.

Is it guerrilla marketing at its best, an in-joke, an entertainment industry curiosity, or … or… who knows what?

Even "The New York Times" ran a story: "Have You Seen It Yet?"

In the months that followed, the "Duckrabbit" story grew into mythic proportions but opinions as to its merits varied greatly. It was hailed as a masterpiece by some of those who were fortunate enough to have seen it or at least claimed to have seen it. Some thought it elevated film making to something like bizarro world brilliance, the "Citizen Kane" of indies. Others thought it was pure dreck, a joke, trumpery of the most pretentious kind.

Regardless of the opinions of the merits of the film, the "Who is Hobsbawm" stories (the credited writer/director) popped up with the regularity of Geico ads. He was (take your pick of rumors), a CIA operative, a disgruntled priest, or any of numerous film directing mavericks including Roman Polanski, Quentin Tarantino, Paul Thomas Anderson, David Fincher, Stephen Soderbergh, Spike Jonez and David O. Russell—just about every director short of Ronnie Howard and Penny Marshall. One blogger opined that he was a she and she was Yoko Ono.

One unsupported rumor that gained notable media traction is that the film was yet another product of Banksy, the pseudonymous film director and painter. He was already famous for his satirical street art and subversive epigrams which appeared on street walls and bridges in scores of cities around the world. It was a logical connection.

"Hobsbawm Unmasked" or some variation of that appeared on

websites and on covers of supermarket checkout magazines.

"Rolling Stone" opined the filmmaker was a professional vandal using film as graffiti, as a weapon for the people, as a spokesman for the underdog.

Various photos appeared in various newspapers showing various people purported to be Hobsbawm. I suppose that sold newspapers but it didn't offer anything in the way of proof.

Not unexpectedly, scores of self-promoting artists/filmmakers/hucksters turned up claiming they made "Duckrabbit" but none could produce details to support their claim.

Despite the relatively few people who actually saw the film, evidence of Hobsbawm mania was everywhere. T-shirts emblazoned with "I Saw Duckrabbit," and "I Can't Tell You The Secret" were big sellers even if in many cases the claim had to be a lie. For a few dollars you could have your very own Duckrabbit logoed coffee mug, keychain, ballpoint pen or baseball cap.

Duckrabbit popped up in badly written country-western song lyrics:
Saw the duck the other day,
Saw it on the side of a big Safeway.

If not Hobsbawm, some entrepreneurs at least were making piles of money. Could it be the filmmaker himself? Could this be a clever form of guerilla marketing? Maybe. Why not release it to the commercial market? Why all the mystery? I don't know about film marketing. Maybe the mystery is how you sell … something. Not tickets, though.

Was I the only person on this planet who knew who made it even if I didn't know where he was?

70

Since the film was apparently about neither a duck nor a rabbit, the question naturally arose, what the hell is a duckrabbit anyway? Or even is there such a thing?

Well, apparently, as I came to learn, a duckrabbit is a concept made famous by the Austrian-British philosopher, Ludwig Wittgenstein. I had heard the name before, but beyond vaguely knowing that he was some kind of philosopher who wrote some kind of complicated stuff, I knew nothing.

With interest in the film sky high, various thankfully dumbed down stories about him appeared in the popular media. There may even have been a "Wittgenstein for Idiots" but I didn't check that out.

Apparently his 1999 posthumously published "Philosophical Investigations" was called by some people who knew about such things, the most important book of 20th-century philosophy. Bertrand Russell, another philosopher I vaguely remembered reading some back in my John Jay days, described him as the most complete example he had ever known of genius as traditionally conceived—passionate, profound, intense and dominating. I looked that up.

The simple version is that a duckrabbit is a picture that can be seen as a duck or a rabbit, depending on how you view it. According to Wittgenstein when one looks at the picture and sees a rabbit one is not interpreting the picture as a rabbit but rather interpreting what one sees. One just sees the picture of a rabbit. But what occurs when one sees it first as a duck and then a rabbit? Wittengstein says he is not sure, and if he is not sure, I sure as hell am not either.

What he does seem to know, however, is that technically, the duckrabbit figure is an ambiguous figure, not an illusion. He says that many illusions illustrate the role of unconscious inferences in perception, while the ambiguous figures illustrate the role of expectations, world-knowledge and the direction of attention. For example, children tested on Easter Sunday are more likely to see the figure as a rabbit but if tested on a Sunday in October, they tend to see it as a duck.

So be it.

I guess we're left to assume the film should be seen as ambiguous and that it can be viewed in two different ways. What ways exactly I don't know.

71

I sifted back through my memory stacks, back to living with Bruns, watching him create his art, listening to him talking about the film he was planning to make. He mentioned the name duckrabbit but I really didn't know what that meant, or frankly at the time cared a whole lot. It was his thing, so I listened politely, nodded appropriately, threw in a few perfunctory questions, but in reality gave it little note. I had long since mastered the art of feigned interest in his projects, and after a while, in him, too.

As best I can recall he said something about how it would be an apocalyptic vision of the collision between two worlds, but for the life of me I'm not sure what those worlds were supposed to be or why it was supposed to be so damn apocalyptic.

He said t was to be an object in moving time, the meaning of which, like all good art, he claimed would be up to the viewer.

Art according to Bruns (I'm paraphrasing here, but I'm not far off.) has no intrinsic meaning. This is, he insisted, its power, its mystery and ultimately its attraction. Art is free, it stimulates the viewer to insert their own meaning, their own value. So any meaning or value the film might have comes exclusively from the beholder. The film's role is to provoke, to raise questions that only the audience can answer. This is the highest value in any work of art, not predetermined meaning, but meaning gleaned from the experience of the encounter. The encounter is what it is about, not the meaning. If meaning is the point, then propaganda and advertising is the form. "I'm not sure as hell in the advertising business," he accurately proclaimed.

So I guess then, in the sense of art the way he meant it, the meaning of duckrabbit is whatever the hell someone wants it to be based on their own … life experiences.

Still, it's hard not to draw conclusions, which is what I think I concluded.

72

Narrative films need actors and a crew and judging by the length of the credits that roll on and on at the end, they need lots of crew including such people as best boys, key grips, dolly grips, gaffers and lead men. I don't know what any of them do except they're either important or union required. Either way, with so many people, it was virtually a certainty that sooner or later, one or more would spill the beans. Celebrity status would certainly follow. Or at least an interview with Cooper Anderson.

I waited.

73

Some time ago I had looked up this Eric Hobsbawm guy, the so-called public intellectual and the name used by Bruns for his art. It seems Eric Hobsbawm (now dead), the famous British Marxist historian had this idea that outlaws were individuals living on the edges of society by robbing and plundering—people who are often seen by ordinary folk as heroes or beacons of popular resistance. He called it "a form of prehistoric social movement," whatever that is supposed to mean. He wrote about men such as Ned Kelly, Dick Turpin, Billy the Kid and Carmine Crocco, all criminals whom some people considered heroes because they were fighters for a kind of justice.

Was that it? Did my Hobsbawm see himself as fighting for some perceived wrong? What wrong would that be? What justice? Maybe Eric Hobsbawm's examples would offer a clue. So I looked them up, too.

Ned Kelly was an Irish-Australian bushranger. To some he was simply a cold-blooded cop killer. To others he was a folk hero and symbol of Irish Australian resistance against the Anglo-Australian ruling class.

Dick Turpin, an English highwayman, became a legend after his execution. Writers romanticized him as dashing and heroic in scores of English ballads and popular theatre pieces of the 18th and 19th centuries and later in film and on television. A Robin Hood type who stole from the rich and gave to ... I don't know who. Maybe his mother.

Carmine Crocco, known as Donatello was an Italian bandit, a robber out to revenge the abuses suffered by his family. He apparently developed a real hatred of the upper class after his brother was beaten silly by a young lord for killing a dog who had attacked a Crocco family chicken. His pregnant mother tried to defend her son but the lord kicked her in the belly, forcing her to abort. His father was later accused of the attempted murder of the lord and was imprisoned, apparently without proof.

Billy the Kid, seen as a friend to the poor and downtrodden, sought justice for the murder of a friend who was killed for opening a store that threatened a corrupt monopoly backed by a corrupt sheriff. It is said that more films have been made about him than any other figure in American history, most portraying him as a folk hero.

So, short of asking the present day Hobsbawm himself, or seeing "Duckrabbit," I had to consider the possibility that he was assuming some manner of a folk hero role, out to right a perceived wrong. A true Hobsbawmian guerilla.

74

I maneuvered Bucephalus through a seedy section of town that appeared as if it had been built that way from day one. More built down than run down. It looked as if a graffiti convention had just taken place. The art of the streetz. Whoever owned the spray paint can concession around there must be sitting pretty. I parked in front of a blue-going-to-gray-going-to-undefinable clapboard house, gingerly picked my way up the broken (booby-trapped?) steps, and knocked on the door.

In a voice that crackled, "Yeah?"

"I'm looking for—"

The door creaked slightly opened. "He ain't here," said a dead-eyed skinny woman, a skinny cigarette hanging from pursed lips. Curlers pinioned her thinning yellowish hair. She was carrying a can of beer; she smelled of beer and tobacco and recently applied nail varnish.

"Who?"

"You're looking for my son." He ain't here," says the woman very obviously blowing a puff of mentholated cigarette smoke in my face. Just as obviously I didn't acknowledge it.

"Do you know when he might be back?"

"No."

Then a man's voice came from somewhere in the apartment. "Whadda you want?"

"Can I talk to you for a minute?"

The man yanked the woman away from the door with a violent tug. If anything, Smudge was even skinnier than the weedy woman. He had not been hard to track down.

"What do you want?"

"I just want to ask you a few questions."

"The cops already been here. Twice."

"I'm sure."

"You're looking for my roomie. I don't know where he is. Could be on the moon."

"The moon?"

"For all I know."

"When'd you see him last?"

"Can't remember."

"Since the thrift shop."

"Another lifetime. Play me fair. Any money on the table?"

"I'm willing to pay for information. Can I come in?"

"How much?"

"Depends on how much you've got to sell."

He opened the door and I stepped in. The place didn't look as if it belonged in this neighborhood. It was filled with expensive looking things—crystal, china, silver. I didn't ask where they came from. House beautiful in the graffiti alley. On the marble (or marble-like) coffee table was a dead potted plant, the leaves of which had turned the color of pie crust. The walls had been painted stop-light orange by someone who was either colorblind or ugly fixated.

A man with heavily tattooed arms was sprawled across the couch. He was either asleep, in a deep drug fog, or dead. I wouldn't want to put a bet on which.

The woman disappeared into the kitchen leaving her smoke behind.

"I've seen you at the store," Smudge says.

"That's a nice piece of crystal," I say nodding toward the coffee table with a cut-glass vase being used as a cigarette butt receptacle.

"Want it?"

"Not particularly."

"Because everything in here is for sale."

"Including information?"

"Only the best."

"Any idea where your housemate might have gone?"

"Could be."

"Care to tell me?

"Like I said, everything is—"

"Yeah."

"for sale."

I didn't have a lot of money but expecting that this creep would be best persuaded by some green, I pulled out my wallet stuffed with $10 bills. I figured that a bigger stack of smaller bills would be more impressive than a smaller stack of bigger bills. Obvious disgust showed on his face.

"A hundred bucks?" he said apparently knowing exactly what a stack of 10 $10 bills looks like. "What do you think that will buy?"

"You tell me."

"Pizza and a couple of beers. Tax and tip extra."

"You said you might know where he is."

"Maybe."

"Then where is he maybe?"

"Maybe he's in San Francisco."

"San Francisco?"

"Maybe."

"What makes you say that?"

"Another hundred bucks might help me remember."

"I don't have another hundred bucks."

"And I don't have any more information."

"All right. I'll ... go get some ... where's an ATM around here?"

"They all got broken."

"OK, I'll be back," I said and headed back to Bucephelus, half expecting it either to be completely gone or be missing a few important components, like the wheels. But much to my pleasant surprise it was there intact. I guess Indian motorcycles are respected in such neighborhoods.

My semi-paid informant was right about at least one thing though: he lived in an ATM free zone. How uncivilized. By the time I managed to find one of the magic money dispensers, and make it back to the orange-walled apartment, the woman—mother—was alone.

"What happened to your son?" I asked.

"Nothing happened to him."

"Where is he?"

"Not here."

"He said he could tell me where I could find—"

"No he didn't."

"…maybe he knew—"

"You can talk to me."

"OK, enough with the goddamned games, where the hell—"

"You have the money?"

"Another hundred," I said, handing over five twenties which she quickly jammed into her pocket.

"San Francisco."

"That's what he said a hundred bucks ago."

"And you asked how he knew. This hundred bucks says he got a phone call from him from San Francisco."

"When?"

She shrugs.

"How do you know the call was from San Francisco?"

"What he said."

"But he could have been in Tibet."

Another shrug.

"Or one or other of the Wallas."

"This time I get a smile."

"You wouldn't know where in San Francisco, would you? It's a big city."

"And hilly."

For such a crummy neighborhood information sure was expensive. I'll have to chalk that up to rampant stooge inflation.

So all I got for $200 is the suggestion that maybe he was in hilly San Francisco from a woman who may be the mother of a man who may be telling me the truth and for all I know, could be an accomplice. I don't suppose that information comes with a money back guarantee. Perhaps I should assume he's anyplace in the world but San Francisco but since I don't have any other lead I figured I might as well enjoy the city by the bay.

75

I flew up to the metropolis of iconic hills, bay, bridges, cable cars and gingerbread Victorian homes. The only city where weed is legal and plastic bags aren't.

Where to start? I didn't suppose he'd choose to make a career of thrift shop dreck sorting again, but I decided to check them out anyway. There were a lot.

I began with the appropriately named Out Of the Closet, and quit when I got to the Minxy Boutique. If he was working at any of them, nobody was talking. Could be a cabalistic fraternity of sock sorters protecting one of their own, but I doubt it.

I guess I arrived in San Francisco's rainy season because I spent so much time puddle jumping that I might have been training to be a ballerina in "Swan Lake."

Had Smudge given it to me straight? I couldn't know for sure but I was beginning to chastise myself for even thinking he might. Why would he? They were buddies, right? Then again the world is filled with snitches (A word made uncool by rappers who wear pink fur coats.) who ditch their friends for less noble causes … such as cash. Since I didn't have any better leads to chase I slogged on through the hilly dankness. Then too, there was always the possibility I would run into a showing of "Duckrabbit," even if the odds on that were long. Or maybe I'd find some blabbermouth who saw it and was willing to break the tacit vow of silence.

I figured the best places to hang out were the lousier sections of town because that's where the lousier sections of humanity congregated and I was looking for a lousy human.

I headed for the tenderloin, an area so named because supposedly the police who were assigned to patrol this area got an extra stipend allowing them to upgrade their beef buying to tenderloin. Although it is adjacent to the touristy tony Union Square area, it is any cities' definition of seedy.

The freebie paper I picked up announced, "Twenty-four-year-old Robin Freeman who fled police during a traffic stop Saturday was shot and seriously injured while exchanging gunfire with police." Sounds promising.

The first place I checked out was the 21 Club, a dive-y joint which after ordering a beer and otherwise being completely ignored I realized was a gay bar, but since I had no reason to suspect the suspect is into the gay scene I left and looked for a dive-ier dive.

There are dives and there are dives. Aunt Charlie's is a dive. "Honkytonk" would be a step up. It even had Conway Twitty on the jukebox and that can't ever be bad. This ain't no hipster cool spot. Like almost nothing else in San Francisco, it ain't no tourist attraction. No, it's a place where professional drunks with that sad unable-to-help-themselves look come to drown away the day beginning shortly after sunrise … at the latest.

I sat at the bar, ordered a beer and … I didn't know what else. Wait I guess. But for what exactly? I'm not normally a procrastinarian but until I got either a stroke of insight or a stroke of luck, indecisiveness would remain my M. O. which is detective lingo for a settled and monotonous routine that is hard to escape. My groove.

After a while, a guy with a hole in the back of his dropping sweatpants plunked down next to me. His Tee-shirt apparently advertised his philosophy of life: It proudly proclaimed: "I only drink on days that begin with the letter 'T.' Tuesday, Thursday, Today, Tomorrow, Tsaurday, Tsunday."

His nod in the direction of the bartender was all it took to bring him his chosen drink—Red Rabbit Irish whiskey. I just woke up and I was already two drinks behind. Life's rough all over.

"I haven't seen you in here before," he said with a clarity and directness belying his appearance. "New in town?"

"What do you do on Wednesdays?" I said while thinking about a quick exit strategy.

He immediately picked up what I thought was a cryptic comment with a rather obscure referent.

"Even God took one day off."

"Did he?"

"Never drank on Wednesdays."

"Is that so?"

"It's all bullshit."

"I'll drink to that."

"I'll drink to everything."

As flea-bitten and woebegone as my bar mate seemed I had the distinct impression there was more here than met the blurry eye.

"I take it you're a regular here," I said not immediately coming up with a better fishing line. He looked at me as if he were saying with dripping sarcasm, wow, how very perceptive you are, my dear.

Instead he said with dripping sarcasm, "I didn't realize it was that obvious."

"I'm very perceptive."

"Perceptive people don't waste their time in dumps like this."

"No? What do they do?"

"They go out into the world and perceive things."

"That's perceptive."

"Ah."

"Wouldn't you say?"

He launched into what sounded as if he'd recited this verbatim before. "I would say that the accepted theory of perception is based on the philosophy that there exists an external world that is real to which we react. However, that is an Aristotelian dictatorship which is imposed on the masses who reside inside the educational system and have been wired up to it like humans wired up to the matrix. In reality it is entirely possible to perceive anything, and believe any construct or effect that arises from the actions which inevitably arise as consequences of those perceptions."

"In other words …?"

"What you believe you become."

"My, my."

"My perceptionalizationality of you is a well-guarded secret. So don't worry about a thing because it's all good."

"Yeah, and what is that, perceptionaliza—?"

"That, my inquisitive drink-Ms, is the degree of perception anybody can express to nobody."

"I'm not sure that makes sense."

"What does?"

"That's too … I don't know."

After another drink my philosophy-spouting bar mate confided that his name was Charlie Brown.

"Really?"

"Unless my mother was lying. Which by the way is a distinct possibility."

"Named after …?"

"Charlie Brown."

"The guy who needs to tell Lucy Van Pelt to fuck off and get a life?"

"The very ones."

"The philosopher."

"The anti-hero, the existentialist."

"Is he?"

"Is he? Poor Charlie Brown. He sits outside the principal's office, waiting to find out what will become of him. He offers up a little prayer, but all he gets is a stomach ache."

"An existential position."

"But then everything we do is absurd, without meaning, isn't it? Take for example that every Halloween Linus faithfully waits by a pumpkin patch in the hopes that he will be blessed with the holy experience of a visitation by The Great Pumpkin. But, oh, The Great Pumpkin never shows up and he never answers Linus' letters. Linus, though, remains steadfast, even going door to door to spread the word of his absent deity. So, does The Great Pumpkin exist? From the existential point of view it doesn't matter if he does or doesn't. The point is that Linus is abandoned and alone in his pumpkin patch."

"And poor Charlie?"

"He is alone, both physically and emotionally. Alienated from his peers he is fearfully awaiting punishment for his actions. In his desperation he looks to a deity for hope and comfort. Ah, but instead his angst overwhelms him. There is no comfort to be found. No hope."

"Kind of defeatist and depressing, wouldn't you say?"

"Except he also demonstrates the optimism of existentialism. Why does he continue to go out to the pitcher's mound, despite his 50-game losing streak? Why try to kick the football when Lucy always pulls it away at the last moment?"

"You tell me."

"Because there is an infinite gap between the past and the present. Regardless of what came before, there is always the possibility of change. It's a double-edged sword. We exist, and we are responsible. This is both liberating and terrifying."

A simple philosophy according to Charlie Brown—the other Charlie Brown.

"The very point of philosophy, insofar as there is any point to philosophy, is to begin with something so obvious and simple as not to seem worth stating and to end with something so paradoxical that no one will believe it."

"So you've adopted his philosophy?"

"In the book of life, answers aren't in the back. So I've adopted the philosophy that I only dread one day at a time. That way I can replace one worry with another."

"And that simplifies everything."

"I'm living the dash. That's all I can do."

"Meaning?"

"All any of us can do."

"I don't know what you—"

"The dash."

"What dash is that?"

"The gravestone dash. That little line between the birth date and the death date on gravestones. It represents a life. A little fucking straight line chipped out of granite or marble or something by a chisel. It's all that shows we were ever alive."

"Never thought of it that way."

"Seems to me anyway."

As the morning wore on he continued to drink, yet the more he drank the less drunk he appeared to be. This Charlie Brown it seems was a former college professor at Berkeley who either drank himself out of a job or lost his job which led him to drink. He wasn't copping to either.

"So tell me, are you the self-defeating stubborn Charlie Brown or the admirably determined persistent Charlie Brown who can never fly a kite but continues trying?"

"Isn't it obvious?"

"What did you teach?"

"Apparently not enough."

Why exactly I stayed I can't figure. I don't even particularly like beer. But there is something compelling about down-and-out cum-existential philosopher Charlie Brown but I can't figure out what that is either.

After a long silence he says, "It's blatantly transparent what I'm doing here, but I don't have a fucking clue what you're doing."

"Wallowing in irony."

"How so?"

"You know, like wearing a Che Guevara T-shirt made by a multi-national corporation—"

"Or bombing for peace."

"Do we do that?"

"It's been said."

"I'm looking for a guy."

"In San Francisco?"

"There must be some."

"Rumors."

So I explained my situation as well as my fuzzy-tongued mouth would permit. I'd have to check an instant replay to see if I was making any sense. Charlie nodded as if either I did make sense or he didn't know the difference and was just a habitual noddist. He offered to help with whatever it was he thought I was talking about.

"What do you know about this guy?"

I had to admit not a lot other than what I had gleaned from our grill-related conversations.

"What would you like to know about him?"

Although I realize the question caught me a little off guard, it really shouldn't have. I was looking for a man I knew little about although I had revealed a fair amount about myself to him. That says something about him, doesn't it? What? What does it say? He's smarter than I am? He may be but more likely it says he's more devious.

I told Charlie Brown everything I had gleaned about Staats from our thrifty encounters. It didn't take long.

"So you're looking for a serial killer," said Charlie with a little chuckle, "a juggalo with a sweet tooth for film noir classics, an advanced education in sock sorting, and a Club Fed alumni card."

"That's about the gist of it."

"The unreliable mother of an unreliable friend says he may be in San Francisco but he could be in Kokomo, Kazakhstan or Kathmandu."

"Not a real strong lead is it?"

"Well ..."

"And I can't say for sure he's a serial killer, but I think he is."

"Well, let's see, what do we know about serial killers?"

"They kill a lot."

"A lot being ...?"

"I'd say three ... or maybe four. I don't know."

"Studies show that more than 90 percent of known serial killers are male Caucasians between the ages of 25 and 35."

"You know that do you?"

"I don't know that. I know that I've read that."

"Because ...?"

"I used to read a lot. Now I drink a lot, two pursuits with about the same efficacy."

"So what exactly did you not teach enough of at Berkeley?"

"Demography."

"I don't know what that is."

"Apparently neither do I."

"What is it supposed to be?"

"The catalog says it's the branch of sociology that studies the characteristics of human populations, and I never argue with catalogs."

"So you know something about serial killers."

"I must."

"Such as …?"

"There are different types. The visionary serial killer usually hear voices instructing them to kill. The psychotic and schizophrenic cases. Your guy?"

"Not that I'm aware of."

"The lust killer is usually driven by sexual motivation."

"Don't think so."

"Thrill killers enjoy the experience of killing."

"Couldn't say."

"Power seeker killers enjoy having total control over the fate of their victims."

"Maybe. I don't know."

"The missionary serial killer often feels responsible to rid the world of a specified group of people."

"Could be."

"Charles Manson for example."

"Sounds like him."

"You sure?"

"No."

"Most are intelligent."

"Check."

"Despite their intelligence they often demonstrate poor performance in school, are socially inept and prefer solitude to social environments."

"Yeah, I guess that could all fit."

"Here endeth the lesson and begineth the next beer, which, by the way, you're buying. It's the information age and information costs."

"So I've been learning."

With the ghettofied hole-in-the-wall bar overflowing with midday boozetafarians we managed to find a booth in the corner to continue our conversation which was proving to be much more valuable than it had originally promised. Despite being a no-smoking environment, several people are. It's not likely though that anyone will call the nicotine police.

"So, you think your guy may be on some sort of anti-religious crusade?" Charlie asks after waiting for the requested beer to arrive.

"On the surface it would seem so, but you know, I'm not so sure … and I don't exactly know why I feel that way."

"Instincts can sometimes prove more valuable than facts."

"What do you think?"

"I try not to."

"From what I've told you, what do your instincts say?"

"Let me put it to you this way, everything in this fucked up world operates according to the laws of nature."

"Which are what?"

"Oh, like Newton's law of gravitation, Mendel's laws, the law of supply and demand and all sorts of things where there is a connection between lawhood and confirmability by inductive inference."

"That's over my head."

"Not likely."

"What are you saying?" Laws determine everything? They are ultimately truth?"

"No such thing. If you think you've got an inside track to absolute truth, you are undeniably doctrinaire, irrefutably humorless and intellectually constipated."

There was probably more to the encounter with Charlie Brown but I honestly can't remember how it went. The fog was moving in—both literally and figuratively.

I know I told him about the film and I know he said he'd heard about it but, naturally, hadn't put it together with the man I was looking for.

After that … it's all fog.

76

As soon as I left the bar, I sensed I was being tailed, a sense developed in the sandbox and mixed with the alcohol made me an absolute paranoid drunkophrenic. The fact that I was listing as I walked probably went completely unnoticed by the many other neighborhood listers. If I was being followed I certainly wasn't making it difficult and this was not a place where I particularly wanted to duck into an alley, dark or otherwise. Perhaps if I had been battle rattle ready… but that was another world, another time. Whiskey, tango, foxtrot.

Who would want to follow me? Lousy question. Why would anyone want to follow me? Lousier question.

I walked a block looked behind me, walked a block looked behind me, walked a block looked behind me. I wasn't seeing too well so any of the street people, either listing or listless, could have been the culprit if in fact there was a culprit.

It was a film noir gray day with clouds brooding rain.

All the girls I saw either looked like Lisbeth Salander or I imagined they looked like Lisbeth Salander when they actually looked like Miss Marple. All the boys were dressed like they had just come off the night shift of Murder, Inc. and were off to their high schools where weapon detectors would be used to check for pocket-sized Uzis. I was feeling a little screwed up.

I may have been drinking in wackaloon dives but I sure as hell wasn't staying in one. My relatively ritzy hotel was a long walk away but I figured I could use the air and perhaps the time to see if someone was really on my tail. I started up a picture postcard San Francisco cable car mined hill which reminded me of some of the slopes we trudged up in the sandbox. It's the last thing I remember before waking up in a white hospital room.

I didn't have to ask where I was. I knew where I was, I just didn't know why I was.

Should I have been surprised that no one in the hospital was paying any attention to me? Probably not. I checked to see what parts were movable. Arms, check; legs, check; neck, hands, feet, all check. What hurt? Pretty much everything. A dull burning pain. I knew the symptom. How's this for irony? Unhurt in Iraq, conked in Winoville.

Stranger than strange while I was out I saw no light, however dim, at the end of a tunnel. No curious onlooker staring down. Rather an an oddish ethereal voice: "Oh, you dubbuh-cwosing wabbit! You twreachewous miscweant. I'm a vegetawian. I onwwy hunt for the sport."

Completely off the hinges. What is it about being down for the count that makes you think you hear cartoon voices? Next thing I know I'll be cuckoo for Cocoa Puffs.

Later that afternoon I was released from the white-walled bizarroland with the caution not to "exert myself" as I was showing "concussive effects." Either that or hangover effects.

Now one of three possibilities has to have been the cause of my headache: I was conked as a random act of violence by someone into random conking, or by someone looking to withdraw cash without using an ATM, or someone warning me to mind my own business and not theirs.

I'm guessing the last option and after checking my wallet, I'm reasonably certain. Then applying my limited but satisfactory inductive skills I conclude that while I haven't found Staats, Staats may have found me. No other who-elses or why-elses make any sense. It's a start.

Maybe ol' skinny Smudge was selling the real stuff. Maybe. If so, what then? Was the attack supposed to be a warning to be followed by …? And the police, where were they in all this—or weren't they? I didn't even know if they knew about the film.

Time for serious evaluation.

As I see it, there are two distinct possible lines of investigation here. One, I suppose I could walk around San Francisco for the next few days hoping that I could get lucky enough to spot the head conker (pre-more conking) but that seemed like a dicey and perhaps painful chance at best. Besides he might move on from conking to something more sinister— like stabbing or shooting. Two, I could continue to look for someone who has seen the film, knows someone who has seen the film, or even happen to see the film myself. This may be a long shot but likely less painful. Would the film even offer up clues? Maybe.

So, how to go about it? After giving that question whatever consideration my dinged up brain could muster I decided to go walkabout while beckoning the aboriginal songline spiritual connection. It couldn't hurt.

Do paranoid people think they're paranoid? I don't know but I figured it couldn't hurt to carry my gun. OK, I had never bothered to get a permit to carry a concealed weapon, but I took my Baretta Sub Compact and concealed it in my pocket anyway. Why take chances?

For several days I wandered up and down the crooked streets of "The City" in all their daily dewiness hoping, I suppose that I would stumble into something or someone leading to something or someone of value in my search. I walked hither. I walked yon. I encountered more funky monkeys than could be found in any barrel of, with nary a boffin in sight. After sunset I would find myself constantly scanning blank walls hoping against hope that I might come across an impromptu showing of "Duckrabbit," but all I saw was dirty brick and enough graffiti to warm the heart of any spray paint can salesman worth his aerosol. A ruinous stench seemed to follow me everywhere.

Maybe I'd even come across Staats himself.

The city looked begrimed, dirty, I suppose because I was looking for the grime and the grunge. Had I been looking for the elegant and sophisticated I may well have seen men not wearing their jeans lower than their underwear and drinking beer from actual glasses, but as I wasn't, I didn't.

As far as I could tell, the new American vocabulary consists of just four words—"omygod," "awesome," and "shit," punctuated at regular intervals with "like" and the ever popular phrase "you know."

San Francisco may well be overrun by the sophisticati but I doubt if I was encountering anyone who could distinguish Monet from Manet, or for that matter, spell either one. On top of that, the weather was what I can only describe as truly dreich which, as my old Scots uncle used to say, means a combination of dull, overcast, drizzly, cold, misty and miserable weather—as he remembered it from the Glasgow of his youth. (He insisted that at least four of the above adjectives must apply for true dreichdom.)

When I checked in with the police to see if any progress had been made on the nun murders, a non-too-helpful detective told me, "we're not giving out any information on that case," which I took to be cop talk for "no."

Despite the initial attempts to keep the story out of the press, it began to get a lot of attention on television entertainment/news shows. Of course it was. They were nuns for Christ sakes. Dead nuns sell Viagra — particularly seven at one time. Mix in the mysterious film popping up willy nilly and you've got what television does best — exploitation disguised as information. The networks were tripping over themselves trying to line up all the "experts" as if they had the keys to the perpetrator's insights.

Pompous Blitzer ran with the story for weeks. And the O'Reilly clown … well, he was sure he understood the psyche of the murderer, but then he would.

I'm guessing the Nielsen rating points/share were, as they say, off the charts.

It is not my wont to admit this freely, but I was at a loss for what to do next. I was also at a loss for income. Normally I'd be tracking down deadbeat fathers and spying on sordid trysts both welcome and not. As it was, I was quickly running out of money, leads and ideas.

77

One drizzly day I was standing on a BART station platform, San Francisco's answer to New York City's MTA. Destination undecided. I was tired of gumshoeing my way around the hilly city. A moving seat seemed like a good idea. After a few minutes of looking for an interesting sign to read (there weren't any), a burst of stale air came rushing into the station announcing the arrival of a train. As a train approached a voice from behind said, "Hey, you don't want to get on that one, it's nuts to butts." I recognized Charlie Brown's gravelly scotch-trained voice—a voice that tinned my ear.

"Crowded you mean."

"Perhaps an understatement."

"What gets you off your stool?"

"You."

"Should I be flattered?"

"Absolutely."

Despite Charlie's caveat, we get on the train which as advertised is chock-a-block full.

"Where are you headed?" he asked raising his voice to be heard over the BART babble.

I looked up at the map above the door. "Millbrae."

"Why is that?"

"That's where the train is going. How did you find me?"

"Wasn't hard."

"Why did you find me?"

"To enroll in your quest. To search for everlasting truth. To find the answer to the question."

"Which question is that?"

"Why?"

"Ah, yes."

"I've decided to be a quester, to help you in your search."

"Help me?"

"In your search."

"Watson to my Holmes?"

"Poncho to your Cisco."

"Or Kato to my green Hornet?"

"It dawned on me in a rare moment of semi-clarity," he said stroking a beard that he didn't have. "A brief interlude of quasi-lucidity that perhaps—and I emphasize the 'perhaps'—an actual goal to chase might prove to be ... I don't know ... more interesting than life on the stool, albeit generating more sweat than I am genetically adapted to accept without considerable and stridently vocal protest."

"Such a sacrifice."

"And I have a tidbit of information that might prove ... worthwhile."

"I'm not proud, I'll take any handouts I can get ... scraps or full meals."

"The film is going to be shown sometime soon in the Haight. I don't know on what building, but how many blank walls can there be over there?"

"And you know this because...?"

"A stoolie on a stool whispered it to me."

"How did he … or she … know…?"

"No idea."

"Why would someone know you were—?"

"I know you can't trust that whisper stream because that stream don't run by everyone like it does by me. But somehow I think this might be the real deal."

"Why do you say that?"

"Hunch."

"That's it? Who is this person…?"

"I'm a little blurry on the details. Actually I'm a little blurry on almost everything but as they say in the detective business, I have to protect my sources don't I? Isn't that what you say?"

"I never have, but I suppose—"

"It's worth a try though isn't it? You want to see the film, I … have a hunch, and unless I'm mistaken you don't have anything, so hunch-hunting is probably better than nothing."

"Let's go to the movies."

78

Ah, the Haight-Ashbury (or as Hunter S. Thompson called it, the Hashbury) was once home to the summer of love be-sure-to-wear-flowers-in-your-hair hippies, now home to rows of neat "Painted Lady" Victorians, a gentrified Bohemian ambiance in its throw-back to the 50s lounge scene, organic and spiritual New Age vibes of the Sixties, punk-rock-politics and computer culture. Only in San Francisco.

"Ground zero during the summer of '67," said Charlie in a tone suggesting either disdain or reverence. I couldn't tell which. Maybe it's both.

The place has a just rolled-out-of-bed vibe with tourists, locals, and panhandlers in about equal numbers. A lot of homeless camp out nearby in Golden Gate Park, so the Haight becomes panhandlers' paradise.

We hadn't gone a block when I was greeted by a skinny panhandler "Hey sweetheart, got a hundred bucks?"

"No," I said doing my best to skirt the bony outstretched hand.

"Then how about a quarter?"

"Not today, bro."

"Well then, shizzle my dizzle, what a bizzo meet me up the gizzo when you get a clizzo."

"I didn't understand a word of that."

"You will," he said and scampered off down the crowded street presumably in search of someone who might.

Only in San Francisco.

"Look for a blank wall," I tell Charlie.

"Any wall left blank for more than five minutes is going to be graffitied over in four."

"Maybe up high someplace."

For more than an hour Charlie and I walked the streets of the Haight looking for blank walls. In a couple of hours it would be dark.

"Maybe we should find a place for a quick drink," said Charlie. "After all, I am a serial swiller."

"Swill on. I'm going to keep on trucking."

"Truck on. I'm going to keep on swilling."

Finding a bar was easy. The Magnolia Pub & Brewery was conveniently located right next to us. Finding a blank non-graffitied wall wasn't.

Had I been looking to get a piercing, grab a burrito, find the latest drum 'n' bass 12-inch, or spend the evening people-watching from any number of nearby cafés I would have had no problem. However, my life never seems to be that simple. Or is it?

79

From behind, a voice that rustled: "I've been expecting you."
The voice cuts through me like a shard of glass. "I know."
"Took you a while."
"Living with your brother?"
"The family that stays together…"
"Does what?"
"Whatever."
The last time I had seen Bruns was when I threw him out. He looked different now. Older, yes, but there was something more. Something in his eyes that looked like it came from someplace else. Someplace far away. Or maybe I'm just flattering myself that I can read such … signals.

"You've made quite a name for yourself without naming yourself," I say. "Really clever self-promotion? The mysterious artist who will emerge some day from the mistiness, fame and fortune to follow? Or something else?"
"When did I ever say I wanted to be rich or famous?"
"I don't know. When did you?"
"You think I'm on a quest for fameification?"
"All artists want to be famous. Why would anyone want to be a secret artist? You show your work. Isn't that what artists do? Show their work?"
"Sometimes."
"And if they become famous enough—"
"To do what, rest in the long term memory caches of others?"
"OK."
"How are you, Cherry?"
"Frustrated, tired, curious."
"You always look so composed.'
He could be, and often was … I don't want to say charming exactly, but … affable, genial. I'll leave it at he could be very friendly.

80

We first met five years ago, believe it or not, at a circus. That was odd because I don't even particularly like circuses. I have sort of a "so what" response to anyone who can spin dinner plates on top of sticks, twist themselves into contorted shapes, or take a close-up look at lions' dentures. Goody-goody for them. I was only at the circus because I was meeting an old college girlfriend who had a thing about elephants who could stand on their front legs.

He was sitting next to me with a sketch pad and a stick of charcoal busily drawing away. I wasn't paying much attention, until he held out the pad in front of me.

"What do you think?" he asked.

I took a brief glance and quickly concluded it didn't look like anything other than black smudgy marks on paper. "What is it supposed to be?" I asked.

"It's not <u>supposed</u> to be anything. It is exactly what it is."

"OK," I said, hoping that would put an end to the impromptu art exam.

He ripped the "exactly what it is" page from his pad and handed to me. "Here, it's for you. It's a present."

"Thanks," I said flatly enough to suggest that I wanted to end the exchange.

"I think you'll agree it captures the elephantness of the elephant while completely avoiding the cliché of representation."

My friend looked over and giggled at the absurdity of the situation. I was caught between wanting to get out of the conversation and not wanting to embarrass this pushy guy any further.

"It's a composition that exists with a significant degree of independence from any visual reference to the real world," he said apparently oblivious to the giggle and what must have been my obvious discomfort.

"You mean it doesn't look like an elephant."

"I don't know about 'looks like.'"

"Well, it doesn't to me."

"It all depends on how you look at it. Someone may see an elephant, someone else may see … something else."

"I guess I'm in the 'something else' category."

Looking at the drawing again, I have to admit that within the maze of black lines I could with some imagination make out the outline of an elephant, although if he hadn't told me I don't think I would have. Maybe a bowl of squid ink pasta.

"Bruns," he said, putting out his hand for a shake.

"What?"

"My name. Bruns."

"Cherry."

I have to admit he was a rather good-looking guy, rugged, with a neatly trimmed light brown beard. But his most commanding feature were his really lively blue eyes. (He once described them to me as being china blue.) Oh, those sprightly eyes, they seemed always to be so alive, so full of … I don't know, potential I guess … anticipation. I could imagine them being the eyes of an explorer excited by what might be around the next corner. But his voice was something else again. I always thought of it as a husky tragedy voice that belied the promise suggested by those eyes. Did this dichotomy suggest a struggle going on someplace behind that beard? I wondered back then; I'm rather certain of it now.

Anyhow that's how we met—over a drawing of an elephant that wasn't.

"We, that is artists, see life in a different way from most people," he said as we were walking out of the circus. "Literally. It's not a choice, it's the way we're … wired, I guess is the way you'd say it today. Something that looks like one thing to you … to a normal person, may look completely different to me … to an artist. But anybody can be an artist. See that streetlight? Don't think 'streetlight,' think something new, something completely different, something a little weird. You can't be afraid of weirdness. It has to be embraced."

I wasn't particularly interested in an art appreciation lesson, and at the time I wasn't particularly interested in seeing him again. But I did.

"How did you get my number?" I asked when he called the next day.

"I read your mind."

"No you didn't."

"You gave it to me."

"No I didn't."

"You're a sneaky son-of-a-bitch."

"So you want to go out with a sneaky-son-of-a-bitch?"

The conversation veered off topic to where we might meet up again and I never did pursue the telephone number question. We agreed to meet the next weekend at an old movie theatre showing an even older movie—supposedly some kind of classic but I have long since forgotten what it was except that it looked like the producers couldn't afford lights. That I remember.

We continued to date for a while, albeit very casually. He was a couple of years younger than I, still in college, and working part time in a gallery downtown. I had graduated, was living on Daddy's money, and was trying to decide what to do with the rest of my post-John Jay life.

When Bruns suggested we move in together I agreed, not because I was in love with him but because it was convenient. Looking back on it, maybe it was because I was bored. OK, maybe that sounds a little callous. Perhaps "looking for excitement" might better describe my situation, and to me Bruns held out that possibility, although I didn't know precisely how or why. I was about to find out.

He moved into my apartment.

Yes, I was supplying most of the rent money, (thank you Daddy) but I understood that when he moved in, and I accepted it. He called himself a "starving artist," although only half of that phrase was even remotely true.

The thing about him that was the most noteworthy is that he acted like he knew everything—and he pretty much did. Well, if not exactly everything, at least a lot of things. He could be arroganic one moment and downright childlike the next. This could be either off-putting or comforting depending on the moment or the situation. For the most part, though, getting into an argument with him was to end up on the pointed end of his verbal rapier or the shattered victim of one of his frequently lofted logic grenades.

All of this made for animated dinner parties and volatile amusements when alone.

I was expecting the artist—any artist—to be compulsively sloppy as befitting the stereotype of the creative, perpetually shambolic artiste. Somehow the idea of order runs counter to the idea of creativity.

However, he was anything but disorganized.

His creative streak betrayed his formal, almost Holmseian, rationalist mien; insatiable curiosity, fundamental discomfort around other people and beneath all this, a deep wellspring of tenderness. As the saying goes, something of a conundrum wrapped in an enigma.

One thing he most certainly wasn't was an overt sentimentalist, a romanticist. Not that he couldn't be romantic, passionate even, but not a romanticist in the way the word is used to represent a school of thought popular in art, writing, and thinking originating in Europe in the 18th century. As I recall from my college days it had something to do with placing an emphasis on untrammeled feelings.

By way of example: I remember once when we were walking along the East River and came upon the cutest damn dog—no collar, obviously hungry. I don't know what kind it was but it looked so forlorn, with a "won't-you-please-take-me-home" look. There was no one else around so he wasn't out on a walk with his owner.

I suggested we take him home, feed him, maybe keep him. To my mind he was of the loveable persuasion with pleading eyes and a longing smile-like snout. Bruns thought otherwise.

"When I was a kid we briefly had had a dog named Fido," he said, "originality not being one of our strong suits. Fido was vicious and he bit. Like other dogs he was part hyena and part wolf, neither of which could remotely be called trustworthy. Both mean, both meat eaters with only their teeth for tools. Dogs are dogmatic; they will refrain from killing only so long as they are being fed. We preferred either the 100 percent complete and balanced nutrition of the quality ingredients in Alpo or the neighbor's cat. Fido preferred meat. No meat thermometer necessary. He wouldn't send it back if under- or over-cooked. Or even cooked at all.

Like all dogs it would only have taken a few lean days for dear Fido to revert to cracking living bone in his teeth. He had enough Doberman lineage in him that he knew to be loyal to his feeders. If we had not fed him, he would have either found new masters or reverted to killing on his own. He was loyal just so long as we killed for ourselves as well as for him, throwing him scraps from the result of slaughters in return for his loyalty. As long as there are dogs with kind eyes we will understand that man is a killer so efficient that he has something left over for his four-footed friend, for it is on the scraps that the bargain is sealed or forgotten, not on kindness. Dogs don't like us, they use us."

"So what happened?"

"To Fido? "My brother shot him with a .22."

"Why?"

All I got in response was a shrug.

This was typical. During our time together we had many long conversations about many things, but the one topic he shut down on almost immediately was anything to do with his family. If I got anywhere near the subject, he'd respond with a shrug—which in time I took to calling the Brunsian shrug. He didn't have to say he wasn't going to go there. The shrug said it all—that he didn't care or at least pretended not to care.

I eventually learned that he grew up with two brothers and a sister. When I asked about his sister: Shrug. "She died a long time ago."

"How?"

"Accident."

When I asked about his brothers: Shrug, "I don't know."

"Don't know what?"

"Anything."

"Where they are?"

"Yeah."

"Were you … close? Growing up—"

"Once."

"But not now?"

"No."

When I asked about his mother: Shrug, "Never knew her."

"You never knew your mother? What happened?" Shrug redux.

When I asked about his father: Shrug, "Let's get Thai. I feel like Thai tonight." Or some patently similar evasion.

The father evasion though, seemed more defensive than the others. Eventually, after persistent cajoling which he probably considered nagging, he told me his father moved away and it took Bruns years to finally find him. Someplace in Texas. Dennison or Denton, I think. Something like that. Worked for a railroad company and was killed in an accident. Must have been a careless or unlucky family—both a sister and father killed in accidents. I knew there had to be more to the story but that's all I dragged out of him.

Most of our days were taken up with his painting, (with nary a drop of pigment on floor, walls, furniture or ceiling) and with me out looking for a job, the stream of Daddy's money slowly being reduced to a trickle.

Among his artistic skills was the ability to draw famous cartoon characters. And he was really, really good at it. His Elmer Fudd and Bugs Bunny you couldn't tell from the real ones. The same with other well-known cartoon figures. He'd sketch them quickly when he became frustrated with a canvas he was working on—like doodling. When I'd mention how good they were, he would toss them away with "That's just craft, simple craft. It has nothing to do with art."

Much to my father's chagrin, I had a degree in Criminal Justice rather than one in finance. Yeah, I know, old story—offspring refusing to follow Daddy into his profession. My brother and I were hardly groundbreaking in our rebellion against parental wishes. Oh sure, more than once Daddy had threatened to cut us off, but he couldn't find it in his larcenous heart to do it completely.

I'd like to think that we opted for a more honorable life, but maybe that's just blatant rationalization. After all, we didn't exactly turn down his tainted money. I suppose we were hypocrites (sort of like eating a veggie burger with bacon) and probably no better than he.

Anyway, I was looking for a job that Daddy reminded me would prove to be dangerous, low-paying and undignified. Daddy knows best. You would have thought New York had enough criminal activity to hire every Criminal Justice major this side of Pyongyang. But apparently not so.

It's not that I was being picky. I didn't even find scraps from which to pick. I ~~knew~~ thought agencies were hiring women now, even small women. They were, however, not hiring this small one. I suppose this put me into a perpetual semi-foul mood, and certainly didn't help my relations with Bruns, which after a few months of living together, began to head south—or at least southerly.

How to put this discretely? Well, he liked the chase and I got tired of running. Sex, he claimed, resembled VIP access, because like all men he had to be invited. "We work for it," he said, "we convince, we campaign, we strategize and pull out all the stops. You women control all access and we're supposed to enjoy the challenge of obtaining this 'invitation.'"

What he meant was that he didn't want to wait for the invitation. He wanted in anytime he wanted in. That didn't work for me and one night

I told him so. He was … pissed.

    He grabbed me. I told him to let go.

    He pushed me down. I told him to get off.

    He pulled my jeans down. I tried to shove him away.

    He saw his action as his right. I saw it as rape.

    Adios amigo. I left that night and hadn't seen him since.

81

Now encountering him again in the Haight brought out both the good and the bad vibes.

"I am going to assume you're looking for me because you want to find my brother."

"Assumption—the mother of all fuckups."

"Is that so?"

"An expression in the Corps."

"Peace or Marine?"

"Marine."

"Were you?"

"Right after we split."

"You always said—"

"You're creating quite a show."

"Am I?"

"With your film."

"I know."

"So, about your brother."

"What about my brother?"

"Where the fuck … where is he?"

"Ah, yes, where the fuck is he? Well, I can say for sure he's not here."

"Here being …?"

"Here, right here. In or at this place."

"I wasn't really interested in where he isn't."

"No."

"So?"

"Maybe you'd like to see the film."

"If that's going to tell me—"

"Something at least."

"the truth about—"

"Everyone around me wants the truth, but as Michael Clayton showed, the truth can be adjusted."

"So I've discovered."

"We are, after all, living in a relativist postmodern world."

"You're mistaking me for someone who gives a damn."

"So you're into the detectifying business."

"The film, where can I—?"

"Stick around."

"Count on it."

"Nice seeing you again, Cherry."

With that he was off down the street at a fast enough clip to let me know that following would be difficult. I thought about going after him but then quickly surmised that there was nothing to be gained. Even if I did catch up, gimpy leg and all, what would I get? He obviously wasn't going to divulge more than he already had. But I took it as a good sign that we were both in the same city. Coincidence? I doubt it.

I went back to the Magnolia where I had dropped off Charlie Brown. Not surprisingly he was still there.

"Any luck?" he asked mid swivel.

"As a matter of fact."

"So?"

"I ran into our stealthy auteur."

"What a coincidence."

"Yeah."

"Did he tell you about the film? When it's going to be shown? Where?"

"No, but he isn't here because he wants to buy a tie-dyed bandanna."

"It would be the place."

"So I'm thinking we're in for a show, if not tonight, then soon."

We knew we had a little time before it would be dark enough to show a film, so we agreed to a post-beer exploration of the neighborhood buildings by splitting up. We agreed to meet back at the Magnolia Pub & Brewery.

It was a clear starry night with nothing to suggest a weather delay might be in the offing. But, just as the daylight was about to give up the daily ghost it started sprinkling. Now this is very odd because it doesn't rain in August in San Francisco except it was. Soon the sprinkle that wanted to grow up to be proper rain did. I headed back to the Magnolia.

I ducked in out of the rain as obviously had a slew of others. The place was fairly packed. I didn't immediately see Charlie so I looked into the row of high wood-backed booths and the various nooks and crannies of the crowded pub even though he was more of a bar stool guy than a nooks and crannies guy.

No Charlie. I was surprised I could get to a bar before Charlie, but I ordered a beer nevertheless and waited among the other standees. Perhaps he had come up with something concrete that had detained him.

The bartender who didn't look old enough to be out of grade school let alone pulling brews told me he hadn't seen Charlie for a while and didn't remember seeing him leave.

The rain turned to a steamy low-hanging fog. Outdoor film night in the Haight seemed to be off.

I left sans Charlie Brown. I'm not sure why I had thought he might be reliable. The eponymous cartoon character is after all the great American un-success story in that he failed at almost everything he did.

Still, the night hadn't been a complete loss and I felt reasonably confident the film would be projected on the next available clear night. Whether it would, in fact show me or tell me something of value in my search, was another question.

82

That night, lying in my far-too-squishy hotel bed, I couldn't sleep. I kept going back to what I thought of as a golden youth lost forever. My brother and I running freely on the slopes of Central Park. Lollipop days.

We spent a lot of time together. Joe was a "blue baby." That is, he was born anemic. Something about being incompatible with Mother's blood type. There was a lot of to-do about it when he was little. I was too young to understand any of the details but I do know he was overly protected by our parents—ridiculously so. He was a sweet kid and we kind of semi-bonded. He didn't really have a lot of friends … other than me. I can remember playing with him on the jungle gym in the park. I remember long hours of us reading our library books under leafy park trees. I remember horsing around … wrestling. Maybe that's what led him to join the wrestling team in high school. He wasn't particularly good, but he stayed with it. The odd thing, given his career choice, is that he never seemed particularly spiritual, didn't go to church regularly, didn't talk about his beliefs in things … religious. When he decided to go the clerical route I was rather surprised, but by then we had gone our separate ways. We attended different high schools and colleges so what influences he had been subjected to during those years I don't know. But whatever they were they led him to … whatever has happened to him.

After he disappeared, the police did a perfunctory investigation and eventually arrested Staats but then in an act of what? Incredible incompetence? They let him get away due to what they called "an act of God," implying, I suppose that God was pissed off at someone working on his behalf—a dubious position at best. OK, maybe Joe had issues, but he was hardly unique among the priesthood.

With time to reflect back on all of this, I remembered once some time ago when living with Bruns that I came across a card he apparently thought he had torn up and thrown away. While emptying the wastepaper basket I saw it and, because I was becoming somewhat curious if not suspicious about whatever had gone on in Bruns' past, I spent some time putting the little pieces of the card together like a jigsaw puzzle. The card was for someone named Dr. Robert Sinnott-Smyth, a forensic psychologist.

I decided to see if I could find the forensic doc. Perhaps he could tell me more about Bruns which perhaps would tell me more about Staats which perhaps would lead me to him. That was a lot of "perhapses" but lacking any "definitelys," I thought I would give it a shot.

He wasn't hard to track down. Thank you Google.

83

He introduced himself and said he would talk with me but that there was a line over which he couldn't or wouldn't go. Something about a "privileged relationship." Other than that he turned out to be a lot less pretentious than his stiff upper lip name suggested. He looked to me like a Simon/Garfunkel combo—a face that reminded me of Simon, hair that reminded me of Garfunkel.

In my experience you can usually look around a person's office and tell something about the person. But this office was pure vanilla. Not even whipped cream or cherry on top. Nary a picture of a family, boat, dog or cat in sight. Nothing on his desk to suggest that he played golf, fished for trout or hunted white rhinos. As far as I could tell, this man was a complete cipher which I guess is exactly what he wanted to imply. A blank slate onto which his "patients' (or are they "clients?") could project whatever they wished.

He started out by questioning me.

--How much do you know about the accident? With the train.

--Only what he told me.

--Which was?

--I don't even know how much of it was true … if any.

--Tell me.

--You already know. You did the questioning. You had him, you questioned him and then you let him go.

--I'd like to hear what you know.

--He called it the "incident."

--Yeah.

--But he wasn't always as forthcoming with answers about his … life and things. Truth wasn't always in his court. But you know that.

--Well—

--You do.

--What else did he say … tell you?

--A man was killed.

--Did he say who?

--He said it was a mystery. Anyway it was for the investigators. For a long time they didn't know. But then they found out that the dead guy had been living under a false name. Someplace in Texas I think. Some Podunk town. I don't know. He was very much a loner and very much an alcoholic. Fact is he was blotto at the time of the accident ... the incident. So he should have seen it coming. The signal that was wrong. If he wasn't drunk he would of seen it. He would of gotten out of the way ... jumped off the train.

--Go on.

--That's it.

--Not who the man was?

--No. Only that he was arrested. You guys held him for I don't know, a while and then let him go. As I figure it, you know who he killed. You've always known. Or at least you've known for a while.

--At first we didn't, no.

--But now you do.

--Now we do.

--So why don't you tell me.

--His father.

--You've got to be shitting me.

--No.

--His own father.

--An abusive father he didn't get along with. None of the brothers did. The father, he was a drinker and had something to do with the death of his own daughter. I don't know the details.

--Then why in hell did they let him go? What, patricide isn't a crime anymore?

--He didn't do it.

--They let him go because he didn't do it?

--That's about it.

--He confessed to throwing that ... whatever it was ... a switch or something. He said he threw the switch. He said he killed the man on the train—his long lost father. He admitted killing his father and you let him go.

--Yeah.

--So now you going to tell me why he confessed?

--He was covering for someone else.

A long pause as she stares at her questioner. Finally ...

--His brother.

--His brother? His brother did it?

--The younger one.

--The one who went into the Marines?

--Yeah. Apparently that's why he took off. As I understand it, he was sent to Afghanistan or someplace, served there for a while and then disappeared, went AWOL. I guess the false arrest and admission of guilt bought the real killer enough time to ... I don't know, disappear into the hills or something.

84

The next day I went back to the dive bar where I had met Charlie Brown. While there I learned two things: One, he wasn't there. Two, courtesy of the seldom courteous young bartender, who I was told was called Tiny Tim, the eponymous Charlie Brown was actually the "Aunt Charlie." It took me a moment to remember that that was the name of the dump. It seems he was the onetime college professor he professed to be but had bought the bar years ago, apparently partially with grant money that was supposed to go for some sort of research. Maybe this place was his research and maybe that was why he was an ex-professor.

Tiny Tim said he hadn't seen Charlie in a couple of days, didn't know where he was, and didn't "give a flying fuck."

For several days I returned to the Haight hoping to see the film. I didn't.

It was time to take stock.

I checked with the police on their progress with the nun murders. There was none. They had no leads no fingerprints, no physical evidence, not a hint of motive other than a general suspicion of anti-clericalism. Ditto the file on my brother.

85

Early one day I was wandering along Van Ness Avenue when I heard, "Damn girl yous is fuckablessed. Shiiiiit."

I recognized the odd-looking panhandler I had encountered earlier even if I didn't understand the language he was passing off as English.

"Cause I know who you be looking for," he continued.

"Is that right?"

"I knowed first time I put my poppin' peepers on you at Smudge's. Seen you from the couch."

"How is that?"

"He ain't normal, you know."

"Yeah, well, who is?"

"Not him anyways."

"So, where is he?"

"Well, shizzle my drizzle, honey, yesterday I bopped into the Harbor Mission. Down by the bay. A sign in the window said," he fumbled in his pocket and came out with a pamphlet and handed it to me.

"Harbor Rescue Mission strives to serve the Lord through all of its services. The aim of Waterfront Rescue Mission is to Demonstrate God's Goodness by Providing Rescue and Recovery Services in Jesus' Name."

"I was hungry," he said. "and they was dishing out wet grub and you could bet your bippy I knew the power of the religious con game. So I slide inside. Another sign it says, *If you haven't got a friend in the world, you will find one here* and I did. It was like coming home. My old roomlump celli mate, Staats. He was ladling out soup to the droolies."

"Did he recognize you?"

"I ain't hard to miss, miss."

"He was working there?"

"Didn't I just tell you?"

"You said he was serving—"

"Working there, yeah."

"Did you talk to him?"

"Yo."

"And …"

"And what?"

"What did he say?"

"Hello."

"What else?"

"Chicken noodle, beef gumbo or mullag … something soup?"

"Soup?"

"It was a fucking soup kitchen, little lady. That what he was doing, pushing soup."

"Did you have a conversation with him? Did he tell you anything about … I don't know … where he was living or anything?"

"Said he'd found true religion … and soup."

"Did he?"

"What he said."

"Did you believe him?"

"Look, sweet cheeks, all I can tell you is that's what he said."

"Did he seem different? From when you guys were in prison, did he seem different?"

"Yeah, he seemed free."

"Looks, I mean."

"He was bald and sleeved."

"I don't know what that means."

"What what means?"

"Sleeved."

"Get an education, carrot-top."

With that he was off down the street, presumably looking for his chemical of choice.

So it was on to the Harbor Mission, which was obviously over by the harbor, which was obviously yet another seedy section of town. I was getting used to this.

86

The Harbor Mission was a storefront facility facing the Bay Bridge, albeit a large one serving what looked like hundreds of free meals in exchange for a little proselytizing. It was a monotone place with neon-lit joyless gray walls adorned with various "We believe …" aphoristic quotes such as *"We believe that for the salvation of lost and sinful men, regeneration by the Holy Spirit is absolutely essential,"* and a few health reminders about things like sharing needles and "better safe than sorry" condom use.

Staats was not there. My understanding was that he worked there either as an employee or a volunteer. But when I ask about him no one seemed to know who he is. I assume he probably used a different name. When I describe him I get blank looks. But then giving out information in a place like this is probably strictly *verboten*—particularly if the asker might be someone in authority. Even though I hardly look like the law I might have been better off dressing down for the occasion.

An older lady wearing a blue jumpsuit and a fuzzy purple hat sat at one of the dozen or so round tables with her Chihuahua terrier. I joined her.

"Chicken, chicken, chicken, chicken, she says. "I'm going, cluck, cluck, cluck."

"The price is right," I say.

"They should serve healthier food."

"Like tofu?"

"What's tofu?"

"I don't know but it's supposed to be good for you."

"I don't like tofu."

"Do you happen to know a man here who—?"

"Nope," she said with emphatic conviction. "You don't happen to have any lighters, do you?"

"Lighters?"

"You know, like Bics. They're little portable cigarette lighters."

"I don't think you can smoke in here."

"Lighters are not toys," she said as if she were reading a prepared statement. "Teach children that matches and lighters are tools for adults, not toys for children."

"Yeah, I'll be sure to do that."

"Keep all matches and lighters well out of children's reach."

"OK."

"See, I collect them. That way the children can't get them to burn down things."

"Makes sense."

"They come in all sorts of colors you know."

"Well, it was nice talking to you," I said as I got up.

The assorted "diners" were serious about their eating. No one looked up from their plates, no one noticed me ... except the man with the collar who appeared to be the man described in the brochure on the table:

"LuTimothy Jones. With an exceptional anointing for ministry and greatness in his veins Rev. LuTimothy J. Jones, Sr. is a 3rd generation Pastor. He is the son of the late, great Rev. Theosophus Jones and First Lady Margaret Jones and the grandson of the founder, the late, great Rev. T.W. Spooner and late First Lady Francis Spooner. Rev. L. Jones' commitment to Christ is a part of the legacy of his mentor and father, the late Theosophus Jones."

I approached him and asked if he knew Staats.

"As far as I'm concerned everyone here is anonymous," he says.

"I'm not police. He might work here."

"You certainly don't look hungry, so why are you—?"

"He knows my brother and I haven't been able to find him lately ... my brother that is. He's sort of ... gone missing, and I thought his friend, Staats, might know where he was."

"Well, you're certainly welcome to stay and see if he shows up."

I thought if I engaged the affable reverend a little he would loosen up and I might be able to get more from him.

He is a small, trim, tidy mocha-skinned cheery collared man with the cheerierist giggle this side of Goldie Hawn.

It wasn't long before it became clear that in any encounter he led with a smile. It was his weapon of choice and it was ChrisRock/Magic Johnson magnificent, gleaming white and wide, a smile that easily burst into laughter. Still, sometimes he seemed to hold onto that smile too long—so long that it became just teeth.

I asked him about the program they were running.

"We have two phases to our program. The first phase lasting about three months, offers a rigorous Bible-based curriculum, individual and group counseling, and a work experience program to help the men rebuild their lives. In the second phase lasting four months, the men move over to our New Horizons Home for Men where they continue in counseling and work therapy, but also work one-on-one with chaplains to address the life-dominating issues that have led to their situation. At the home, they also have the opportunity to work toward their GED certificate."

As far as I knew, Staats didn't have any addiction issues and certainly didn't need a GED and probably didn't have the patience to teach a GED class.

"Most of the men … and a few women … who work here came through our program."

"But not all?"

"I don't think so."

"When you hire someone do you do anything like … like background checks?"

"Everyone here has a background … issue. That's why they're here. We're here to help not judge. No, we would never check."

"It's really great what you're doing," I say in an attempt to keep him engaged.

"It's probably one of the hardest challenges I've ever faced" Jones said, "but, nevertheless, it has brought more value to my life, to my understanding of where our obligations need to be as a community. I know now that we can collectively overcome what all odds says we can't."

"It's truly wonderful that we have people like you. I mean look at all these—"

"If we weren't here I don't know where these souls would get help. Did you know there are over 6,000 homeless people in San Francisco and almost a thousand are youths?"

"Why so many?"

"Oh, lots of reasons really. When Reagan was the gov he closed most of mental hospitals statewide which put scads of people on the streets, people who are not able to care for themselves. Then, too, the cost of housing here is very high and our weather means that people can live on the streets year-round unlike say New York. And we're in a very liberal city with more programs like ours to help the homeless and destitute than most cities, so they come here. Of course, the government should be taking care of them but really they're not. Our whole social services, the San Francisco Human Services Agency … well … they're not doing the job. I'll leave it at that."

"At least they have you."

"If anyone has material possessions and sees his brother in need but has no pity on him, how can the love of God be in him? Dear children, let us not love with words or tongue but with actions and truth. John 3:17."

"Amen. I guess I didn't mention my brother was a priest … is a priest."

"What was his name?"

"Joe … Father Joe."

I am not a mind reader; I'm not clairvoyant. I am somewhat intuitive, however, and as soon as I mentioned the name of my brother, I was hit by an overriding impression that I had struck a nerve. He knew who I was talking about. He knew my brother, or he knew about my brother. I was sure of it and as a detective you have to go by gut impressions.

"Do you know him?" I asked.

The big smile disappeared instantly. "I doubt it," he said. "Look, it was nice talking to you but I've got things I need to attend to, so if you'll excuse me. If you'd like to make a donation, there are some forms you can use on the table by the front door."

Donation? Was he implying that if I made a donation to the shelter he might offer more information? No, surely not. Well … maybe. It sounded like it. If so, information inflation seems to be rampant.

He went into a little office off the dining room. There was a small window through which I could see him. He was sitting at a desk talking on the phone. Every few seconds he looked out, looked at me.

I milled about as the free lunch bunch thinned out. There was a connection here with my brother's disappearance (Should I just come out and say "murder?") and the more time I spent at the Mission the more convinced I became.

The diners were, to say the very least, an eclectic crowd—mostly men, a few women, a few beyond my ability to determine.

I had a short but bizarre conversation with one man who insisted that Lukas Hammer was very active in San Francisco. I have no idea who Lukas Hammer is, but the man insisted that he was "responsible for the Nazi Warsaw design that killed so many people and he is doing it again in San Francisco."

I had no intention to argue the point. For all I know he might be right.

I was about to leave when Rev. Jones returned from his cubby-hole office.

"I think I need to come clean," he said. "Isn't that the right phrase? Detective talk for ... explaining things."

I never said I was a detective. Either it was that obvious or he had been forewarned.

"I do know the man you're looking for. Staats."

"Tell me about him."

"He's harmless."

"Surely you jest."

"He's a ... well, he's hard to describe."

"You telling me."

"For the last few years he's been a semi-regular at our devotional services. He's worked here ... helped here as a volunteer ... helped prepare and serve meals."

"You sure we're talking about the same man?"

"I know it seems ... a stretch, but he really is a man of ... well, I was about to say, faith, but I know he's had his share of doubts and they show up in his ... what shall we call them ... flights of fancy."

"You'd better define that."

"Imagination. Maybe overactive imagination."

"Tell me you don't think he's violent."

"No more than you or I."

"Speak for yourself."

"I am."

"He killed my brother."

Rev. Jones stopped, took a deep breath turned, walked a few steps toward his office and then turned back. It was obvious that he was wrestling with what to say next.

"Please excuse me for a moment."

He went back into his cramped office. I could see through open slats in the window blind that he was sitting quietly. I assumed he was praying, probably for divine guidance. Should he tell me more? Apparently he received an answer because in a few moments he returned.

"He is a middle-aged man with a paunch, ponytail and a runaway imagination. He suffers from the same malady not unknown to some famous clerics of the past. Men like Luther, Calvin, Knox and I don't know how many popes. He lives his life too much in his mind, in his imagination and comes to the point where he can't tell the imaginary from the real.Look, he's perhaps a little delusional. He's in his own world wherever in Walter Mitty land that might be. He's actually the mildest mannered man you'll ever meet, temperate, docile."

"Are we talking about the same man?"

"I know it doesn't seem that way sometimes."

"You think?"

"He's very … complicated."

"Nuts, you mean."

"I don't know. It's very possible to be delusional without accompanying prominent hallucinations or significant thought or mood disorders. Apart from the delusions, people with delusional disorder often continue to socialize and function in a normal manner without their behavior seeming odd or bizarre in any way. They can remain coherent, sensible and normal."

"But he still can be nuts."

"I know this may be hard for you to believe but he's really a spiritual man, a believer. Well, in essence he is, but in his self-searching for … I don't know what you call it … peace, I guess, doubts creep in and so he fantasizes about another self, the one you think you know."

"What do you mean fantasizes?"

"Makes up stories."

"You're losing me here."

"He wants to know if he could be the man he … makes up. The man who murders believers. He wants to put himself in that position, in his mind, that is."

"Are you trying to tell me didn't kill my brother."

"I don't think he did."

"Then where is he, my brother?"

"That I don't know. He's talked about a few others, too. A man in a parking lot, some others."

"How do you know he's not telling ... that he didn't really do them?"

"I've talked to him a little, gotten to know him some."

"Except he's got a hang-up about religion ... religious figures."

"He's testing. He's a believer, albeit with doubts. That's really not so unusual. Lots of religious figures have them."

"You?"

"Sure, at times."

I couldn't be sure if the reverend was giving it to me straight or not. Was he covering up something? Protecting Staats? What he was telling me didn't align with my impressions of Staats. Not by a long shot.

"The motivating force in his life is unbridled boredom. He called it the slump duck—boredom in the existential sense. Sort of like Schopenhauer. You know Schopenhauer?"

"Only the name. We had to read him someplace along the line but I don't remember anything other than he was hard going."

"Well, he as well as his existential buddies claimed that boredom was not inconsistent with the propensity to meet it with various religious activities, not because religion is wont to associate itself with tedium, but rather, partly because boredom may be taken as the essential human condition to which God, wisdom, or morality are the ultimate answers."

"Bored or not, he has decidedly anti-clerical leanings."

"Does he really?"

"Seems to me."

"There's a lot of that going around, particularly among orthodox liberals and in so many novels movies, television and the mainstream press."

"Some of it is justified, though isn't it? Child abuse and all."

"Sure. That's appalling, so has been the bungled, often corrupting responses by men in the hierarchy. It's no wonder that they have provoked expressions of anger in words unmatched since the 1920s. Those crimes are abominable, as the anger of enormous numbers of clergy and lay leaders dramatizes. The bottom line is that we've acknowledged it, we're dealing with it, and we're moving away from it."

"It's growing, though, isn't it? The opposition to the influences of the clergy in public affairs."

"I suppose it is. There's something I'm going to tell you that ... well, you'd probably figure it out anyway," he says with an excessively affable smile—there's something rather carnivorous in this overdone amiability. "Maybe not, but anyway I suppose you should know."

"I'm listening."

"I know what he says happened to those nuns—the ones who were found hanging. It was mass suicide."

"How could that possibly—?"

"They had help. Someone assisted them, probably with a ladder and then took the evidence away."

"You mean Staats?"

"I don't think so. Somebody else, maybe another sister or one of the clerics."

"That doesn't make any sense, why would they ... suicide? Mass suicide?"

"Apparently."

"Because ...?"

"Some kind of mixed up eschatology. I don't know exactly, but it had something to do with the belief that with the second coming of Jesus Christ believers will be raised from the earth to meet him in the air."

"What, they were trying to get a head start?"

"They were apparently ... confused ... deranged."

"All of them?"

"Maybe one held sway, convinced the others. That's not unheard of. Jim Jones like."

"That's a sin, right? Isn't suicide a sin in any religion?"

"Well, it wasn't always. Not according to the Justinian code for instance in the Middle Ages. Some others, too."

"But today it certainly is. Thou shall not kill and all."

"Unless you translate the sixth commandment as 'thou shall not murder,' in which case it doesn't necessarily apply to the self. So if God has given us free will, then taking one's own life doesn't violate God's law any more than ... I don't know, curing disease or something. And the Bible, too, there is no dire condemnation of God's followers in the Bible."

"What do you think? Where do you stand?"

"Personally?"

"Yeah."

"I'd say it is a sacrosanct right of anyone who has rationally and conscientiously come to the decision to end their own lives."

"Even if they're young and healthy?"

"Why not if they're competent to make the rational decision."

"I suppose you could argue that if God gave us the gift of life, we shouldn't give it back. If it's a gift … you don't give gifts back."

"You mean God would think it rude?"

"Wouldn't you?"

Jones' broad smile turned into a chuckle. "I guess so. It's hardly unknown, though. Japanese Kamikaze pilots, Irish hunger strikers, the entire Jonestown population. Heck, thousands of Japanese civilians took their own lives in the last days of the Battle of Saipan. Jumped off Banzi Cliff if I recall. There are tons of other examples, too—Heaven's Gate, Solar Temple."

"I sort of remember the Heaven's Gate mess."

"They believed that by committing suicide, they were exiting their human vessels so that they could get on a spaceship believed to be following the Hale-Bopp comet. Some of the men even underwent voluntary castration in preparation for a genderless life to which they believed they were headed."

"Who knows, maybe they got it right."

"May have, but I'm going to hang onto my jewels."

"And there was that group in Uganda. Some 800 who took their lives … something about emphasizing apocalypticism."

"You think it's just us? I mean, do you think animals can commit suicide."

"Oh, I know they do. Of course, they do. Some kind of aphids when threatened by lady bugs explode themselves which protects their aphid mates and can kill the ladybug. Some kinds of termites can also explode covering their attackers with sticky goo."

"Why do you know that?"

"I don't know, but I do."

"Do the police know about the suicides?"

"I don't think so."

"If you do, why don't they?"

"The church authorities … they don't think it would send the right message."

"Which is what, suicide is bad for your health?"

"For whatever reason it was their decision."

"So it leaves the police chasing ... wasting resources looking for ghosts."

"That's about it."

"So that leads me to one crucial question."

"Yes."

"How do you know? Because Staats told you that? And you believe him?"

"My job is to listen to those who come here to—"

"Maybe a good lie for a hot lunch is a reasonable deal."

"Except we all tell lies, don't we? Every day, many times every day. Some of these may be biggies, like 'I never had sex with that girl,' but more often they are little lies we usually call white lies, like 'yeah, I really like your hair cut that way.' Not all deceptions are lies, though, more like comb overs like nodding when you're not listening. Then, too, there are the lies we tell ourselves for all sorts of reasons. Maybe maintaining our self-esteem. The thing is, I don't think he knows the difference. His lies, his fiction,—call it his art—they are one and the same. He is his film. He makes up adventures, he ascribes significance to them and then lives them. He lives in his own film, makes his own clock tick in a clockless world."

"That's crazy."

"I don't know. I see all sorts of people come in here and ... well, let's just say it's not always easy to separate the real from the fantasy. It's not A or B, black or white, yes or no. Life's more complicated than that, more complex. But to Staats, his reality and his fiction are the same. At least he wants them to be the same. He fights that battle but in the end fiction has narrative shapes and a coherence that life frequently ... usually lacks. In fiction seeing contrasts between light and dark is rewarding. It emphasizes story and character, but in real life ... well, experiencing those contrasts is an absolute bitch. It's the old innocence/experience predicament, a sort of Catch-22. Even so, we have to accept that even if it means suffering metaphorical bloody noses."

"Or not metaphorical."

"There's a thought that it's all relative. All truth is relative. There is no God of relative truth. Morals are relative to the social group within which they are constructed; considerations of right and wrong are dependent on the situation."

"Do you really believe that?"

"I don't, but I know he does."

"What do you think?"

"It doesn't really matter."

"I'm interested."

"OK then, I think that there is such a thing as absolute truth that our culture is abandoning. We want to avoid the truth of right and wrong. Our judicial system, for example struggles to punish criminals, our entertainment industry continually pushes the envelope of immorality and indecency, our schools teach evolution and social tolerance. All over, people are accepting homosexuality, pornography, fornication and all manner of sins that once were considered wrong but are now not only being accepted but are being promoted on a big scale. Oh, and if you speak out about this 'anything goes' philosophy, you're labeled an intolerant bigot. Pure hypocrisy! The truth is that too many people today are promoting the idea that all points of view are true except for the views that teach moral absolutes, an absolute God, or absolute right and wrong."

"Staats."

"It would seem. Look at our lives one way and they are reality; look at them another way and they're pure fiction."

"The film."

"Look around, many of the characters in his film are here."

"You've seen it?"

"I have."

"His film, or his brother's film?"

"The brothers, all three of them were in on it. I don't know exactly what each one of them did but I know they were all involved."

"You said the characters in the film are here."

"As Shakespeare said, all the world's a stage, and all the men and women merely players. They have their exits and their entrances."

He proceeded to point out several of the diners including the man I had already met. He called him "Tootsie Pops." He identified another one as "Trashcan." He told me they were all in the movie, that Staats used the people he came into contact with as characters in his film story.

"How long has he been coming here?"

"I don't know. He was around when I got here a year ago."

"Are you saying none of the stories he told me about his background, growing up and all that … that he made all that up?"

"Only he knows that.."

"You're saying he has fooled me all along?"

"I'd say there are a couple of ways any of us can be fooled. We can believe what isn't true or we can refuse to believe what is true."

"Ah, but to know the difference."

"Yeah."

"And you think you do."

"I am the Way and the Truth and the Life; no one comes to the Father but through me."

"Truth as an attribute of God?"

"It is."

"How do you know?"

"The Bible says so."

"Which is without error?"

"It is without error."

"Staats' brother insists art is truth, the avenue to the highest knowledge available to us … a kind of truth impossible to attain by any other means."

"God shows himself in many ways."

"Getting back to Staats' … truth. His version of truth—"

"Comes out in his film, yes. It was all about a movie, making a movie. He wanted to live his movie. Write it from the inside. He would do certain … things … and then explore them in his movie."

"His victims, how did he choose them?"

"Assuming there really were some, they were probably related to some key figure in past traumatic events."

"Like his father."

"I think that's a reasonable assumption."

This made me wonder about my brother. If Staats did kill him, and knowing what I did about Joe, it raises the suspicion that perhaps Staats was molested by his father as a child. Perhaps all three brothers were. Did that turn Staats to symbolic revenge murders, Bruns to expressing his emotions in art, Hyde to running off to war? I didn't know the answer but it was a question worth considering.

"Did he ever tell you that?" I asked the pastor, doubting that he wouldn't say even if he knew.

"Not directly, no."

"You … inferred it?"

"You asked about his possible victims and I offer that as a reasonable supposition."

"Then he did say something—"

"I know this. I know that it's very difficult for most victims of sexual abuse to ever talk about their experience of the abuse. They bury the trauma deep someplace within, but the memories … they haunt and they mark the victims for life. If they ever act on their pain and anger it may come out as violence or as is often the case, as some form of developmental disability."

That could certainly explain Hyde.

"What do you think about artistic creativity and … emotional disorders? I asked.

"I know that some people argue that artistic creativity and mental illness are somehow inevitably linked, that emotional disorders sometimes come with a built-in creativity boost."

"Do you believe that?"

"Not completely. I think that can be, and sometimes is the case, but clearly that stereotypical viewpoint and the stigmatizing statements that often come along with it … well, that idea should have been put to rest a long time ago."

"But it's not inconceivable that in a given situation they could be connected."

"Sure."

This was starting to add up. The brothers as victims. The brothers as injured. Could be an explanation. I queried the pastor about what, if anything he knew about Staats' father. He said he didn't know anything. He said Staats never talked to him about his family. That I could believe. Bruns didn't either, but there was that story about killing his father in that train wreck.

The pastor had given me a lot to chew on. How much I could believe I didn't know.

87

For the next several days I stopped by the Harbor Mission but there was no Staats. Perhaps the reverend warned him off. Perhaps Staats had seen me there and was now avoiding the place.

I decided to avoid the Mission for a few days hoping that if Staats was keeping tabs on me he might have decided I was no longer looking for him there.

Then one night I was heading to Aunt Charlie's to see if the eponymous owner might have returned.

The street was greasy with rain. What little light there was bounced off puddles. I couldn't really tell what I was looking at. It looked like … it looked like three men in silhouette. Hard to see. It's raining, it's dark, it's shadowy. Three men. The brothers? Staats in the middle, Bruns and Hyde on each side? Looks like them.

I'm not about to take chances. I pulled my Baretta while the tapes played in my head—Hyde in the sandbox telling me everything was FUBAR, Bruns in our apartment telling me his X was a higher truth, Staats in the thrift shop telling me he didn't know which the hound liked more, the chase or the kill.

For what seemed like a full minute but was probably only a few seconds, I was frozen in place looking at them as they stared back. It was raining and windy enough that the rain was coming directly into me. I had to wipe my eyes. After I did, they were gone. Maybe they weren't ever there. Had I become so obsessed with them that I was seeing shadows in the rain? Was I losing my grip on whatever passed for reality?

No, it looked like them as silhouetted as they were. Was this supposed to be some kind of threat like when I was knocked unconscious? I had come to the conclusion that that may not have had anything to do with them. Random attacks aren't uncommon in big cities, but I may never know for sure.

Either way, I ran to where I had seen the three figures, or where I thought I did. On the right there was an alley. Bad things happen in dark alleys, but I started down it anyway. I remember Staats talking about his love of film noir. This was a film noir alley if ever there was one. What little light there was came from a couple of windows high up on both sides. I edged my way along the brick-sided alley dotted with trash bins and several large cardboard cartons serving as homes for the otherwise homeless. I held my gun down by my thigh. I didn't want to use it but I would if I had to. A scrawny cat ambled by. And then another.

Down near the end of the alley I could see a metal door that looked as if it wasn't completely pulled shut. Did they leave it open as an invitation to go through it, a dare to go through it? Or maybe somebody just forgot to close it. I moved next to it to see if I could hear anything inside. I couldn't. I looked in. It was dark but there was a light on. Not much. Not overhead but enough to see that it looked like a kitchen restaurant. I reached out and pushed the heavy door open wide enough that if I chose to I could get through. Still no sound from inside. I waited a moment, took a deep breath and crouched as I slipped in.

Nothing.

I ducked behind a counter, stayed still for some time trying to decide whether to move, call out for Staats, make a hasty exit or …

I heard footsteps and then fluorescent light flooded the kitchen. I peeked around the counter to see a man—could have been Chinese or Korean—carrying a big sack of … something. When he saw me he let out an exclamation in a language I didn't understand but took to mean something like, "What the hell are you doing here, lady?"

It quickly became apparent that Staats wasn't here. Neither were his brothers. If they ever had been they had left through the restaurant.

When the sack carrier saw my Baretta he let out what was certainly an expletive and boogied back into the restaurant. I grabbed a fortune cookie and returned to the alley.

My shadow chasing was over for the night.

As I walked down the alley I opened the fortune cookie: Looking for your brother will prove dangerous.

What the …? That's not possible. Did I misread it? Just then a gust of wind jetted down the alley blowing away the little slip of paper with the fortune on it. I started to go after it, but I would have to have been a bird to catch up to it.

88

Maybe I was seeing things, imagining things. Maybe my chase to find Staats had affected me to the point that I was no longer completely dealing with reality. In the parlance of the day maybe I "was losing it." A distinct and increasing possibility.

In the days that followed I began cataloging the increasing symptoms of … I don't know what. I noticed bodily sensations such as a crawling feeling on the skin. I heard sounds that may not have been there. I heard whispers. I saw patterns of lights where there shouldn't have been any. I smelled foul odors without a source.

The divide between reality and illusion was becoming blurry.

All life is an illusion. Somebody said that. I don't remember who, but somebody important enough to make into one of my college textbooks. Or is that just wishful thinking on our part? Maybe we can't handle too much reality so we grab onto our illusions even as they contradict the obvious.

But if all life is an illusion then every experience we've ever had, every person we've ever cared about is an illusion. On the other hand, maybe reality is not an illusion but rather our version of reality is an illusion so that we perceive reality not for what it is, but for what we wish it to be.

Still there has to be a difference between what something is and what we think it is. Actually what we think is completely inconsequential to what is. That's what I think anyway.

I kept asking myself how we can know if illusions are creating reality.

Ah. That's the deal me thought. We can't while we're under their spell. When we understand the difference between reality and that which we inject into it through our thoughts and beliefs we realize that much of our despair … anger was fueled by these misperceptions. It seems to me most of our conflicts in life stem from our illusions, but then, who the hell really wants to live in reality? Maybe Staats is more comfortable living in illusions under the assumption that the gain far outweighs the effort needed to eliminate them.

89

Back at Aunt Charlie's I again asked churlish Tiny Tim if he knew where Charlie was.

"Try the San Francisco city morgue."

According to him, after Charlie hadn't shown up for some days, one of the waitresses went to his apartment, knocked, got no answer, found the door unlocked, went in, found Charlie on his couch looking as if he had been there for several days stone dead.

"The way he drank, what the hell else could he expect?" said Tiny Tim.

"Yeah. They do an autopsy or anything?" I asked.

"What for?"

"To see what—"

"There was no family, nobody to look into anything. We're the closest thing to a family he had, me and the girls and we know what happened. Charlie's gone, that's it. Goodbye Charlie. Tip one with the big guy."

"So what about the bar? Who owns it now?"

"Damned if I know. I'm just gonna keep working here, take my pay from the till until somebody stops me."

"Was there ... I don't know, a funeral or something?"

"Beats me."

So Charlie Brown was gone and nobody gave a shit. I kept thinking about his 'living the dash' remark.' Somebody should put up a marker someplace with his name and that dash. I suppose I could.

"Do you know when he was born?" I asked the bartender.

"Nope."

"Do you know where he was born?"

"Nope."

"Do you know why he was born?"

"Yeah, his father fucked his mother."

I guess that summed it up pretty well.

"His stuff is in the back room," he said. Me and the girls, we went over and got it before they cleared it out. Go and look if you want."

Now I'm not the most sentimental soul who ever came down the pike and I can't say I knew Charlie for long or well, but I couldn't help feeling a little emotional as I looked over the detritus that he left behind.

Naturally there was nothing of any monetary value. I don't remember if he wore any jewelry or a watch. I imagine if he did the firm of Tiny Tim and girls would have hocked it by now.

There were a couple of books. I picked up one: "Introduction to Social Macrodynamics: Compact Macromodels of the World System Growth." I put it down quickly.

There was a Berkeley catalog. I remember he said he once taught Demography there, so I checked the faculty listing. There he was.

Charles Brown earned a B.A. in History from Yale, and M.A. in Demography and Social Sciences from the Ecole des Hautes Etudes en Sciences Sociales, Paris and a Ph.D. from the Department of Demography, UC Berkeley. His research interests include: long-run demographic and fiscal stochastic forecasting; intergenerational transfers; macro consequences of population aging; evolutionary theory of the life cycle; and population and economic aging.

The catalog was a couple of years old. Why he chose to leave or was thrown out I don't know.

There was a pile of his logoed tee-shirts

We are all born ignorant but one must work hard to remain stupid.—Benjamin Franklin.

Knowledge is knowing tomato is a fruit. Wisdom is not putting it in a fruit salad.

And there were numerous well-worn drinking shirts:

The liver is evil and must be punished.

Wine is proof that God loves us and wants us to be happy.—Benjamin Franklin.

Finish your beer. There are sober people in China.

My Life is a very complicated drinking game.

Drink … Pee … Repeat.

So clearly, Charlie Brown, Ph.D. was a really bright guy, a lush with a sense of humor, and … not much else. Was he married? Was he ever married? Did he have children? Will anyone (else) regret his death? Former students maybe? I'm doubting that there was even an obit to let them know he was gone.

I'm feeling sorry for a man I barely knew.

While sifting through the unremarkable pile of effects I came across a folder with "Duckrabbit" scrawled on it. Inside were a few yellow quad pad pages with handwritten text—apparently Charlie's. I sat and read.

"Notes on Staats, Hyde, Bruns:"

George Washington, The Joker, Dracula, Julius Caesar, Robin Hood, Hans Solo, Superman, Buddha, Goldfinger, Vlad the Impaler, Spartacus, Tarzan, Joan of Arc, King Kong, Jesus Christ, Huey Newton, a couple of popes I didn't recognize, Christopher Columbus, Martin Luther and Martin Luther King, Jr., Freddy Krueger, Bonnie and Clyde, Mao Tse Tung, Idi Amin, The Wicked Witch of the West, Moses, Lassie, Mohammed, Robespierre, Virgil Tibbs, Hitler, Popeye, The Terminator, Alexander the Great, Caligula, The Toxic Avenger, Osama bin Laden, Bernard Madoff, Nero, Jim Jones, The Swamp Thing, Dr. Hannibal Lecter, Darth Vader, Ghandi, Abraham Lincoln, Norman Bates, Indiana Jones, Atticus Finch, Butch Cassidy and his sidekick, Patton, Obi-wan Kenobi, Michael Corleone, Captain Bligh, Batman, various Martians or other aliens, Lex Luthor, The Penguin, The Thing, Ivan the Terrible, Pol Pot, Stalin, Genghis Khan, Himmler, the Dalai Lama. Elmer Fudd."

That was all. I looked around to see if there might be additional pages somewhere else but there weren't any.

Charlie Brown, you were a mass of contradictions piled on paradoxes, surrounded by ambiguities.

What were you getting at? Or were you too high to be getting at anything? Were you ever anything more than an oxymoronic boozer/intellect? Did your woozy life amount to anything more than unfulfilled promise?

90

if i could of come back i would of but i cant. not after i took out them creeps that killed our own. im glad i did just like i done to pops on the train. somebodys got to see that things are made right. goodbye bros you probably wont hear from me again but dont worry none. i can take care of myself.

91

It was probably the time to give up the chase, let it go. My brother was gone, the nuns were dead. I kept telling myself to move on. I had done all I could. Except, the drive for the truth had become so powerful as to render any other activities I might have pursued meaningless. I felt all inner development was ceasing, that I was being choked because a single idea was filling my entire being. I was obsessed to the point that I couldn't walk down the street without looking at every passerby to see if it might be Staats. My anxiety level was sky high. I wasn't sleeping. I was barely eating. I was so completely preoccupied by my search that no logic or reasoning dulled my obsession. I was becoming unhinged, quite possibly delusional and I knew it.

I began seeing Staats everywhere. Give it up I kept telling myself. Go back to New York. That would have been the rational thing to do but rationality had long since stopped being my modus operandi.

If I asked anyone at the Mission about Staats I drew nothing but blanks. I rattled every cage I could think of but all I got back was the snarl of beasts.

92

Then I saw a poster in the window of a little book store advertising: *Noir City. The 15th San Francisco Film Noir Festival. Featuring 25 Cinematic Samplings of Murder, Mayhem and Mystery. January 16-25 at the Castro Theatre.*

The poster showed a typical film noir shadowy scene with a tough looking man with the noir obligatory gun, hat pulled down low and dangling cigarette.

At the bottom of the poster: *If you want to know the meaning of life, don't study Shakespeare, don't peruse Plato. Everything you need to know in life you can learn from film noir. And everything you can learn from film noir, you can find at Noir City.*

Inside the store was a little brochure listing the titles, dates the films would be shown and a statement about the foundation: *The Film Noir Foundation is a nonprofit public benefit corporation created as an educational resource regarding the cultural, historical, and artistic significance of film noir as an original American cinematic movement.*

They also had postcards: *Greetings from Noir City. If you want fresh air, don't look for it in this town.*

This is promising. Knowing Staats' fixation on film noir, if he's still in the city he'd likely turn up there. So would I.

I traded my Stetson for a San Francisco Giants baseball cap and on opening night of the festival made my way to the theatre.

The Castro Theatre is like no theatre I had ever seen. I guess you would call it Spanish Baroque. The inside is incredibly luxurious and ornate with both convex and concave walls and ceiling and a mighty pipe organ they play before the films begin.

Film noir must be more popular than I thought because the place is jammed. "Sold out" read the sign in the box office window. There was, however, a scalper who sold me his extra ticket for $20.

I moved across the street where I could see the noir buffs arriving. Most were young men who weren't even alive when many of the films were made. Some were wearing "costumes"—trench coats from the 50s, brimmed hats, double-breasted suits. There were young women, too wearing 40s or 50s dresses (I can't tell the difference) and hair styles to match.

A few minutes before 7:00 when the film was scheduled to begin, a large crowd moved in. I thought I saw Staats but I'm not actually sure. I didn't want to get too close because he would surely recognize me. My red hair if nothing else.

I'm about the last person who went in. I found a seat in the back row where, if it ever got light enough, I could see the audience in front of me, although since it was film noir that could take a while.

After a few welcome remarks by the festival organizer, who apparently was dressed up to look Sam Spade like, the film started. It was an oldie—"Silent Night, Bloody Night."

A young girl walks through the woods and comes upon a house. *This house was built by Wifred Butler in the 50s*, she says.

I spent more time, more scanning of the back of heads in front of me than watching the film.

Soon they will tear it down and I will be left with only memories.

I think I see Staats in about the fifth row. It's hard to tell for sure because typical of the genre most of the film is dark, but I think it's him.

He never lived there until one night.

I watched him intently to make sure he didn't leave. He doesn't budge during the entire film.

I, Wilfred Butler, being of sound mind and body … at least what the world considers sound do hereby leave this world as I found it with all its inhumanity and cruelty.

The man I thought was Staats was still there as the credits rolled. I am stunned by what I see.

The principle character in the film is a man named Wilfred Butler. He is represented by three different actors at different times in his life. The actors are named Staats, Bruns and Hyde.

93

I waited as the audience filed out—everyone except that man whom I could then see was in fact the man I had long been searching for. He remains seated, staring forward. When everyone else has left he gets up and without turning walks forward and through a door next to the screen. He was inviting me to follow. Why else would he be acting this way?

As I go through the door, it closes behind me. The room led to another and then another. They were storerooms, utility rooms of some sort.

It was dark. I took out my Beretta.

"Can I interest you in a George Foreman Grill?" came his voice from someplace in the dark.

"Only if you show me how it works."

"It comes with instructions. Turn on. Cook."

"That's over my head."

"Work on it."

"Come on out. Let me see you. It's been awhile."

"Put your gat down."

"My what?"

"Noir talk for gun.

"OK," I said putting the gun on top of a nearby cardboard carton.

He stepped out from behind a metal rack holding film cans silhouetted by a dim shaft of light coming from a barred window high up. I could tell, though, that the ponytail was gone, replaced by a shaved head. I couldn't see if he was holding a weapon.

"You've led me on a merry chase," I said.

"Never chase a lie. Let it be, and it will run itself to death."

"A lie then, is that it? Not reality?"

"That all depends from which side you look at it."

"I'm looking at you."

"Personally I like to look reality straight in the eye and then deny it."

"Is that what you do when you think about my brother?"

"I don't think about your brother. At least I haven't for some time."

"Oh, but I think about your brothers."

"And just what do you think about them?"

"Now how could I be so lucky to meet all three of you in one lifetime?"

"Pure serendipity."

"Is that what you'd call it?

"Something pleasant or useful found while looking for something else. Inspired by a Persian fairy story, "The Three Princes of Serendip.""

"Hyde. What happened to Hyde?"

"He went AWOL, which in his case either meant 'absent without leave' or 'a waste of life.' Most likely both."

"Because of what happened in Afghanistan? What we saw?"

"I'd guess that was part of it, but then he couldn't really come home anyway, could he?"

"I don't suppose."

"Because you know the story. You know the truth."

"Anyway what Bruns told me, but putting "Bruns" and "truth," in the same sentence requires a leap of faith I'm not always willing to take."

"Coward."

"So, do you know where he is? Hyde."

"Nope. And probably never will."

"And Bruns?'

"He is his art."

"What is that supposed to mean?"

"What it says."

"So where is his arty self?"

"Art is everywhere. The X is ominpresent."

"You might as well—"

"I guaran-damn-tee it," he said bolting for a back door.

I always had quick reactions and I was on him before he got out. I tackled him as deftly as an NFL safety and then landed a blow to his stomach with a well-placed knee. I learned a lot in the Corps. I bound his hands behind him with my belt, dragged him up to a kneeling position, shoved him, none too gently, against the wall. He didn't say anything.

His face showed what I can only describe as a smirk tending toward a simper. I little blood dripped from the corner of his mouth, his nose looked as if it no longer centered his face.

For some seconds he stared at me, said nothing. Then, "Enjoy that?"

"I told you once I'm into violence. Yeah, I enjoyed it. It's good fun. Let's you know you're alive. I told you that night we had dinner in my apartment. Remember?"

"And all along I thought you were coming on to me."

"Is that what you thought?"

"I figured you were into ponytails."

"You don't have a ponytail."

"I did then."

I gave him another swift kick to get the smirk off his cynical face. The smirk/simper segued to twisted anguish.

"So where do you want to take this?" he asked. "You can't arrest me. You're not police. You don't got no stinking badge."

"But I do have really pointy cowboy boots," I said as I delivered another on-target kick. "Don't underestimate me. If you disappeared, who the hell would miss you? Who would give a shit?"

"Me, for one."

"I want to know about my brother. I want to know all the details."

"No, you don't."

"Let me see if I can convince you," I said as I came down hard on his ankle.

He slumped to his side, took a moment to recover, then said, "Torture is illegal. Didn't you get the United Nations Convention Against Torture memo? It went out to all the assholes."

'Last I heard murder was illegal, too."

"Now you tell me."

"My brother ...?"

"Your brother the brother?"

"My only."

"You know about him. You must."

"What's that?"

"What he did to little boys. Lots of little boys. Lots of little boys lots of times."

I didn't know. I had suspicions but maybe I didn't want to know so I never pushed him into talking about his private life. Maybe the failing was mine, not his.

"Who appointed you judge and jury?" I said barely resisting the impulse to impart more pain.

"The boys in absentia."

"We have a legal system to—"

"I heard them."

"take care of—"

"You want to know what happened to your brother, ask him."

"I hardly think that's possible."

"Oh, but it is. If you can find him. You think I killed him. I didn't. I threatened to expose him, to tell the church, the police, the boy's parents your father, anybody else who gave a diddly. The church might not have done anything, but yeah, I confronted him, I told the sick son-of-a-bitch that he had three choices: He could confess, he could kill himself, he could make himself invisible. I was hoping he would off himself, but unlike his little sister he seemed to have an aversion to violence. So he invisibilized himself."

"I don't believe you for a second."

"Truth and belief don't always go hand-in-hand."

"Don't I know that. You and your brothers, as far as I can tell, you've been prisoners to lies for so long you've practically become institutionalized."

"You're wight."

"What?"

"Right. I mean you're right. Of course I mean you're right. About the lies I mean, but not your brother. I didn't kill him. He just … I don't know where he went. Undercover. I guess that's what you'd say—undercover. He went undercover when I threatened to expose him."

"You didn't kill him?"

"I never killed dat wabbit."

"My brother. I'm talking about my brother. They arrested you for that."

"Indeed, indeed."

"And you got away because of an act of God."

"Was that what it was?"

"Or dumb luck."

"Luck."

"I'd say."

"Ah, yes, luck—life itself."

Is there a shred of reason to believe him? I can't come up with one. He may be, probably is, a liarholic. Does he even know it? Is he so self-deceptive that he can't tell fact from fiction, delusion from truth?

Another long pause is lightly punctuated by the sound of rain dripping off the roof hitting a garbage dumpster. An endless, repetitive whispering sound spreading sullenly through the small storeroom.

Staats' eyes look a little sad, downcast. His lips are dry and he has a growth of beard on his chin. His protruding eyes make him appear slightly stupid although he is hardly that.

"You know, I learned a lot in Afghanistan. Among the things I learned a really lot about was torture, particularly waterboarding. I'm guessing you've heard about that, maybe even seen YouTubes or something."

"Yeah."

"We got good at it. Of course, we denied it, but we got it down to a fine art. Want to hear about it?"

"Not weary."

"Not really? Well, tough shit. Here's how we did it. First we'd get some sort of board. Let me see if I can find one around here someplace. Oh, look, here's a little table. I bet I could knock of those spindly legs. Then I'd have a board."

It didn't take much. I knocked off the boxes sitting on the top, lifted the table over my head and then brought it down hard on the floor. After several attempts the legs did snap off.

"Now I'll want to set it at an incline of about 15 to 20 degrees so that when I tie you to it your feet will be above your head. What did you say? Did I hear you say something?"

"How dare you twy to mistweat me, you miscweant."

I found a cart with a lower shelf that as soon as I blocked the casters, fit the bill. I put the board in place. Perfect.

"Now you can either get on the board nicely or I can put you on it un-nicely."

"I twied and I twied to tell you the twuth."

"Your choice."

I yanked him up and he got on the board with a shit-eating, the-hell-with-you grin.

"Now this is optional but I always liked it. You can either put a damp cloth over the face to keep the water clinging to the face—the towelheads choice—or put plastic wrap over the mouth but not the eyes or nose so as to prevent water from escaping the throat and sinuses—the CIA technique. This is not essential to the procedure. Consider it a bonus intensifier. See, if you try to blow the water out of your throat or mouth, the wrap will catch the water and keep it in. Sort of a one-way valve to let more out and then close again to prevent inhalation. Eventually you'll end up with empty lungs, collapsed lungs with no ability to inhale more air, a throat, mouth, and nose that's still full of water. And no ability to get water out since you're already fully exhaled."

I could have used a plastic bag but fortunately there was a box of Saran Wrap. I ripped a piece off.

"You trying to kill me? You can't kill me, I'm already dead."

"Then it won't matter."

Before I could put the bag in place, he said, "Sawan Wap is the twade name for a number of polymers made from vinylidene chlowide along with other monomers."

"Now I'll pour water onto your inclined face so that the water will run into your upturned mouth and nose. The water will stay in your head, filling your throat, mouth and sinuses with water."

Experience has shown that his lungs wouldn't actually fill up with water so he wouldn't asphyxiate, but he would surely feel his entire upper respiratory system from trachea filled with water, simulating drowning— drowning from the inside, filling the head and neck. The lungs would stay out of the water, keeping oxygen in the blood and prolonging the glubbing.

"Now from actual firsthand experience I can tell you that on average the subjects last 14 seconds, or roughly the amount of time they can exhale through the upturned nose. This will keep the water out temporarily but when your breath runs out the water starts flowing in. Admittedly there are a number of variables I could play with: the board's angle, the amount of water, the pressure of the wrap, maybe a couple of others. We used to say we had to walk a fine line between allowing waterlogged wheezing and deep gurgling. Asphyxiating is, of course, quite possible, but over in the sand pile we usually had doctors on hand with blood oxygen monitors to make sure the poor slobs stayed oxygenated enough to remain conscious. If they didn't, the doctors had at most five or six minutes to resuscitate before brain damage occurs. I'm afraid we don't have any doctors here so you'll just have to trust my … judgment. Oh, and by the way, doctors on our Behavioral Science Consultation Team who reviewed interrogation procedures and trained the interrogators determined that inhaled liquid is an immediate life-threatening situation that will kill you faster than other interrogation historical favorites such as third degree burns or severed limbs. Yeah, I learned a lot of valuable things in the Corps."

Staats lay still on the board looking strangely composed.

"So, what do you think? Want to tell me the truth? Want to tell me what you did with my brother?"

"I told you, I talked to him."

"Life doesn't mean much to you, so I guess when I take yours it won't mean much either."

"Nary a whit. A veritable yoctosecond in eternity."

"What the—?"

"A septillionth of a second, or a decimal point followed by 23 zeros, then a 1."

As I fill a pitcher with water, he sings.

A shimmewing wight
Gweem of a bwade
And the debt was paid
When the ax comes down
A chewing sound
Steel against the head
Another wabbit's dead
I'm a wabbit swayer
An ideal preyer
With a nasty habbit
Kill the wabbit!
(Hah hah hah)
AhhhaahooOhhh

"I want the story. The whole story. Skip the adjectives, just give me the dirty details—the unadorned story sans self-serving adjectives, whether hyphenated or not but skip the embroidery. Keep it simple."

"Just the facts ma'am."

"Facts, yeah."

"Did you know there are no adjectives that may be used to describe nothing, but any adjectives, and all adjectives may describe everything."

"That so?"

"Could be."

"I'll take your word for it."

"Life demands answers, but sometimes there just aren't any. There are door mats and there are matadors and never the twain shall meet. Somebody said that."

"Who's that?"

"No idea."

"Cut the crap."

"The Siamese twins—good and evil. The victim may be as guilty as the victimizer. The point of view is that of the villain. His nature is the same as his fate. The worst people in your life know all of your secrets and all of your lies and use them to get you. No matter how noble your intention, there is always a snake in paradise, a worm in the apple, a monkey in the wrench, a gorilla in the mist ready to strike without warning."

"What are you talking about?"

"Don't you know about film noir?"

"Apparently you do."

"In the beginning was the word and it came out of the mouths of babes named Lily, or mugs like Jake, or Dix. Nobody is melba-toast, Jello, PG rated, Wonder-bread. It's not a 'honey, I'm home' life. There are no white picket fences. Everything is in the shadows, everything is bigger than life—"The Big Heat," "The Big Clock," "The Big Combo," "The Big Steal," "The Big Carnival," "The Big Knife," "The Big Sleep," "The Big Lebowski."

"You think you're Sam Spade?"

"See, Mr. Gittes," he says screwing his face into a caricatured 'tough guy' face, "most people never have to face the fact that at the right time and the right place, they're capable of anything.'"

"Think so?"

"Says John Huston."

"You may see yourself as the hard-boiled Sam Spade, that tough and shifty guy able to take care of himself in any situation, but in reality you're nothing but the pathetic Elmer Fudd. Don't you know, Fudd may be out to kill Bugs but he always ends up seriously injuring himself?"

"Oh you scwewy wabbit."

"He's a cartoon. He's' not noir. He's—"

94

I got the bunny.
     — Farley Granger, "The Naked Street."

I ended her smug, lopsided leer by bringing my tied together feet up with force enough to send her sprawling across the room. Presto, zippo my hands slipped through my ties. I grabbed my shotgun. Aimed it directly at the red head of the dickless dick.

Ohhhh...
And there won't be any more wabbits awound!
No more Wodger Wabbit
No more Peter Wabbit
And no more Pwayboy Bunny Wabbits!
Ah ha ha ha ha!
Be vewy vewy careful. Oooh...
Cwazy wabbits...

"Bang, bang, bang! Come out of your holes, you cowardwy wabbits! Bang, bang! And I'll bwow you to smitteweenies! Come on out now, and let me see the cowor of your spurting bwood! Oh, what have I done? I've killed the wabbit. Poor wittle bunny. Poor wittle wabbit."

95

A soft, enervating drizzle has settled over the Haight. It's neither rain nor mist but a kind of sticky floating wall that moves sluggishly in whitish banks. The water vapor is so dense that the saturated air seems to have liquefied.

There on the misty wall: a film.

96

I'm a big fan of murder. I stare at a wall mirror looking deep into my eyes, and just slightly to the left of each retina I can make out the gates of hell. They are ajar.

97

Fade in on Staats.

DUCKRABBIT